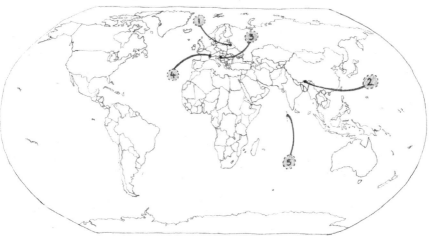

City names that Del thinks are swell

1. Minsk (Belarus)
2. Thimphu (Bhutan)
3. Zagreb (Croatia)
4. Bern (Switzerland)
5. Malé (Maldives)

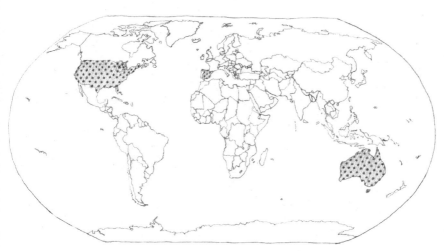

Rosa's Faves When It Comes to Cafés

1. FLYWHEEL, Sydney Aust
2. Gorilla Coffee, Brooklyn, NY
3. Taberna Matritum, Madrid, Spain

COUNTRIES WHERE THE GIRLS THINK
CHARLIE McFARLANE IS DARLIN'

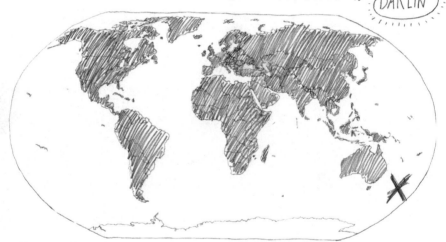

GET IT TOGETHER,

Delilah!

ERIN GOUGH

CHRONICLE BOOKS
SAN FRANCISCO

First published in the United States of America in 2017
by Chronicle Books LLC.

Originally published in Australia in 2015 under the title
The Flywheel by Hardie Grant Egmont.

Library of Congress Cataloging-in-Publication Data available.

ISBN 978-1-4521-5187-8

Manufactured in China.

Design by Jennifer Tolo Pierce.
Typeset in ITC Galliard.

10 9 8 7 6 5 4 3 2 1

Chronicle Books LLC
680 Second Street
San Francisco, California 94107

Chronicle Books—we see things differently. Become part
of our community at www.chroniclebooks.com.

For Emma Kersey

As far as English teachers go, I could do worse than Mr. Hammer. He's a smart guy with a good haircut and an admirable passion for punctuation. He's taught me since the start of high school and I have only two misgivings: his views on the semicolon and the fact that he ruined my life.

To be fair, when he paired me with Georgina Trump for a class project, ruining my life probably wasn't his intention. Class Harmony is Mr. Hammer's big thing, and I understand that bridging the gap between those in the class who carry pink clutches and those who don't is a legitimate part of that.

It was in a similar spirit of goodwill that I decided to make an effort with Georgina. This was despite the fact that when Mr. Hammer said, "Georgina, you're with Delilah," she pretended not to know who I was, even though we've gone to school together for over four years now.

So when she giggled stupidly at things that weren't remotely humorous, I was tolerant. When she eye-rolled with her friends across the room, I refrained from strangling her. I even lent her my study notes when it became clear she hadn't read the book.

Little by little, she began to laugh at my jokes, and not with her fake giggle but with a slightly embarrassing (and therefore endearing) snort. I began to make more of them, just to hear it. People started to notice how well we were getting on. Our friendship seemed so unlikely, so against the usual order of things, that they started talking, and speculating.

I'd heard the words before. Of course I had. Lezzo. Dyke. Some were actually quite creative, but that didn't make them easier to hear being muttered by a netball player as she shoved me hard against a locker.

Soon this kind of thing was happening more than once a day. The words, once they'd been said aloud, seemed to multiply. I heard them whispered from the back row in biology. The hockey squad captain slugged a few at me as she steered me out the changing room doors. They traveled on the breeze from the windows of the tuckshop, along the sports field, and through the choir stalls.

And my new best friend, Georgina? She threw "obsessive stalker" into the mix and asked to change English classes.

So much for Class Harmony.

1. FLAMENCO HOUR

When life throws up in your lap, my father is fond of saying, *find yourself a distraction from the smell.* For him, this means watching *Horse Feathers* on a loop in a darkened room in his pajamas. It's how he spent a whole month after my mother, June, ran out on us the January before last.

Not that the Marx Brothers ultimately did him much good. Dad's still a ball of quivering mush. That mother of mine really stomped on his heart. I'm hoping the overseas trip I've made him take—his first in the twenty years he's spent running our family cafe—will knock the misery out of him once and for all.

As for me? In the past month, I've had insults about me scrawled on school desks, and I've been called too many names to remember. But with the Flywheel to run, a recuperative vacation is out of the question, and some '30s slapstick flick isn't going to cut it.

Lucky, then, that I've found my own diversion from the reek of proverbial vomit.

I call it Flamenco Hour.

Six nights a week my schedule is more or less like this:

7:51 p.m.: My heart begins racing in anticipation.

7:52 p.m.: My legs do this thing where they go numb along the insides.

7:53 p.m.: Out of the corner of my eye, I see the stack of washing up on the Flywheel counter. I ignore it.

7:54 p.m.: I toss my tea towel on the kitchen floor and sneak upstairs to our flat.

7:55 p.m.: I wade through the junk in Dad's bedroom to the window that looks out over the street.

7:56 p.m.: I peer into Charada, the tapas restaurant across the road.

7:57 p.m.: I look at my watch. Not long now.

7:58 p.m.: I keep my sights on the figures making their way through Charada: two girls in flamenco skirts and a boy in high-waisted pants.

7:59 p.m.: The three of them take their places on the scuffed boards between the tables. A loud crackle erupts from a speaker and a man's warbling voice starts singing in Spanish.

8:00 p.m.: They begin to dance.

The tall girl with the red skirt is Angeline. Ramon, all in black, is her brother. The other girl, her dark hair parted down the middle and fixed with a tortoiseshell comb, is their cousin. Her name is Rosa Barea, and she is the reason I stand here watching: watching and imagining, as she dances, her arms around my waist, and my hands on her hips.

The music stops and for a moment I am still there with her, still charged with the rhythm of the dance and the warmth of her body. For a moment it doesn't matter that I'm the butt of a hundred hallway jokes while she is an elegant goddess with the greenest eyes in the Southern Hemisphere. For a moment Rosa Barea loves me despite all of it, with all her heart.

While the fantasy lasts, I forget about the misery of the last four weeks. I'm in the arms of a beautiful woman, and we're dancing.

Then I catch my reflection in the window. An ordinary girl in a dirty cafe apron looks back. It brings me down to earth.

Who are you kidding, Delilah? I sigh, my breath hot against the glass.

2. A SUDDEN GOODBYE

In the real world, I spend too many hours stuck indoors at the Flywheel with Hamish Creel, Laziest Person on the Planet.

It's four o'clock on Saturday and one of his neglected customers is waving a hand in front of my face. "I ordered a coffee half an hour ago. From that man." I follow the inevitable direction of his finger past the uni students on the couches playing poker. Past the cake counter. All the way to the coffee machine, where Hamish is chatting away to one of his mates.

"Sorry," I apologize. "Leave it to me."

I march across the cafe floor to the kitchen and put the plates I've been carrying into a sink of dirty dishwater Hamish should have emptied an hour ago. I walk back past the uni students. One is doing a victory lap around the tables. The others have thrown their cards down in disgust.

When I reach him, Hamish is still talking to his friend. "This place is okay, but it could be *great*," he's saying. "If you knocked down that wall and got rid of the storeroom you'd have nearly twice as much space." He flicks one of his massive dreadlocks nonchalantly over his shoulder.

Charlie and I have our theories about what Hamish keeps in his nest of unwashed hair. Spare change, perhaps? A family of mice?

I clear my throat loudly. Hamish and his friend turn and stare at me, as if I have interrupted a very important conversation, not just Hamish's latest scheming about what he'd do with the Flywheel if *he* was in charge.

"Can I have a word?"

"What is it, sweetheart?" Hamish asks in the patronizing tone he always uses with me.

"You forgot the order for table nine."

"Oh." He turns around again.

"It's the third time today," I say, raising my voice.

"Take a chill pill. I'm on it." He flicks a switch on the coffee machine with a casual finger.

When I finally convinced Dad to take a break from the Flywheel, it was not my idea to run the place while he was gone, believe me—there was year eleven to consider. Dominic, our full-time manager, said he was happy to take care of things during the week as long as I could help him out on weekends, and with the assistance of a couple of part-time kitchen hands, I figured we could handle it. We had to: Dad's broken heart was proving bad for business. The regulars had started calling him Groucho, and not just because he loves the Marx Brothers. *Take six weeks,* I told him. *Take eight. We'll be fine!* And I truly believed that—until a month ago, when Dominic ran a red light on Parramatta Road in the Flywheel delivery truck.

This would have been okay in any ordinary circumstance: for example, if Dominic had a driver's license and an Australian working visa. Trust my father to hire a guy without checking his credentials.

So Dominic got sent home to Dublin and I stepped into the manager role and hired Hamish to help out.

Clearly my recruitment skills need some honing. The good thing about Hamish is that he makes a damn fine coffee. It's a pity he's lazy, can't cook, and has his attitude dial set permanently to Sneering Contempt. Ever since he asked if he could DJ for the Sunday lunch crowd and I knocked him back, he has transformed into one long Frontier of Sneer. I'm pretty sure Hamish's unpleasantness is beginning to affect our daily profits as well.

I'm counting the days until Dad is home. Just fourteen to go now. I sometimes wish it wasn't school holidays so I'd only have to work with Hamish on weekends, and that's really saying something after the hideousness of school last term.

In the kitchen, I cut two slices of sourdough and hurriedly prepare the Flywheel's famous HAT sandwich (haloumi cheese, artichoke, and sun-dried tomato). My favorite band, Rushmore, is playing on the cafe's speakers as usual, so I turn it up and start dancing while I wait for the sandwich to grill. I love nothing more than dancing to Rushmore. Unfortunately my limbs don't really coordinate and my hair, which is messy at the best of times, flies in every possible direction. But none of this matters in the privacy of your own cafe kitchen.

When the grill light turns green, I extract the sandwich and deliver it with a strained smile to our patiently waiting regular, Mandy, who runs the physiotherapy practice down the road.

"Hang in there, Del," she says, raising her fist in solidarity and giving me a cheerful grin.

I mime strangling Hamish with my tea towel and she laughs. I make my way back to the coffee machine.

"One cappuccino," Hamish says.

I grab the coffee from him and wind my way past a group of backpackers whose collective body odor wafts unpleasantly into my path (the plumbing at the youth hostel must be on the blink again). Finally I place the cappuccino onto table nine, carefully wiping away the small drips that have landed in the saucer.

Mr. Table Nine looks down at the cup and frowns. "I ordered a flat white," he says darkly.

I should have guessed. Hamish has made the wrong coffee on purpose, as revenge for me telling him off. To calm myself, I spend a few seconds picturing him lying dead under the front wheels of a semitrailer.

"I'm so sorry," I say.

"That's not good enough. This isn't the first time." Mr. Table Nine's frown deepens. "I'd like to speak to the manager."

Oh, no. Here we go.

"You're speaking to her," I tell him, straightening my apron.

"What?" he says, just as I knew he would. "How old are you? Fifteen?"

"Seventeen," I say, unable to keep the defensiveness out of my voice. "I'm short for my age."

Mr. Table Nine laughs, but it's the kind of laugh that has no humor in it, only disbelief at the sorry state of the world. I can see him wondering if there's some government agency he can phone to report this latest instance of child exploitation. I can already see the headline: CHILD SLAVERY RACKET AT INNER WEST CAFE.

"You know what?" He glances down at the unwanted cappuccino and back again. "I've changed my mind. I don't feel like coffee today after all."

"Wait!" I really don't want him spreading this around. That's the last thing we need right now. "I'll make it up to you!"

But Mr. Table Nine is already getting to his feet. The Tibetan cowbell Dad sent me clunks dully above the door as he strides out into the cold street air.

That's it. Hamish is done for.

I march back to the coffee machine.

Not there.

I untie my apron straps and burst into the kitchen.

Not there, either.

It's only as I'm heading back through the kitchen doorway that I spy him. He's standing at the other end of the cafe near the open cash register, presumably getting change for a customer.

Except there are no customers nearby.

I watch his shadow move beside the stencil on the wall behind him: Chico, Groucho, and Harpo Marx in a silhouette of slapstick. The outline of his protruding dreads makes his shadow-hair look as clownlike as theirs. When Hamish moves to the left, and then to the right, the outline of his hair swoops across the wall. It is so distracting that I almost miss him slipping the fifty into his back pocket.

He shoves it down, but when he moves his hand away it slips back up, one pineapple-colored corner protruding like a flag.

Breathe, Del. But all I can think about is how poor our daily take has been since he started.

I consider my options. Grievous bodily harm—that's one.

Fortunately for Hamish there are too many witnesses. I walk cautiously forward along the stenciled wall until I'm standing behind him. "Why are you taking money from the till?" I ask stonily.

Hamish jumps. He turns around, smiles a placating smile. "Come on, babe," he says in a reasonable tone. He seriously barely skips a beat. "You can't expect me to make the coffee *and* run the kitchen for what you're paying me."

"Why not?"

"Why not, she asks." Hamish laughs, turning his head to an imaginary audience, dreads slapping against his shoulders.

"I'm paying you more than most cafe workers get," I continue, reciting Dad's usual spiel to rubbish workers. "And you know why? Because investing in good people is the key to success in the hospitality industry. Good people who understand the importance of trust."

He looks surprised. He didn't expect a schoolkid in her dad's cafe to lecture him like this. He probably thought he'd get an easy ride, being hired by someone as young as me.

"You can't be serious," he says, laughing still, but I can tell he's beginning to feel uneasy. "You don't even know how to manage a business. This place is going down the gurgler.

If you knew a thing or two you'd be jumping at my DJ idea. With a couple of music sets a week the Flywheel would rake it in."

"So you'd have more cash to pinch?"

I consider my options. Two weeks isn't such a long time to run the Flywheel by myself. Not during school holidays.

Hamish narrows his eyes at me disdainfully. From the mild flicker of panic behind them I can tell he's trying to come up with a way out. Either that, or a clever retort.

He fails to find either. "You're crazy," he says.

I smile sweetly. "You're fired."

3. THE LURE OF MONGOLIA

I have a confession to make. I've been lying to my father for weeks. He phones from overseas pretty much daily, and ever since Dominic got deported I've been telling him the following:

Dom's still running the Flywheel (Lie #1);

we're packing in the customers (Lie #2); and

we're killing the opposition (Lie #3).

What choice do I have? If I gave Dad even a hint that something was wrong he'd be on the next plane home, and home is the last place he needs to be right now.

There's just one other tiny fib I'm spinning:

School's going well, no problems there, Dad, honestly everything is absolutely fine (Lie #4).

Giving him some time off from it all—fathering as well as the cafe—is the least I can do after everything he's done for me. For seventeen years Dad's been my rock: the steady, reliable parent who packed my lunch every day, made me brush my teeth, and helped me with my homework. Sure, June can be a lot of fun. She's the queen of dress-ups and midnight feasts. She's called him a stick-in-the-mud for years and I've always agreed with her. Turns out when it adds up, I'd rather have a stick-in-the-mud who sticks around than a volatile whirlwind who, after twenty years of marriage, abandons her husband and only child to run off with some new guy to Melbourne.

But it was time to give Dad a chance to step out of the mud, rinse off his feet, and take a little wander.

So when he called from Hanoi a fortnight ago, I lied. And then I lied last week when he e-mailed from Colombo, and yesterday when he Skyped from Ulaanbaatar. *The customers are banging down the doors*, I said. *Things could not be more awesome.*

The problem is, he's home in two weeks. I've been getting Charlie to do Dom-like background noises when Dad calls ("That screeching? Oh, that's just Dom making coffee/blending a smoothie/strangling a customer," etc.), but I don't think the sound effects will be quite as convincing when Dad is actually standing in the room. So now that Hamish is out of the picture and not likely to be replaced in the next fourteen days, I think it's time to finally tell my father about the whole Dom deportation situation.

I open my laptop. The screen lights up, a bright square in the darkness. I log on and, as I wait for the page to load, crawl into bed. It's almost midnight. I can hear the hum and whirr of the industrial dishwasher downstairs and the murmur of cars on Parramatta Road.

Five new e-mails. The first one is from Charlie wanting to make plans for the weekend. I write back to tell him I've fired Hamish—he will definitely high-five me for that. There's also a message from Lauren, with study notes attached. It's typical for Lauren to be studying over the holidays. If the entire Eastern Seaboard blew up, you'd find her floating among the debris, thumbing through a critical essay on the gothic elements of *Frankenstein*.

And of course, between a Viagra ad and a Nigerian scam, there's a message from Eugene Green himself.

Dearest child o' mine,

How were tricks at the Flywheel today? Was the lunchtime crowd as big as yesterday's? Things really seem to be going from strength to strength. I almost wonder if it would be better for the Flywheel if I stayed away longer!

I know you'll say I'm wrong about that, but you *have* got me thinking. You and Dom are handling things so beautifully, and a great opportunity has just landed in my lap. I've met some wonderful people who have offered to take me through the desert in Mongolia!

You keep saying I should make the most of this trip and, well, maybe you're right. The guys I'd be going with are very experienced—they know the area and the people well.

If I do accept their offer, though, I won't be back in a fortnight like I intended. In fact, it could be as late as mid-September. That's why I'm e-mailing you. Darl, if you have any doubts at all, I'll get on that plane and head in your direction at once. You are what I care about most. You have a big year at school and if Dom can't cut you some slack on the weekends to study then it's a no-go.

Think about it. As I've said, one word from you and I'm home.

Love, Dad. xx

September! Sure, if Dom really was here that might be fine. But he's not. And running the Flywheel by myself for two weeks during school holidays is one thing, but for over two months of the semester?

Then again, I *have* told Dad he should make the most of this trip. It's obvious he really wants to do the desert trek, and who am I to stop him? He deserves a shot at happiness.

Maybe I can use the extra time to get the Flywheel back on track.

First things first. I need to find a new full-timer, and fast.

4. NO SUDDEN MOVEMENTS

In a life of uncertainty there is one thing I can rely on. No matter what the occasion, I will always arrive later than Lauren.

As I round the corner on our first day back at school, dread emanating from my every pore, I see she's waiting for me at our usual meeting place, jogging impatiently on the spot to keep warm. My oldest friend is the only person I know who would get to school early if she could. We're told they lock the gates until eight-thirty for security reasons, but I know it's really to stop Lauren Crawley from stalking the teachers before roll call.

"Sorry. Flywheel emergency."

"Mr. Kosnik is going to kill us," she moans, picking up her bag from the footpath. "What kind of emergency?"

"I'm down a full-timer and can't find a new one."

Lauren frowns. "Wasn't your dad due back on Saturday?"

"He extended his trip."

"Does he know you're short-staffed?"

"He doesn't need to know. I can handle it." This might even be true. Since firing Hamish two weeks ago, I've kept the cafe under control. Just. I'm trying to pretend that this won't change now that school's on again.

"God, Del," she says.

As always, I practically have to run to keep up with her. We've "walked" to school together ever since year seven, yet it's as if Lauren has never noticed that her legs are twice the length of the average human's and therefore three times the length of mine. Neither my panting nor my visible sweat patches have ever made the slightest impact on the swiftness of her stride.

"How could we not have seen each other all holidays?" she calls back across the meters that already separate us.

"I know. Crazy, huh?"

"Did you get a chance to read *The Aunt's Story* for English? I got through the Judith Wright poems but I didn't get to *The Aunt's Story*."

"I didn't know we had to read it," I pant.

"That's probably because you missed the last three classes of English," she says crossly. "What about your overdue essay on the Tomb of Reneni? You finished that, I hope?"

"Nup." I stop to catch my breath. "Things have been a bit hectic."

"You do know we're in year eleven now?" Lauren asks in a teacherly voice that isn't even ironic. "Stuff *counts* now. You've got to stop skipping classes and do your assignments. The marks you get this term will affect your HSC."

When Lauren gets like this about Higher School Certificates and stuff, I know she's channeling her parents. They're pushing her to get into law. In a way I'm sympathetic; June used to go on about how she never had the chance to have a tertiary education and how she would hate to see me limit my options. When she ran away to Melbourne, though, I realized that these remarks really were just another way to put down Dad about the choices he'd made.

Her new boyfriend, Mungo (yes, that is actually his name), is some sort of professor. He spends his life in a book-lined office ruminating about the Socialist Aspects of an American Something or Other. What a great contribution to society.

Lauren's red ponytail swings in front of me. She's implausibly skinny and a lot taller than me. In fact, she's taller than the average seventeen-year-old boy and some members of the Australian netball team. The giraffe jokes started after her first growth spurt in year nine, so she began to slouch in an effort to disguise her height. The hunchback jokes started in year ten.

Another point of difference is our dress sense. I have none, which places me in a slightly better position than Lauren, who has adopted her mother's idea of Young Professional Chic. This means that on the weekends, when I'm knocking about in the first item of clothing I laid eyes on, she's wearing pencil skirts and heels like she's trapped in an episode of *Law and Order*.

The superficial stuff aside, I've been wondering lately whether we've got what it takes to be friends after high school. For most of my life, we've been inseparable—always hanging out together after school and on weekends, always sleeping over at each other's houses. We've ridden bikes together and gone to the movies together and mooned over the same film stars together, and when I've needed someone to have my back—against my parents or some feral classmate—I've always been able to count on Lauren.

But in the past year we've grown apart. The lesbian thing has something to do with it. When I told Lauren last year that I thought I liked girls she said she was okay with it, but we never really talked about it beyond that. I don't know what I was expecting. Maybe that she'd ask me how it felt, or how I knew, or what my parents thought. (Dad was cool with it. He went out and bought one of those rainbow pride flags for the Flywheel window, which was nice but totally embarrassing. June is still treating the news like I'm going through a phase, which is typical of her, but also, whatever.) But Lauren didn't really ask anything, and her silence opened up a gap between us that's still there. It meant that when I started getting picked on last term, I didn't feel I could talk about it with her. Now it's like we spend our time waving at each other with a canyon between us. No matter how madly we wave, we can't actually reach each other.

"You did the extra reading for Geography though, yeah? The stuff on ecosystems?" Lauren is dogged.

"No, Lauren. I didn't. I haven't done *anything*, okay? You should try running a business sometime and see how *you* manage to do your reading on the side."

This finally stops her. She waits at the street corner for me to reach her. "But you love Geography. It's the one subject you actually love."

"Not anymore," I snap.

She looks at me sadly. Can't she tell I don't want to talk about school? I'm actually trying to pretend that we're not on our way there right now, just so I can keep putting one foot in front of the other. Unless some alien force miraculously erased everyone's memories over the holidays, I know exactly how the next seven hours will play out.

If only Lauren would forget about school for a moment, I might even consider telling her the real reason I was late this morning.

It's true I'm down a staff member, but that's not what held me up.

I was late because Rosa Barea was late.

Lauren is not the friend to tell this story to, though, as much as I'm bursting with it. The friend I'm dying to tell this to is Charlie.

Charlie and I haven't known each other nearly as long as Lauren and I have. We only met halfway through last year. It was like we just clicked. We don't go to school together, and on the surface we don't have much in common. He grew up in the eastern suburbs, I grew up in the inner west; he was born with a silver spoon in his mouth, I spend my life hauling stainless steel ones out of the dishwasher. But he understands me better than anyone. Plus we talk about girls, which is something I definitely can't do with Lauren.

Lauren is always asking about Charlie. This is either because she's jealous I have a new friend or, like most girls, she thinks he's hot and has a massive crush on him.

I consider calling him now, before school starts. I'm keeping an eye on my phone as often as possible anyway, waiting for the perfect candidate to ring me about the cafe job. So far the only bites have been from a student with no experience and a seasoned cafe hand who wants more money than I can pay her.

I pull out my phone at the same time as the bell rings a block away. "You go ahead," I tell Lauren, and I dial Charlie's number.

Charlie is well aware of my Rosa obsession. I've recently begun talking to him about her a lot. A lot. Having a crush is such a good distraction from reality. So he already knows that over the last few weeks Rosa has been dropping her parents off at Charada on her way to uni in the morning. He also knows I've developed a habit of waiting for her car each day, hoping to catch a glimpse of her.

What he doesn't know, and what I'm dying to tell him, is that today I got especially lucky. I'd just given up waiting—I had actually crossed the road on my way to meet Lauren—when Rosa pulled up, five minutes later than usual. She was helping her mother out of the passenger side and practically opened the car door into me!

As the door scraped the curb and I stumbled backward to avoid it (stepping onto the foot of a woman pushing a stroller, who cried out in pain and limped off), I looked straight at Rosa and our eyes met. And she smiled at me.

I obviously need Charlie to know this, but he isn't answering his phone, so I leave him a message to call me back urgently.

There's nothing left to do now but take the long route to roll call, damn it. The heavy feeling I woke up with settles on me again. Focus on the positives, I tell myself.

I'm not spending the day with Hamish Creel. That's one.

Two: . . .

That is literally the only positive I can come up with. OK, new strategy. I will make myself as inconspicuous as possible today: No sudden movements. I will speak to no one unless they speak to me first. I won't meet anyone's eye.

If I follow these rules, with any luck I'll make it out alive.

5. A DANGEROUS IDEA

The morning goes better than expected. I manage to slip into roll call at the precise moment Mr. Kosnik is tearing strips off Carl MacDonald for calling Bridgette Leong a filthy wench. Carl is retorting with a lame argument about how he was simply quoting *The Merchant of Venice*, Bridgette is doing some high-pitched sobbing, Mr. Kosnik's head is exploding, and Carl's friends are sniggering. There's just enough time after that for me to sign the roll beside my name before the bell goes for first period and I'm out of there without anyone except Lauren even noticing I've arrived.

Maths is the usual drone and Biology proceeds almost without incident—although at one point I see Sophie Murray and Clare Ando staring at me and whispering to each other and my stomach turns. I pretend to be deeply absorbed in a handout on prokaryotes and viruses, and I don't look up till break time.

Usually I would head straight to our spot on the Road Lawn via the sports field to meet up with Lauren and our friends Misch and Lucas, but today I go the roundabout way via the staff block and the undercroft. Going by the sports field would mean passing the field-side girls, Sophie Murray and Clare Ando included, and there's no point in risking that.

The Road Lawn is a narrow strip of grass next to the main road that nobody else would bother sitting on, let alone naming. We like it because it's tucked away from the rest of the school and we have it to ourselves. Lauren is there when I arrive, of course. Misch and Lucas are there, too, Misch flat on her back, her head resting on *Core Biology*, drinking bottled juice through a straw. She gurgles a hello.

Misch and I became friends after Mr. Hammer sat us together in English in year eight. She has a round cherubic face inherited from her Sri Lankan mother that always looks perfectly composed, so for the first week and a half I was fooled into thinking she was just another well-behaved study-head like Lauren. Then I noticed that the notes she was taking were not about juxtaposition but in fact limericks about the field-side girls, each one with an impeccable rhyme scheme. That's when I began to get an inkling of how smart and funny she is.

Misch puts her juice aside. "You make it here okay? I saw the Evil Bitch was by the field already."

I feel my face go red. I should have expected someone to mention her sooner or later. I give a halfhearted laugh and stare at a traffic jam beyond the fence. "Was she? I went the other way."

Misch nods. "Along with Clare and Sophie. And that cow Ella."

Ella is queen of the field-side girls. When she wears a skirt over jeans, the rest of them wear skirts over jeans. When she calls Misch "fat Misch" or Lauren "Lauren the Loser" to their faces, guess what the field-side girls call Misch and Lauren. "Pity you're not in our History class. It was epic," says Misch. "Ella was being rank as usual, but she was nothing compared to the Evil Bitch."

I know Misch is trying to be supportive, but every time she calls her that I flinch. No one seems to notice, though. Lauren is focused on unwrapping her muesli bar. Lucas simply makes one of his trademark noises in agreement—a cross between a snort and a burp.

"She was trying to argue that Hitler started the First World War!" Lucas grins. "She was utterly convinced."

This is a comment Lucas can only make in our company. Ever since he made the mistake of bringing his ornamental spoon collection to school at the start of year seven, his loser status is so well established that if he'd dared to even

28

smirk during class he would have been called one of the various names the field-side girls have for *him* (a lot of unfortunate things can be made to rhyme with "Lucas"), or shoved over a park bench by one of the sportos, which is what happened the last time he laughed at somebody he shouldn't have.

"That's hilarious," I say halfheartedly. I wish they'd change the topic. I check my phone, wondering when Charlie will ring. It's not as if he has school today—the posh schools don't go back until next week.

"Don't let someone catch you with that," Lauren warns.

"Such a stupid-arse rule," says Misch.

"You know I have to keep it on me today," I say to Lauren.

Misch sits up. "Recruiting a new full-timer, I hear."

I nod. "No luck yet."

"That sucks balls." Misch falls back again. "You've got too much going on." She looks contemplatively at what's left of her juice. "Know what I'd do if I were you?"

"Nope. What?"

"Quit school." She grins, pops the straw into her mouth, and slurps contentedly.

Lucas cackles.

Lauren looks horrified. "Don't listen to her, Del."

"It's standing in the way of your life," says Misch. "After everything that happened last term, I'm surprised you could even stomach coming back today." Lauren shoots her a look, which she ignores. "Who would blame you if you didn't? You know your dad would *love* to get you on board full time. How old is he? In his fifties or something? Who's going to take over the cafe when he gets senile dementia? A full-time salary," Misch says dreamily. "Terrific work experience. You could make a career of it, without even finishing year twelve."

"I don't know about that."

Misch grins, her cheeks dimpling. "Look at Tamara Howard. She quit at the end of last year and she's already got a job in the marketing department of her uncle's accounting firm."

Lucas smirks. "Tamara Howard who flunked English? Let's hope she's not required to actually write anything down."

"Del doesn't want to spend the rest of her life running a cafe. She's got too much potential for that," says Lauren. "No offense to your dad, Del. But really, this is a ridiculous conversation that should end right now."

As if to back her up, the bell rings.

Only four hours left to endure.

6. HELL, POPULATION 1

My afternoon turns out to be roughly a thousand times worse than my morning. The living hell begins in third period, History, with Ms. Shanker demanding to know the whereabouts of my essay on the Tomb of Reneni. She gives me her signature stare-down, followed by a caution that if I don't hand it in by the end of the week she'll dock my marks by ten percent a day. Unless I find a replacement for Hamish who can start by, well, yesterday, the chances of me tapping out a thousand words by Friday are precisely zero.

After third period I make the mistake of going to the bathroom. There I find Sophie and Clare standing in front of the mirror, reapplying lip gloss. They turn as soon as I enter.

I pause for the briefest second, a pounding in my ears. But I can't let them own the bathroom. So I head to one of the cubicles and go to close the door—only to have someone jam her foot in it. Sophie. "What are you doing?" I ask, face burning.

"I'm sorry, but we can't let you go in there." Sophie's voice drips with fake sympathy.

"I'm sorry, but it's a free country." I mimic her lamely, trying to keep my voice steady. I attempt to push the door shut again but she won't move her foot.

I hear a group of chatting girls enter the block, then their chatting stops abruptly. "What's going on?" one of them asks with interest.

"Delilah's trying to perve on Georgina," Clare tells them smugly. "She's gone into the cubicle next to hers and is refusing to leave."

Georgina Trump, a.k.a. my former English project partner, a.k.a. the Evil Bitch. It was only a matter of time before we ran into each other.

The group of girls who have just come in start making "ew" noises. "O.M.G. Spying on someone when they're on the toilet? That is really sick."

"I didn't know she was in there!" I call out, but my voice sounds small and pathetic, even to me.

Sophie scoffs. "As if, Stalker."

"You okay in there, George Porge?" Clare asks with exaggerated concern.

Theoretically, this is Georgina's chance to stop me from being crapped on by half of year eleven for the rest of human existence. If, for example, she were to say, "I'm totally fine. Leave Del alone," the madness would stop.

But, surprise, that's not what she says. What she says, complete with upward inflections and panicked voice, is "I can't believe she is still doing this? Can you get her to leave, please? Having her here is really stressing me out?"

My heart sinks. For her allies, those words are enough. Georgina has spoken, and they will fall into line. There's no way I'm going to win this skirmish.

I step out of the cubicle. Sophie smirks triumphantly. I wish more than anything I could think of a smart remark to hold my ground. No doubt the perfect comeback will occur to me ten minutes from now. Instead I push past her, heart thumping. I keep my head down and ignore the rest of the gaggle. Then I dash to the loo beside the art room.

Fourth period is Geography with Mrs. Cronenberg. Mrs. Cronenberg is also the counselor for our year. She knows a lot more personal stuff about each of us than any of us are comfortable with. Today she's wearing her usual awful capri pants and jumper combo. Her jumper has a hole in the sleeve and there's a coffee mark on her pants that is roughly the size and shape of South America. The fact she is a geography teacher is not a valid excuse for this.

Misch and I head to our usual spot in the middle near the wall heater.

"I hope you all had a scintillating break," Mrs. Cronenberg begins dryly. "Let's start with a quick quiz to check you haven't forgotten everything I taught you last term."

The class groans.

"Mr. Chang," she says to Leigh Chang, who has groaned the loudest. "Name two factors that have negatively affected the ecosystem of Kangaroo Island."

Leigh looks at her blankly.

Farming and tourism, I think.

"Come on, Leigh," she says impatiently. "We spent two weeks on this."

"Is farming one?" he asks.

Mrs. Cronenberg smiles. "It is indeed. Sheep farming, dairy farming, wine growing, even beekeeping have resulted in the removal of native vegetation and soil compaction. Who can name another one?" She scans the room. "Delilah?"

So much for staying under the radar. I consider my options. If this were the start of the year, I wouldn't hesitate to answer straight away. Since last term, though, anything I say attracts ridicule. So I opt for no words, and shrug.

"Come on, Delilah. I'm sure you know this one."

A few people are whispering behind me. In my head I am cursing Mrs. Cronenberg very loudly. What makes her so sure about what I know and don't know?

"A high rainfall?" I say to annoy her. I hear sniggers to my left.

Mrs. Cronenberg's mouth goes tight. "Tourism is the answer I was after." She turns away from me. "Next question. What industry is associated with the New South Wales town of Tamburlaine?"

Sighing, I slide down in my chair. Thank god that's over.

My relief is cut short by the sound of my phone trilling loudly from the vicinity of my pencil case.

The entire class turns to stare at me.

"Probably her girlfriend," I hear someone murmur, and a whole row cracks up.

"Delilah Woolwich-Green," Mrs. Cronenberg says with deadly calm from the front of the room.

Great timing, Charlie. Of all the days for this to happen! And Mrs. Cronenberg is renowned for confiscating phones. How am I going to recruit new staff without my phone? I hate this Monday above all other Mondays in the history of my life.

"You know better than to have that in here," Mrs. Cronenberg says with such disappointment you'd think I'd smuggled in an AK-47 and a kilo of cocaine. I give her the coldest stare in my repertoire.

Her resolve seems to waver. She drops her gaze. "Turn it off and put it away. Right now, before I change my mind."

I'm still fuming as we head out of class.

"Don't worry. They're all losers," Misch assures me. "Road Lawn?"

"Definitely."

"Okay. Let me just grab lunch from my locker, then we can bounce."

I peer down the corridor. Bodies are spilling out of multiple classrooms in waves. I spy Ella, who sees me and nudges one of her field-side minions.

"How about I meet you there?" I ask Misch.

"Are you kidding? I'll be like, one second."

So I wait nervously while Misch ferrets for her lunch beneath a pile of books. Turning to face the bank of lockers, I pull out my phone and call Charlie. He answers after the first ring, and the moment I hear him say my name in that unmistakable voice of his, with its trace of poshness mixed with enthusiasm, I'm able to pretend for a moment that I'm hanging out with him, far away from school.

"Thanks for almost getting me kicked out of Geography," I say, grinning. "Not all of us are trying to get expelled, you know."

Charlie's been expelled twice from one of the most exclusive boys' schools in Sydney (his father convinced them to take him back the first time—*big* mistake) and suspended once from another.

"You're at school?" Charlie asks, shocked.

"Relax. Only the public ones are back."

"I know. But who's running the Flywheel?"

"One of the part-timers. He has uni for the rest of this week, though, and I still haven't found a replacement for Hamish." I glance at Misch, who has finally retrieved her lunch, a squashed sandwich, and is fingering it with a look of disgust. "Misch reckons I should quit school and do it myself."

"Maybe you should," Charlie says in a reasonable tone. "Your dad's not back till September now, right?"

Lauren, who's just emerged from French, appears beside me. "Is that Charlie?" she mouths.

I nod.

"Say hi from me."

"Lauren says hi," I tell him.

"Who?" he asks blankly.

"Don't worry about it."

Lauren looks outraged. She must've heard what he said. Then I notice Misch is suddenly looking furious as well.

"I've got to go," I tell him. I hang up just as Misch begins waving her squashed sandwich in the air like she plans to launch it at someone. "Hil-*ar*-ious," she calls down the corridor.

A creeping feeling tells me I should *not* look in the direction she's yelling. I should go directly to the Road Lawn instead. But Misch is actually *yelling*. I haven't seen her this worked up since Carl MacDonald spilled Coke on her autographed copy of *Cloudstreet*. Lauren is standing perfectly straight for once, rigid with anger.

So I turn and look. And what I see is a line of flyers, eleven by seventeen inches, taped to lockers all the way along the hall. Lauren is marching over and ripping them off, but Ella, Clare, and Sophie are sticking them up faster than she can tear them down.

One of the flyers has fallen on the ground. I pick it up. At the top of the sheet, above what appears to be a still shot from a video, are two words in bold letters. At the bottom is a website. In the middle, a contorted human figure looms large, eyes rolling, face screwed up, arms crooked with motion.

The background is the Flywheel kitchen. The words along the top: DANCING DYKE. The person in the picture is me.

A pounding starts up in my head. Every atom in my body suddenly weighs twice as much.

"That bitch," Misch mutters, studying her phone screen. I can't see what she's looking at, but I recognize the Rushmore track that's playing.

"Who, Ella?" I ask croakily.

"No," she says, as if it's obvious. "Georgina."

The chatter in the hallway grows as people reach their lockers. People are studying their phones and casting looks in my direction.

I reckon a teleporter would come in handy right about now.

I try to watch the video over Misch's shoulder.

"Lady, I don't think you want to see this," she says, clicking the screen off and hiding it from view. "When was this?"

"No idea. I'm always dancing in the kitchen," I say helplessly.

"And I respect your right to do that. But maybe you should invest in some blinds?"

Suddenly there is a commotion down the corridor. I turn and see Mark Wellington, a kid from my Maths class, on his toes, his arms at his sides, twirling in an exaggerated parody of bad dancing. The fast-growing crowd around him is looking from me to him and back again to gauge my reaction.

I breathe in slowly, breathe out again. Mark Wellington isn't even a sporto. But as he flaps his arms like a sick bird, throws his head from side to side—everyone around him is in stitches.

In the middle of the crowd I glimpse pale skin and long blonde hair. I can't see her face, but I know it's her.

What I should do at this point is obvious: Walk away. I should leave them to it and head quietly and calmly to the

Road Lawn. I know this in my head and in my heart, but the message clearly hasn't reached my feet yet, since I find myself walking toward the crowd instead. It parts to let me through.

It's Georgina my feet are apparently looking for. She edges backward as I approach. "Tell me you had nothing to do with this," I hear myself say in a low voice, holding up the flyer.

She flushes. Her eyes slide away from mine. Ella and Sophie come up beside her, Ella cradling a stack of flyers against her chest. "Is she hassling you, Georgie?"

"Why are you doing this?" It's my voice again, and this time it's almost a whisper.

Ella laughs, a dinner party trill. "What did you just ask her?" Her tone is incredulous.

With Ella backing her, Georgina grows bold. She fixes me with a hard stare and a cold smile spreads across her face. "Now you know what it's like to be perved on. Perv." She spits the word.

That's when I become aware that Mark Wellington is hovering beside me. He grabs me suddenly by the wrist and puts his arms around my waist.

"Get your filthy hands off her!" Misch shouts from the back of the crowd.

I wriggle to free myself, but his grip is too tight. He spins me hard. Someone starts up a chant in the crowd:

"Dancing dyke, dancing dyke." I lose balance and stumble, hitting the ground to the sound of laughter. A couple of people even clap. Pain shoots up the arm I've landed on. I can't believe I let myself think this semester would be any different.

"Mark," booms a familiar steely voice. "Collect your lunch and take it outside."

Oh, great. This is just what I need.

"Delilah, come and see me in my office. Everyone else," says Mrs. Cronenberg, looking around darkly, "show's over."

The crowd scatters reluctantly.

"Fuckwit," mutters Misch viciously after she and Lauren have battled their way through to me. She offers me a hand up.

"What a dick," Lauren adds, which is particularly strong language for her. She pats me awkwardly on the shoulder.

I scrape grit off my limbs and swipe away the tears at the corners of my eyes. "I don't think I can do this anymore." My jaw is aching. I realize I've been clenching my teeth.

"It's going to be okay," Lauren says hastily. "Mrs. C will be able to help with all this . . . stuff."

Why won't she acknowledge how messed up this is? Why can't I talk to her about what's going on? But I'm not up for a fight with Lauren, not after what's just happened. Instead I shake my head angrily. "No. Mrs. Cronenberg will only tell me off again."

41

"What about?"

"Oh, you name it. Not answering her stupid quiz correctly this morning. Having my phone in class."

"You know what she's like," pleads Lauren, who is in Mrs. Cronenberg's other year eleven class. "If you don't go to see her, she'll come and find you."

"No way. Misch, tell her about how she got stuck into me in class today."

"I actually thought you got off lightly. She let you keep your phone."

I shoot her a betrayed look and she shrugs.

"Go on, Del," Lauren says. "She has your best interests at heart."

"That's not the impression I got last term," I tell her. I'm still bitter.

"We'll meet up with you afterward," says Lauren.

It's the last thing in the world I want to do, but I head to Mrs. Cronenberg's office, careful to avoid eye contact with everyone I pass—the first person in history to be peer pressured into obeying a teacher. How typical it is of her to make me go to her office when I'm the one being picked on.

I reach her office and peer in the window. She's on the phone, dabbing at the coffee stain on her pants with a wet handkerchief. She sees me and holds up a splayed hand. Five minutes.

I curse her under my breath. She doesn't have time for me, when she's the one who's requested I come? Well, I don't have time for that.

If Mrs. Cronenberg knew how to help me, she'd have done it already. Instead she's just made things worse. I peer in her window again. "Just hold on for one more minute, Delilah," she calls. "There are a few things we really need to discuss."

I feel like screaming. What am I waiting around for? For her to sit me down in her comfy little chair reserved for meaningful chats and give me her spiel about my great potential and how I'm apparently strong enough to cope with all of this? When she said all that last term I wanted to believe her, but now I know she's wrong.

Something occurs to me: an exhilarating thought. If I walk out right now, Mrs. Cronenberg can't stop me. I could just turn around and leave the building. What does an afternoon off school matter in the scheme of things? She can shove her counsel down someone else's throat. By the time she gets off the phone I'll be blocks away.

I swivel on the linoleum. I hover there, facing the direction of the street. Then, very slowly, I begin to walk away from her office. People are passing me but I don't look at any of them.

I pick my pace up.

Past one classroom, then another. Past the cleaning closet and the boys' toilets. I take the steps at the end of the corridor two at a time, hitting the concrete at the bottom with a bounce, then follow the path that runs along the side of the basketball courts.

It's easy. By the time I arrive at the open gate I'm feeling lighter than I have for weeks. I look through it, that inviting gap. Beyond it, the school grounds end and the world begins.

Behind me I can hear the familiar racket of kids playing basketball. But in front of me is the beautiful clamor of everything else: cars speeding down the road, planes roaring above, and, on the footpath, people walking freely.

School can manage without me for the day.

I step out into the street.

I am away.

7. WHAT FREEDOM FEELS LIKE

Before Dominic got deported, I liked to watch him bake. I'd sit by the Flywheel oven to see his orange poppy-seed cake rising inside it until it cracked open at the top and the crust came away from the edges of the tin.

At eight o'clock on Tuesday morning I have the same expanding feeling as that cake in the oven. The reason?

I'm skipping school today. I need a mental health day. I'll go back tomorrow.

Anyway, I've got a cafe but no one to staff it. I have to don the apron or lose a day's income.

So I put Rushmore on the Flywheel stereo and turn up the volume.

I'm bopping along to the song's soaring chorus when I sense someone watching. An image of Mark Wellington in the corridor yesterday flashes into my mind. I turn around quickly, heart pounding. But it's only Charlie, hands cupped to the glass. His yellow hair flops across his forehead. He's wearing a black woolen scarf with his favorite Bonds T-shirt (he reckons it shows off his biceps), pre-faded jeans, and boots.

I turn down Rushmore and poke my tongue out at him, which Charlie reads as permission to enter. A burst of cold air follows him in, and the Tibetan cowbell crashes against the glass. He bounds toward me and grabs me by the waist.

"You're here! I thought you'd be on your way to class by now." He grins. "Taking my advice, are you? Giving up the study?"

He gives me a quick hug, but when he pulls away I glimpse a flash of broodiness.

"Are you okay?"

"I'm fine!"

"Charlie, what is it?"

"What's what?" He smiles, unwrapping his scarf.

I've known him long enough to tell he's faking it. Before I can interrogate him though, the Tibetan cowbell clinks again. It's Lauren, wearing her hair in a way-too-neat braid and her face in a look of bitter disappointment.

"Hey," I say, as casually as possible.

Lauren eyes my cafe apron disapprovingly. "Del, you can't be serious about this."

"I told you last night. It's just a day. I don't have a choice."

"Well, I'm here to convince you to change your mind."

I knew she'd be like this. "You remember Charlie, right?" I say to divert her attention.

Her expression wavers. "Of course!" she says brightly. She gives him a little wave, before dropping her hand quickly.

"Hey, Karen," says Charlie. "Good to see you again."

"It's *Lauren*," says Lauren, smiling bravely.

"You want some breakfast?" I ask her. "We've got those raspberry and white chocolate muffins you like so much."

Lauren's expression shifts again. "What I *want* is for you to come to school with me," she says, shooting sideways glances at Charlie, who is now leaning on the counter with one elbow, positively *exuding* brood.

I begin to take upturned chairs off tables. I can tell Lauren's impulse is to help me, but she resists it. Instead she stands there, her arms crossed, her face troubled. "They're just a bunch of stupid idiots, you know," she mutters. "You shouldn't care what they think."

I feel my ears turn red. "Lauren," I say sternly. "This is about the Flywheel, okay? What am I supposed to do? Leave Charlie in charge?"

We both look at him. He's started making himself a sandwich at the counter and has already managed to splatter guacamole on the coffee machine.

Lauren frowns. "This doesn't have anything to do with Misch's joke yesterday, does it? About quitting? Because she will feel absolutely terrible about it if it does, believe me. She'll be very upset if you don't turn up today."

I pull out my phone and show Lauren the message I received earlier this morning. *GOOD CALL GIRLFRIEND,* it reads. *Enjoy your day of freedom!!! XX Misch*

"Fine," Lauren snaps. "But you still have an hour before roll call if you change your mind. I hope to see you there." She marches out.

I walk over to Charlie. He is eating his sandwich with an air of tragedy.

"Come on. Fess up."

"About what?"

"Cut the crap, Charlie."

He falls into an orange vinyl armchair and the cushion sighs. He runs a hand through his hair. "You know that history tutor I've been telling you about? The one who comes on Tuesdays?"

This is a stupid question. Charlie has yakked on about this history tutor more times than I can count. I know far more about her than it's natural to know about someone you've never met. I know, for example, that she's writing a thesis on European conflict in the twentieth century and is six months behind schedule. I know she wears green bobby pins in her hair. I know she's a Roosters fan, an espresso drinker, and a Gemini. "Of course. You never shut up about her."

"Oh, right. Well, anyway . . ."

"What is it?" I ask warily.

Charlie slumps dramatically in his chair. "I'm in love with her, Del."

History is one of three subjects Charlie's dad has paid for him to be tutored in. I guess he's particularly nervous about Charlie's "prospects," given Charlie's doing his Higher School Certificate this year and hasn't exactly been a model student. It's probably also his way of making up for the fact that he never spends any time with his son. He's too busy flying all over the world as the chief financial officer of one of the world's largest trading companies.

Charlie's mom was the same. She was a buyer for an international cosmetics outlet and spent her spare time overseas, at board meetings for various charities she was involved with, or playing competitive golf. But she's not around anymore. She died of cancer before Charlie and I became friends.

I pull up my favorite green velour chair next to Charlie and sit down, ready for the lovesick spiel. Since I've known him, Charlie's been in love with about fifteen women, and it's the same each time. First he tells me how madly in love he is, next he tells me he's never felt this way about anyone before, and then, after a few weeks of passionate embroilment, he's over her and pining over someone else.

"What's her name again?" I ask reluctantly.

"Sarah."

"And she's beautiful?"

Charlie nods. "Very beautiful." He winks. "You'd like her."

"How old is she?"

Charlie mumbles something behind his hand.

"What was that?"

"Thirty," he repeats quickly.

"*Thirty?*" I say, trying to keep my voice level. "You didn't say she was *thirty*."

"So what if she's a little older?" says Charlie. "What about Rosa? She's older than you, and that doesn't stop you lusting after her."

"Rosa's nineteen," I say. "That's a lot different than thirty. Thirty's middle-aged!"

"A twelve-year age difference is nothing," says Charlie defensively. He leans forward, pushing his hair back. Here we go. "I've fallen for her, Del. I've never felt like this before," he begins. "She's so beautiful. And smart as well." Charlie stares past me dreamily. "To be honest, I don't care how old she is. When it's true love, what does age matter? Going out with people your own age is just another one of society's stupid rules. You of all people should appreciate that," he concludes, with more than a hint of accusation.

I shift my feet, feeling guilty. Charlie has always been supportive of my crushes. "You're right. It shouldn't matter," I say. "I'm sorry. If you decide to go for Sarah you have my full support." I smile. "Age, schmage, hey?"

"Exactly," says Charlie. But instead of returning my smile, he frowns.

"What's the problem, Romeo?"

Charlie sighs again. "She thinks I'm too young for her."

"She does?" I ask innocently.

"She thinks I couldn't possibly have proper feelings for her because I'm only eighteen. It's so unfair!"

"When's your next tutoring session?"

"That's the other problem. We had our last one this week. I may never see her again."

"Then you've got to *find* a way to see her," I tell him. "To prove to her that she's wrong."

It takes less than two hours for Charlie's internal havoc to wreak an external course. While I handle the lunchtime crowd—prepare food, serve coffee, and generally work my butt off—Charlie sits in the orange armchair, gazing forlornly into the middle distance. I have no one to help me with the sandwiches today and my coffee-making skills are proving patchy, judging by the half-finished cups left on tables.

I'm glad to be busy, though. It distracts me from the message I got from Mrs. Cronenberg earlier this morning. In my outrage that a teacher would take the liberty of calling my cell, I deleted the voice mail without listening to it. Of course now I can't help but wonder what she said.

I find myself thinking about what classes I'm missing. I have an Ancient History double on Tuesdays. Right now I'd be getting a lecture about my Tomb of Reneni essay. Working here is definitely better than that.

At one o'clock Charlie announces he has a Brilliant Plan. This is bound to make things worse.

"We have only one option," he continues.

"We?"

"You're right. I've got to show Sarah this is the real thing. We're going to visit her tonight."

"We?" I say again. "Why do you need me there?" I'm beginning to regret my offer of unconditional support. I have an eight o'clock appointment watching the dancing across the road.

Charlie is insistent. "You're my wingman, Del. You were the one who told me I had to find a way to see her. If you don't come with me I know I'll chicken out. I'm going home to sort a few things out, but I'll be back here to pick you up at seven-thirty."

"Are you sure you want to do this tonight?" I ask, in a last-ditch effort to change his mind.

"Seven-thirty, Del," he repeats sternly, walking out.

For the next few hours I juggle coffee and lunch orders and try to think of a way to get out of going with Charlie. My reluctance has to do with more than just Flamenco Hour. I do want to stick around for the dancing, but I also have a bad feeling about this plan—a stomach-twisting, gut-wrenching *bad feeling*.

I'm still trying to think of a way to talk him out of the whole thing when Rosa Barea walks through the door.

All at once my heart is in my mouth, and I forget about Charlie and his plan altogether. She greets me with a casual smile. Today she's wearing a denim jacket over a black leotard and wide-legged pants and, in her hair, colored rags threaded with sequins that flash in the light. She's carrying a heavy-looking shoulder bag, no doubt full of textbooks. Rosa is in her second year of political science and, as far as I can tell, she studies hard. Whenever she comes in here she spends a lot of time tapping away on some essay or other, while I spend a lot of time giving her food on the house and trying to be witty in a way that seems nonchalant.

"Hey," she says to me.

I blush. "Hi there. Um, how are. Would. What can I do, I mean, get—"

"A latte would be great," she says, smiling.

"Gotcha." I swallow thickly. "One latte coming up."

She slips into a seat and I head to the coffee machine, determined to make the best latte of my life. Despite my track record this morning, when it's done I'm pleased with the result. The coffee smells fresh and strong, the crema is smooth. I've made a mess of myself in the process but I don't care. After a poor attempt at wiping the milk drips off my pants, I walk the coffee over to Rosa.

She turns sideways in her chair and looks up. "That guy with the dreads not in again today? Haven't seen him for a while."

"He's, ah, not working here anymore."

Rosa nods. "Probably just as well," she says, matter-of-fact. "His coffee was good, but he was kind of rude."

I'm relieved she's not disappointed at Hamish's departure. Her patronage is something I definitely don't want to lose. "Yeah, well. We did have a few complaints."

I place her coffee on the table. Or try to. Somehow I've misjudged the length of my arm or the angle of my elbow and in the process of lowering the cup and saucer, coffee spills over the lip of the cup. The fern pattern I've made on the crema dissolves. The saucer is now a moat.

I fling my coffee-stained cloth at the saucer in an attempt to soak up the mess. This action sends coffee splashing onto the table and across Rosa's front.

Rosa looks down at her leotard.

"I am. So. Sorry," I say in a whisper.

"It's fine," Rosa says, with a wave of her hand.

I grab the coffee-stained dishcloth again and make for her front with it. Rosa puts her hand out. "It's okay, really!"

"I'll get you a fresh napkin. And another coffee."

She shakes her head. "Don't worry about it. You can't even see the mark. And there's plenty left in the cup."

"Almost as much as there is in the saucer," I say gloomily. "You want a straw?"

This cracks her up, and I breathe out, relieved. She swivels further in her chair to face me properly. Her eyes are incredible, a flawless green. She holds my gaze for a moment, long enough for me to wonder whether she is seriously contemplating my offer. "Actually, there is one thing you could do for me."

"Name it."

She rifles around in her bag and pulls out a handful of flyers. "Could I leave some of these near the door?"

I read the flyer. HELP SAVE OUR LOCAL LIBRARY, it says in bold. RALLY ON THE LIBRARY FORECOURT ON SATURDAY 3 AUGUST AT 1 P.M. At the bottom in italics is the slogan RESOURCES FOR ALL, NOT JUST THE RICH!

"The council's decided to merge its libraries," Rosa explains. "They're going to sell off three-quarters of the books, and most of the buildings, and shift everything to the Leichhardt branch. Can you believe it?"

"That's terrible!" I attempt to sound suitably outraged. I try to think whether I have ever used the local library. I try to remember where it is.

"Everyone from young kids to old people *relies* on that library," she says.

God, I love her passion. "Leave as many as you like," I tell her. "Put a few on the pin board as well." Wallpaper the walls with them. Tape them together and I'll wear them as overalls.

She tilts her head at me. "Your dad won't mind?"

I wave my hand. "I could e-mail him if you like, but I'm not sure his Mongolian yurt has Wi-Fi."

Rosa frowns. "Still away, is he? Are you running the place by yourself?" Perhaps I'm delusional, but I'm sure I detect a hint of concern in her tone. Could Rosa Barea really be concerned about me?

"It's all right," I reassure her, attempting to sound relaxed. "I can handle it."

"But you've got other things to think about, don't you? Like school exams and stuff? You should really consider hiring someone else."

As she says this, she stretches out her hand slightly. Suddenly I realize she is *touching* me. For at least half a second—maybe even a whole one—*her* fingers are on *my* wrist.

I swallow hard. "You're not looking for a job, by any chance?"

She smiles, shaking her head. "'Fraid I've got enough on my plate with this and uni and my dancing." She waves the stack of flyers. "Thanks heaps. I'll leave some on my way out."

8. A CRUISE WITH MR. SMOOTH

I still haven't fully recovered from this encounter when Charlie rolls up in one of his dad's cars three hours later. It's the 1975 Mercedes-Benz with refurbished cream leather seats. With all the Rosa excitement I've practically forgotten my earlier doubts about his crazy plan.

I open the passenger door and see he's wearing a black blazer and tie. "Well, well, well. If it isn't Mr. Smooth," I say admiringly. "Hey, guess what?"

"Jeez, Del," cries Charlie, staring at me as I clamber in. "Here I am, going to all this effort, and you look like you've just spent a week in a garbage disposal unit."

What he says is unfortunately true. I still have on my cafe wear—the Flywheel apron over black pants and black collared shirt, all stained with various consumables, and my hair tied messily in a knot at my neck. It's possible that I stink a little, too. But I'm still too thrilled about Rosa to care.

"Rosa touched my wrist," I blurt.

"Hey, that's great!" Charlie says, his tone turning enthusiastic immediately, as I knew it would.

"We had a proper conversation and everything."

"About what?"

"Oh, you know, saving the local library, that kind of thing. About how there should be public resources for everyone, not just the rich," I say sagely.

"It sounds like she really likes you," says Charlie.

I turn toward the window so he can't see how pathetically wide my grin is.

"All right," says Charlie once we're on the Anzac Bridge, handing me a piece of paper. "Here's the list."

"The list?" I look at the paper. On it, in Charlie's messy handwriting, are thirteen addresses. "What is this?"

Charlie glances at me guiltily.

"Don't tell me you don't know where she lives."

"Of course I do," he insists. "She lives in Rose Bay. I'm just not exactly sure of the actual street. Or the street number. But I looked up all the Joneses in the suburb. So it's got to be one of those."

Rose Bay is a residential suburb on the water, with views of the city, private jetties, big houses, security systems, and plenty of guard dogs.

"We're going door-knocking? In Rose Bay?" This is an even more terrible idea than I thought.

"It's an adventure, Del! It'll be fun."

"Now I understand why you've dragged me along. So you'll have someone to talk to. In prison."

"Don't be like that."

"Couldn't you at least have picked someone with a more unusual name?"

"The heart wants what it wants, Del. That's how it is."

We drive along in silence for a while, Charlie concentrating on the road and me fuming. But I've seen him like this before. Once he gets an idea into his head, there's no stopping him, no matter how ridiculous it is. "Here we are. Beaumont Street," he says, turning right. "Can you check which number?"

Beaumont Street is winding and dark. Every house is hidden behind tall hedges or sandstone walls, but one house stands out from the rest. Its porch lights blaze through the dark and along the driveway, two rows of tea-light candles flicker in paper lanterns.

"That's number fifteen," I murmur as we drive slowly past. "The address on the list."

Charlie grins. "They must have known we were coming."

After parking between two very expensive-looking cars, we climb out onto a neatly mown strip of grass and walk up the long pebbled driveway. Our footsteps answer back from the sandstone walls on either side of us.

Just as we reach the porch steps, the front door swings open.

"Oh, thank GOD."

The woman standing in the doorframe is in a velvet dress, its train bunched at her feet like miniature sand dunes. She is, it appears, immensely pleased to see us. She beams, clapping her hands violently as if we have just performed a dangerous high-wire act and landed safely on the ground. "Half an hour late, but that's fine, you're here now. I almost—well, let's just say *panic* is not a strong enough word," she says. "Miles had me breathing into a paper bag. I nearly threw up in the laundry sink!" She gives a trill laugh. "But that's past! That's history! Crisis averted! Aren't *you* a honey," she exclaims, taking in the sight of Charlie in his tie. She reaches out a perfumed hand to stroke his cheek. "My, my. Anita never said."

Charlie tenses up, his mouth in a half-smile, half-grimace. Like me, he's clearly wondering what this woman is going on about.

"Now," she says, suddenly businesslike, grabbing Charlie's wrist. "The goose. Is it ready? And the fig and pancetta tarts? The guests arrive in half an hour. Do you need help unloading the car?"

Charlie looks at me. I look at him. He looks at the woman and she, in turn, glances back in my direction. I suddenly realize what she's thinking. With Charlie in his penguin outfit and me in my cafe blacks, she's under the impression we're the hired help for a party. If I don't reassure her, I'm worried

61

that in her fragile emotional state she could do anything. And I don't have any paper bags on me. "No, no," I say quickly. "We can manage by ourselves, thank you."

"Excellent." The woman smiles.

She turns to go back inside and I'm about to breathe a sigh of relief at our lucky escape when Charlie clears his throat. "Will, ah, Sarah be here tonight?" he asks.

The woman looks at him, confused. "Sarah? Anita never mentioned a Sarah." She frowns. "Perhaps you mean *Sara*, with no h? Jacob Levine's third wife? But Anita doesn't know Sara so I don't . . . or are you thinking about *Sasha*. Anita's goddaughter . . ." Her complexion suddenly turns pale. "Oh *god*. I haven't invited Sasha. I completely forgot. I assumed she was still in Prague . . . but you're right. She's probably back!"

I can actually see the droplets of sweat forming along her upper lip. "Oh *god*, oh god oh god oh god," she gasps, clutching at her throat. "Anita is going to *kill me*. I am as good as *dead*. Oh *Jesus*—"

"Sasha *is* still in Prague," I interrupt her, thinking fast. "She wrote to me last week." I slap Charlie on the arm and glare at him like he is an idiot. This requires zero acting skills.

Charlie, catching on at last, whacks a palm against his forehead. "Prague! Of course!" he says with an exaggerated laugh. "Sorry. Silly me."

The woman in the velvet dress bends over in relief, her hands on her knees, and begins breathing in and out slowly. "*Oh. Thank. God,*" she murmurs.

"We'll just grab the food from the car." I yank Charlie off the porch steps. "Back in a minute!"

Halfway down the driveway we break into a run. Luckily the crunch of our feet on the pebbles is loud enough to cover our laughter. By the time we're on the street again I have stomach cramps and Charlie has tears running down his cheeks. Wheezing, we lunge toward the Mercedes.

"Lucky escape," I say once we're safely in the car. "No thanks to you!"

"But no Sarah," pants Charlie.

"Which is a total relief." I put on my seat belt as Charlie turns the key. "Imagine if that *was* Sarah's mother. Then we'd have to explain why we'd come to her party dressed as her tardy caterers."

"I told you you should have changed out of your work apron."

"You're the one in the suit! God, we might have even been forced to cook a goose!"

"But no Sarah," says Charlie again, more despondently than the first time, and we pull out from the curb.

There's no Sarah at Spencer Street, either, nor at Ian Lane. There's a Janet at Wilberforce Avenue who has incredible legs and an honors degree in Egyptology, but annoyingly Charlie is not satisfied with either of these credentials. Nor does he like the look of Dennis at Dover Road, who offers us Iced VoVos and a cuppa to stay and watch the footy with him.

Let me say at this point that Charlie is not, nor has he ever been, a violent person. I would even go so far as to say that he is a pacifist. I know this because Charlie and I met when we both skipped a karate class a year ago, when Dad sent me to karate lessons to help me "release" some of my rage about June leaving in a healthy, nonconfrontational way (as he put it).

Charlie was also there against his will. His father had insisted since Charlie had refused to join any of the sports teams his high school offered. According to Charlie's father, "a fit body leads to a fit mind." Maintaining an exercise regime, he believes, is one of the behaviors that will enable Charlie to Get Ahead in Life.

Charlie, as it turned out, felt differently. Ten minutes into the first class, I came across him in the park behind the community hall where the lessons were being held. He was sitting on a bench with his elbows on his knees, lighting a very large joint (which, I have since learned, is the activity that got him expelled twice from school).

Charlie looked up as I approached, his thumb on the lighter wheel. "Want some?" he asked.

"No thanks," I said, thinking, *I'd rather keep my brain cells.*

Charlie cocked his chin at me, eyes sparkling, and flashed his very white teeth. "You feel strongly about the subject."

I realized then that I hadn't just thought it; I'd muttered it aloud.

"It's okay," he said, considering it. "I kind of like that you said it. It's what my mum used to say."

"What does she say now?"

"Not a lot. But that's not unusual for a dead woman."

"Oh."

"I'm Charlie, by the way." He smiled.

"Delilah." I sat down next to him.

Close up, I saw how smooth his face was. Not a zit in sight. Even the shirt he was wearing, with its cuffed sleeves and crisp collar, was classy. Most pot smokers tend to look at least a little bit grungy. That Charlie looked like he'd just come from a Sunday school picnic intrigued me.

"You go to a private school, don't you?"

Charlie grinned. "Correct."

"Lucky you."

"Private schools aren't everything they're cracked up to be, take it from me."

"I was being sarcastic."

"Oh, right," said Charlie, unfazed. "Are you supposed to be doing karate right now, too?"

"Yep."

"So what are you doing out here talking to me?"

"I'm not really into sports."

"I'm with you on that one," said Charlie.

I glanced at him. Was he being serious? He looked pretty athletic to me. "Come on. You're a rugby player or something, aren't you?" I said skeptically.

"Nah." He waved his hand dismissively. "I hate rugby."

I regarded him a second time. "Then it's soccer. I bet you play for the state team."

"Soccer? Give me a break. Soccer's for gays."

"Oh, is it? If only someone had told me." I shook my head with exaggerated solemnity. "To think I could be running around in little silk shorts butting a ball with my head, instead of sitting here with you."

He glanced at me. I waited a moment for the penny to drop. "You mean you're . . . ? Sorry!"

I shrugged.

"It's cool if you're into chicks." He grinned. "I am as well, you see, so I totally understand where you're coming from."

"Uh-huh."

"Shame, though. I was hoping you might be interested in a bit of . . . you know."

I raised an eyebrow.

"What?" he said, with a casual shrug. "You're cute."

"For someone with disproportionately short legs, you mean," I said, blushing furiously.

Charlie looked at them. "There's nothing wrong with your legs. Except for those shoes. You should retire those shoes."

"Gee, thanks. What's *your* excuse for skipping class, anyway?" I asked, to change the subject. "Apart from hating sports?"

Charlie flicked back his floppy hair. This, of course, is a sign that Charlie is about to commence one of his Rousing Speeches, although I didn't know that then.

"That is a factor, yes," he said, suddenly serious. "But most importantly, I am ideologically opposed to violence."

"Really?" I asked incredulously.

Charlie nodded. "I'm not surprised you don't believe me. Most people don't, particularly the ones who know I spent five years learning kickboxing. But that's exactly what made me realize," he said, looking at me intently. "There I was, laying into a punching bag twice a week, in preparation for what? Doing it one day to a person?" He shook his head in disgust. "You think about all the assassinations, the terrorism, the wars throughout history. All we seem to do is fight, but where has it got us?" He stared out across the park. "People used to talk about having a war to end all wars, you know? But it's never going to happen. The Great War didn't cut it. It was barely over and we were having World War Two.

Did you know that there are almost a dozen political conflicts going on in the world right now, each one causing thousands of deaths per year? Just how many Somalis, and Pakistanis, and Mexicans, and Afghans, and Sudanese, and Iraqis, and Syrians have to die before we can learn to get on with one another?"

I listened to him, stunned. He hadn't struck me as the kind of person who would care this much about anything. "Violence leads to more violence," he went on. "So what's the use of learning karate, or kickboxing, or whatever martial art is the new thing? Teaching people, teaching *kids*, how to fight normalizes fighting, and that solves nothing."

This is how I know that Charlie's not a violent person. Of course, Charlie not being in any way violent makes what happens at Faraday Avenue rather difficult to account for.

It's the second-to-last address on our list, and by this stage even Charlie is losing hope. This door-knocking around Rose Bay is beginning to feel like a wild goose chase. His spirits rise, however, as soon as we turn into Faraday Avenue.

"That's her car, Del!" he says excitedly, pointing at a red Corolla. "Right outside number thirty-four!"

We park and get out. Charlie rushes up to the car.

"Look—that's her bag on the backseat!"

I look. It's one of those vintage leather satchels that half of Sydney owns. "Are you sure?"

"Positive. It's scratched along the front, see? That's from when she scraped it on a magnolia branch outside our place."

"You recognize a *scratch*?"

"You bet." He opens the gate.

It's ten-thirty, far too late to be making house calls, but Charlie won't be dissuaded now that he's convinced we've finally found Sarah. We ring the bell and wait, Charlie tapping the doorframe impatiently.

The man who answers is in his fifties: gray hair, a carefully clipped beard, and the shadows of crow's feet. He's wearing a navy jumper over a business shirt and pin-striped pants. In one hand he's holding a bowl of what smells like curry and in the other, a silver fork. A gold Rolex winks on his wrist.

If it wasn't obvious from the bowl and fork that we've interrupted his night, it's clear from his expression just how annoyed he is at being disturbed at ten-thirty on a Tuesday evening.

"We're here to see Sarah," blurts Charlie.

Rolex Man gives him a sharp look. "What's your business with her?"

Charlie's eyes grow bright with hope. "I'm—we both are—friends of hers. We need to see her urgently."

Urgently? If I didn't know him I'd be guessing at this point that Charlie was some deranged drug addict desperate for a hit.

Rolex Man appears to come to the same conclusion. He dips his fork into his bowl. "What about?" he asks skeptically, placing a forkful of food into his mouth.

Charlie begins to rock from heel to toe in agitation. "Could you please just let us talk to her?"

Oh, Charlie, is this the best you can do? I can't believe we've spent half the night knocking on doors and in all that time my love-struck friend hasn't thought to come up with a credible excuse. If he thinks the truth won't cut it, he should have prepared a watertight lie.

But maybe I can talk us out of this situation. "We . . . um . . . found something of hers that we want to return," I say, smiling winningly at Rolex Man.

Strangely immune to my considerable charm, he frowns. "What exactly did you find?"

"Something valuable," Charlie leaps in.

"I'm not aware that Sarah is missing anything valuable," says Rolex Man doggedly. "Tell me what it is and I'll ask her for you."

You have to give the guy points for seeing through our bluster. Were Charlie half as clear-eyed as Rolex Man at this point, he'd realize what has become obvious to me: It's time to cut and run. We're getting nowhere here. We need to retreat and regroup.

But Charlie goes up to bat once more. "I can't say what it is," he says with an air of unconvincing mystery.

Rolex Man cocks an eyebrow. "Whyever not?"

"It's . . . it's private."

If there were a lump of concrete handy I'd bang my head against it now.

Rolex Man chews his food slowly, deliberately, looking suspiciously at Charlie and me. I tug at Charlie's shirt hem and take a step back from the doorway in the hope he'll take the hint and follow. But he's too stubborn and desperate to pay me any notice. He's looking behind Rolex Man with that hungry look he gets when he's waiting in the queue at Catarina's for a flat chicken burger, and believe me, he really loves those burgers. He's itching to barge past this guy and into the house.

Rolex Man swallows his mouthful and I think he's about to give us a verdict. But then he secures another piece of food on his fork, places it in his mouth, and chews. We may look suspicious, but this guy is definitely rude.

"Please?" Charlie tries again with a tone suddenly so sweet, so plaintive that for a moment I think it might work.

Rolex Man pauses to consider him. "Let's see," he says evenly.

Charlie nods, his eyes fixed like a dog waiting for his bone.

"You knock on my door at ten-thirty at night," Rolex Man says, jabbing the air with his fork, "without apologizing for interrupting my evening"—another air jab—"and demand to see Sarah, 'urgently,' on the grounds of some wishy-washy story about a mysteriously unnameable item of value. And you expect me to trust my daughter with you?"

To his credit, Charlie flushes.

Rolex Man leans forward and squints at him. "How old are you, anyway? Does your mother know where you are at this hour?"

That's when I know all bets are off.

If only Rolex Man had been satisfied with the success of humiliation! He has said the unsayable. A strange animal noise comes out of Charlie's mouth. My stomach drops like a shot dog and my best friend launches forward. Rolex Man tries to close the door, but Charlie clutches the frame with one hand and shoves a foot through the doorway so that it's impossible to close it entirely.

This is seriously bad. It's been a long night, Charlie has worked himself into a frenzy of passion, and this stranger has now made the mistake of mentioning Charlie's dead mother: Things are going to get ugly if I don't pull the plug. "Let's go," I tell Charlie, and pull his hand.

Rolex Man looks down at Charlie's foot, occupying territory illegally. "Get out of my house," he spits, and opens the door slightly to allow Charlie to retrieve his foot. But Charlie chooses to take advantage of the opening door to step forward and wedge more of himself into the gap instead. Rolex Man tries to close the door again, and the door whacks hard against Charlie's elbow. He yelps in pain and thrusts the door back open, clipping Rolex Man. Something crashes loudly. Shards of chinaware and globs of curry skid across the floorboards inside.

I gasp.

Rolex Man is standing in the doorway, shirt splashed with curry, face dark with anger. With both hands, he shoves Charlie roughly in the chest.

I watch Charlie grip the doorframe to stop himself from falling over. I watch Rolex Man shove him a second time. This last shove sends Charlie backward off the doorstep and crashing into me. And then I watch, helpless, as Charlie pitches forward again, swings at Rolex Man with a clenched fist, and knocks him to the ground.

9. THE SIGHT OF BLOOD

A pained grunt leaves Rolex Man's mouth as he hits the floor. Blood begins to ooze from his lips and nose.

Charlie doesn't even seem to notice. "Charlie!" I say. He's still looking straight past the figure sprawled in the doorway. But we've got to get out of here.

"Sarah!" Charlie yells, as I haul him down the driveway. "Saa-raah!"

"Shut up, Charlie, you idiot!" I yell back, pulling him down the street away from the house. "Let's go!"

But Charlie's a lot stronger than I am, and I know he'll win the tug-of-war if that's what it comes down to. So I knee him in the balls, hard.

He doubles over in pain and I push him toward the car.

We've almost reached it when, above the noise of our pounding feet, I hear moaning. I glance back. Rolex Man is struggling to his feet.

"Get in." I grab the keys from Charlie and unlock the doors.

I launch myself into the driver's seat and Charlie falls into the passenger seat. "Sarah," he groans.

I turn the key in the ignition and swerve out into the road.

As soon as the car is moving, relief begins to wash over me. It's going to be okay. This can all be sorted out in the morning, when everyone's calmer.

I peer into the rearview mirror. Rolex Man is running down the middle of the road behind us. With one hand he is clutching his face. With the other he is waving angrily at our car. He is waving, and he is shouting loudly. And although his voice is muffled, his words are clear.

"Don't think I won't be pressing charges, you little prick!"

I hate the sight of blood. Even a glimpse of the red stuff makes me woozy in the stomach, not to mention wobbly on my feet. Just as well, then, that when I open my eyes the next morning I am already lying down.

The first things I see are the drops on my freshly washed pillowcase. Then I spy the dried blood in the knuckle creases of the hand that lies motionless on the mattress beside me.

Charlie's hand.

In my small bedroom above the cafe, with its familiar clutter and the sun streaming in through the blinds, it's a particularly disturbing sight. I can't stop staring at it, fascinated and disgusted.

I swallow hard. I've never had blood on my knuckles before. But then I suppose I've never punched someone.

Quietly, without waking him, I get up and head to the window. This is not as easy as it sounds. Clogging up floor space between it and me is the duvet that Charlie has kicked off during the night; an old banana crate full of shoes I don't wear anymore, beneath a pile of dirty clothes I wear all the time but haven't gotten around to washing; a curled-up Rushmore poster that has come unstuck from the wall; a bamboo hat Dad posted from Vietnam last month ("Perfect for a day in the rice paddies!" his note had said, as if I might stumble upon one on my way to school); a pile of textbooks; and three half-eaten bowls of muesli.

I push back the curtain. Outside, a steady flow of cars sails along the street. I can hear the clatter of roller doors as shops begin to open. Just down the road, kids are streaming through the gates of the primary school.

I look across at Charlie again. I had planned to go to school this morning, but how can I now? However cross Lauren will be, I can't just leave him in this state.

I think about what I'll be missing if I decide to skip classes again. In English, Mr. Hammer will be starting us on bush ballads, which will be a complete yawn. In Geography, it's agriculture in Cambodia. Mrs. Cronenberg will probably spend the lesson banging on about monsoon seasons and forced-labor camps in the Pol Pot era, things I know about already.

It's weird to think how keen I was on geography not so long ago. I was one of those brats who actually made an effort to read stuff that wasn't on the syllabus. I even went through a phase of boring people with random facts about other countries, like how in Japan they grow square watermelons so they're easier to store in the fridge. Georgina laughed hard when I told her that one.

Another weird thing to think about: that there was a time, only last term, when I could make Georgina laugh instead of run a mile in the opposite direction. That in those few weeks after Mr. Hammer paired us for our English project, her eyes would actually light up when I entered the room. Pretty soon she'd always have some goofy joke or story for me, stuff I'm sure she'd never share with Ella, who's far too cool for that kind of thing.

"Forget about her," was Lauren's advice before the holidays.

"She doesn't deserve you," Charlie agreed.

"Forget her name altogether," said Misch. "From now on, think of her only as the Evil Bitch." She made me repeat "Evil Bitch" three times.

In an attempt to obey Misch, I turn my attention back to the window. Around the corner in the laneway is a reminder of the more immediate mess I have to deal with. Charlie's dad's Mercedes is badly hidden under a torn blue tarpaulin Charlie found in a Dumpster last night—not the most cunning disguise.

I come back over to the bed. "Charlie," I whisper, lightly shaking his shoulder. "Charlie. Wake up."

Charlie sits up abruptly. His hair is ruffled from sleep, his pants are crushed, and the T-shirt I lent him to sleep in, which is about three sizes too small for him, is skew-whiff across his chest. "What's happening?" he cries, looking wildly around the room.

"Calm down," I tell him. "It's morning, that's all."

I watch his expression change from alarm to relief to horror as he remembers what happened just hours ago. Letting his head fall into his hands, he lets out a low groan. Then when he brings up his head again he catches sight of his bloodstained hands, and his face turns pale. He swings his legs over the side of the mattress and rushes to the bathroom.

Moments later I hear him vomiting loudly into the toilet bowl.

When he emerges, he's still looking pale and is shaking slightly. He sits down next to me on the mattress again, and I rock lightly against him in sympathy.

He shakes his head. "Shit, Del. I've ruined everything, haven't I?"

I consider how to reply. The last thing Charlie needs to hear in his fragile state is the truth: That what he's done is worse than both of his expulsions put together; that when his dad finds out he'll probably send Charlie to a reform school; and that when his beloved Sarah Jones finds out, if she doesn't know already, she will hate him forever.

Lie, I tell myself. *Tell him everything will be okay.*

"You're an idiot, Charlie," I blurt. "What the hell were you thinking, laying into a perfect stranger like that? Do you have any idea what this means? Assault is a criminal offense. And that's even when you *don't* break somebody's nose. I thought you were supposed to be a pacifist."

"He started it," Charlie says. "You saw him shove me!"

"Uh, only after you rammed him with his own front door! Plus, you were being really creepy. He was bad news, but I wouldn't have let you speak to my daughter."

Charlie's expression is gloomy. "Sarah's going to hate me now, isn't she?"

"If that was in fact her father, then yes, she'll probably hate you. And her dad? He'll probably want to kill you. You need to go back and apologize. Today."

"Oh no, I can't do that," Charlie murmurs, peering distractedly around the room. "He'll have me arrested. You heard what he said last night."

"Listen, Charlie," I say in a calm voice. "He's going to find you anyway. He knows what car you drive. And if he *is* Sarah's dad, and she *was* home, she'll know it was you. Don't you think it would be better if you fessed up, rather than wait for the police to come to you?"

"Not if I make sure they can't find me," he says.

"What are you going to do? Skip the country?"

"Nah, it'll be easier than that," Charlie says, a glint in his eye.

The glint makes me nervous. "If this is another one of your grand plans . . ."

"There's nothing grand about it. It's simple, actually. All I have to do is stay here for a while. The Flywheel can be my hideout."

I roll my eyes. I suspect that Charlie has watched too many Matt Damon movies and I am now paying the price. "What about school? You're supposed to be back next week."

"They'll cope without me. Just like your school's coping without you," he says pointedly.

"Then what about your dad? Won't he want to know where you are?"

"He's in Beijing," says Charlie dismissively. "If he calls the house, I'll get Petra to say I've gone for a run or I'm at a study camp or something."

Petra, the McFarlanes' housekeeper, has worked for the family since Charlie was a baby and loves him like a son. She also harbors a handy disapproval of his father's hands-off parenting style. This wouldn't be the first time she's helped Charlie out with one of his crazy schemes.

"But what about the car?" I persist. "If Sarah's dad saw the license plate the cops will be knocking on your door by lunchtime."

"Come on Del, I just need to buy some time, okay? Just until I figure out what to do. It's better if I stay here for now. I could sleep in your dad's room."

"Theoretically, yes. But there's nowhere to sleep in there. I lent Dad's mattress to Mandy," I say triumphantly.

"What did you do that for?"

"She broke up with her boyfriend. He moved out when she was at work one day and took all of their stuff, including the bed."

"Well," he says, looking unfazed. "Then I guess I'll be sleeping with you."

10. HIDING OUT

"It's been three whole days and we haven't heard a peep," I say, trying to sound reasonable. "Surely you're out of the woods by now."

"Three days is nothing," Charlie scoffs.

Over breakfast on Friday in the upstairs kitchen, my well-reasoned arguments against Charlie continuing to hide out at the Flywheel are falling on deaf ears. I actually can't believe it's only been three days. The time might be nothing to him, but for me it's been excruciating.

In three days, I've learnt that my best friend is not only a night wriggler, but a snorer as well; that he spits toothpaste on the mirror; and that his shoes smell. To make matters worse, Charlie's so paranoid about the cops he hasn't left the flat even once. He hasn't so much as loitered at the top of the stairs, let alone poked his head out the window for some fresh air.

Naturally it's been left to me to bring him supplies. Every time I come upstairs he's lying on the bed with the blinds down, staring at the ceiling, pretending he hasn't been smoking pot in my room. Like I can't smell it.

I push my breakfast bowl aside. "Come on. This has to stop."

"It's too soon," he mumbles through a mouthful of my scrambled eggs. "I've got to wait at least a fortnight until I can safely leave this flat."

"*Two weeks?*"

He nods decisively. "They're looking for me, Del. I know it."

There's a knock on the side door downstairs. Charlie ducks under the kitchen table.

"Oh, for god's sake, Charlie. Who is it?" I call out from the landing.

"Lauren!"

She's been turning up at around eight o'clock every day. I'm beginning to wish she'd leave me alone. I whack Charlie on the head. "Get up, ridiculous boy. I'm pretty sure Lauren is not undercover for the New South Wales Police."

I take my time going down. The knocking starts again. When I open the door, Lauren's fist is poised for another round of percussion. As always, she looks remarkably fresh for this time of morning.

"Nope," I tell her before she has a chance to speak, joining her outside. "I was hoping to today but Charlie's still here, and I still haven't found someone to manage the cafe. . . ." The words sound lame even to me. It's been almost a week now since term started and I've missed three and a half out of four days. But the fact is, going back to school seems harder and more pointless the longer I stay away.

Lauren hunches forward and stares at me intently for a moment, like she's trying to see something very small from a long way away. "Mrs. C hassled me all day yesterday about you. She says she's been leaving messages on your phone, but I suppose you knew that already."

"Was it you who gave her my number?" I say angrily.

"Of course not! It's probably on your file. Do you really think I'd do that?" She looks hurt.

"I don't know," I say. "Would you?"

"No!"

"Well, I'm glad to hear it," I reply sulkily.

She grips the straps of her backpack. "Misch and Lucas are coming over this arvo if you still want to come."

We do this English study group thing at Lauren's on Fridays. It basically consists of Misch talking at great length and with stunning insight about whatever book we're studying while Lucas and I pretend to understand what she's saying and Lauren recites her class notes. Then we order pizza.

"I don't know . . ."

"What if we agreed to order the tandoori chicken?"

"You all hate that pizza."

"Well, obviously. Tandoori chicken on a pizza? Plus, you know, Lucas is vegetarian. . . ." Then she remembers her point. "It's your favorite, though."

I butt a shoe against the gutter. "I promised Charlie we'd hang out tonight."

Lauren stares hard at the footpath. "I think you should speak to Mrs. C."

"Thanks for the message."

"They got in massive trouble, you know," she says after a pause. "Sophie, Ella, Georgina. Even Mark. The girls might even be banned from netball this term."

My stomach plunges. "Great. That's going to make them hate me even more."

Lauren turns red. She is possibly also clenching her jaw. "Anyway," she says helplessly. "I'm going to be late if I don't go now, so . . . I'm going," she says, without moving.

"Okay."

"Okay."

"Okay . . ."

There is a short pause.

"Okay, well, bye, I guess."

I watch her hurry toward the main road and, with an uneasy feeling, I head back upstairs.

Charlie is sitting up at the table again. "How's Karen?" he asks.

"It's *Lauren*."

"You know, these eggs are kind of watery."

"You're rating my cooking now?"

"What did you put in them?"

"I don't believe this."

"What did you put in them?"

"Pepper. Some salt. Is that all right with you?"

Charlie smiles winningly and pushes his chair back. "Watch." He goes to the fridge, where he takes out another four eggs, some butter, some cream, and some parsley. He cracks the eggs into a bowl, adds cream, and stirs the fork about. "Want to make some more toast?" he says over his shoulder.

"Are you sure you don't want to teach me how to slice the bread first?"

I slice a couple of pieces and place them in the toaster. Charlie pours the egg mixture into the pan with some melted butter. He adds another dollop of butter and stirs gently for a few minutes.

"Here, try some." He offers me a forkful.

The eggs are incredible: creamy, moist, and full of flavor. "Cooking *and* juvenile delinquency? Quite the all-rounder, aren't you?"

Charlie shrugs. "Petra has taught me a thing or two over the years. Not that being better than you at cooking is a particularly big achievement."

I somehow can't bring myself to launch an attack on him like I normally would when he's being rude. He's right: My cooking is not cafe standard. I certainly don't have the skills of Dad or Dom, and Charlie's unexpected culinary prowess has given me an idea.

"If you're going to continue to play fugitive in my flat, Charlie McFarlane," I say, "you and I are going to have to make a deal."

"What kind of a deal?" he asks skeptically.

"I need help downstairs. You know I do," I say, taking a large spoonful of egg from the saucepan. "The part-timers are unreliable. Our customer count is dropping every day. I'm struggling to pay the bills. And as you so helpfully point out, I can't cook, let alone clean and make coffee and manage the business side of things all by myself, even with the part-timers. It's exhausting. So, it's only fair: How about you step up to the hot plate in exchange for food and board?"

I see panic in his eyes. "What if someone recognizes me?"

"You'll be in the kitchen. No one will see you in there. I'll handle the customers."

"What about when you go back to school?"

"Don't worry about that now. For the time being, you manage the food and I'll manage the floor."

"What if someone walks past the door?"

"You could always grow a mustache."

Charlie looks horrified.

I burst out laughing. "It's either that, Charlie, or I kick you out altogether."

He must see from my face that I mean it. "Fine," he says finally. "But no mustache."

11. FUTURE SMALL-BUSINESS PERSON OF THE YEAR

After we've finished the eggs and cleaned up, Charlie follows me tentatively downstairs. The regulars—all two of them—are already waiting outside. I smile at Tom Vuong, who works as an accountant for the engineering firm around the corner and always comes to the Flywheel for his morning coffee. We have a deal with Tom. He helps us balance the cafe's books in exchange for free coffee. It's just as well, since I can't make head or tail of our accounts, which would be no surprise to every single person who has tried to teach me maths.

Next to him is Mandy Pollard, no doubt awaiting her usual HAT sandwich, which she'll wolf down at lunchtime during the ten-minute break she takes between her physio clients. A couple of backpackers from the hostel are there as well, slumped against the door clutching their oversized rucksacks with pained expressions on their faces, as if they've just swum across the Pacific to get here and not simply ambled down the hill.

Tom is looking scarily neat, as always, in a pink shirt, light-gray vest, and dark pants. He gives me a small, polite smile.

When he first started coming to the Flywheel, I was a little wary of Tom. Given I'm the kind of person who wouldn't know an iron if it dropped out of the sky and knocked me unconscious, neat people make me nervous. I can't shake the suspicion that they're not people at all, but rather cyborgs designed to shame the rest of us out of our shabbiness. This theory of mine seemed further justified when I first met Tom because of his clipped, expressionless way of talking.

A typical exchange between Del and Tom:

Me:	Tom! Great to see you! What a beautiful day it is!
Tom:	Hello, Delilah.
Me:	How are tricks down at Engels?
Tom:	Fine, thank you.
Me:	Keeping the bastards honest, are you?
Tom:	[*silence*]
Me:	[*awkward laugh*] Lots of customers on the books at the moment?

Tom:	[*silence*]
Me:	I must say, you're looking smashing today.
	Orange is definitely your color.
Tom:	[*brief embarrassed pause*] I'll have one skim flat white to take away.

Since I've gotten to know him better, though, I've realized he's just more reserved than most people. Recently I've even managed to make him crack a smile a couple of times.

Mandy is a different story. She's a very open, very friendly type of person who always shows an interest in the crazy soap opera that is my life. Lately, though, since her boyfriend dumped her, she's been miserable. She puts on a brave face, but it doesn't take a genius to see that her heart is breaking.

I hold open the door for them. At the sight of customers Charlie scurries into the kitchen.

"Charlie's helping out now?" Mandy asks, spotting him through the kitchen door immediately.

"Just for a while."

Back at the counter I'm greeted by an unpleasant waft of body odor: One of the backpackers has draped himself across the register. "Got a question for you, love," he says. "Can you tell me how to get to Bondi Beach from here?"

"Bondi Beach?" I say, scratching my chin. "Never heard of it."

The backpacker sniffs. "Ha bloody ha."

"There's a bus that goes from the main road, down the hill." I point through the window. "You have to catch it to Central, then hop on another bus."

"Two different buses to get to your biggest bloody national attraction? What a palaver," he moans.

"Bondi Beach is hardly our biggest attraction," I say angrily.

He puts his hands up in surrender. "Can't blame a guy for asking."

"Is there anything else I can help you with?"

"Just a cappuccino," he says morosely.

I turn to the coffee machine.

"Make that two cappuccinos," says a voice behind me.

I turn back and blink. Standing at the counter is Adrian Hibbert, manager of Crunch, the latest installment of a chain of cafes that have been popping up all over the place. As well as coffee, they serve the usual spread of oily burgers, soggy potato wedges, and sour-cream-soaked nachos. This new location is just down the road from the Flywheel, and I took an instant dislike to Adrian the first time we met. He has the outward appearance of being neighborly and caring, but beneath it all he's just your run-of-the-mill competitive slimeball.

Today, as usual, he's wearing a white shirt tucked into jeans and a very ugly tie. Purple and pink are the prominent colors of today's pick. The tie is because Adrian likes to think of himself as a future Small-Business Person of the Year. He runs a lot of business workshops and events in the area and even has a business column in the local paper that they publish with a close-up photo of his smarmy face at the top.

He rests his elbows on the counter and gives me my own close-up. "Slow morning?" he remarks with faux sympathy, gazing around the near-empty room.

"Sugar?" I ask.

"Usually, yes. But don't worry about it. From the look of things you have more than enough to worry about already." He makes a tutting sound. "It's not your fault. A girl your age should be at school, not running a business. I have a mind to write an article about this very issue for my column next week."

"That's three-fifty," I snap.

"I see you have one of those pride flags in the window," Adrian remarks, handing over a crisp five-dollar note. "Do you find it helps to attract customers?"

"It's about letting everyone know this is a safe and welcoming environment, actually."

"Of course. I understand how important that is for you people. Some folks can be very cruel."

I open the cash register and fling his change in small coins across the counter.

Adrian shakes his hand at the money. "Consider it a tip. We're actually doing quite well at Crunch at the moment. We're even taking on new staff."

"How nice," I say, trying to rein in the sarcasm. I wonder what kind of bigoted moron would want to work for him.

"You might know one of our new employees, actually," Adrian croons, taking the cup from the counter. "Does the name Hamish Creel ring bells?"

12. THE PALAVER AT CHARADA

There can only be one thing better than watching Flamenco Hour through the Flywheel window, and that's watching it from inside Charada itself. I have so often imagined sitting back in a chair at one of the long restaurant tables on a Saturday night, a selection of chorizo, patatas bravas, crumbed eggplant, codfish croquettes, Spanish olives, lamb skewers, grilled quail, calamares fritos, and zucchini rebozado laid out before me, while nearby, on the naked floorboards, Rosa and her cousins dance till the walls shake.

Tonight, however, my imagination doesn't have far to stretch, given that I'm actually sitting at one of those long restaurant tables right now, with a crazy number of those tapas dishes in front of me, wondering, among other things, why Charlie has ordered so much food.

All that's left to complete the picture now are the dancers. In just ten minutes the clock will strike Flamenco Hour and the bliss will begin.

It was Charlie's idea to come. He wanted to cheer me up because I'm feeling stressed about the Flywheel. If I put on a line graph my estimate of the number of customers we've had per day over the last two months—like Mrs. Cronenberg got us to do in class last term to show how many Hmong people are born in Southeast Asia each year—it would look like this:

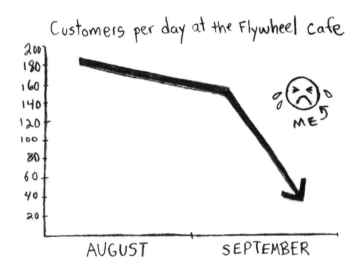

After Adrian came into the Flywheel yesterday, I decided to ask around about how things are going for him down the road. From what I hear, in that same period, business at Crunch has gone steadily uphill:

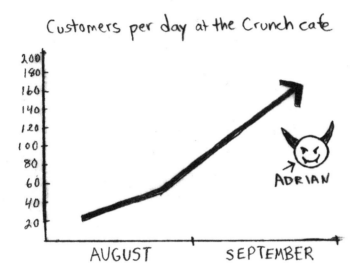

Customers per day at the Crunch cafe

ADRIAN

AUGUST   SEPTEMBER

It's a concerning trend, and the bad luck we've had recently with the supply orders hasn't helped. Our providers, the Fresh Foodies, have made a total mess of our last two bulk deliveries. Last week we ended up with salami instead of haloumi, twice as much milk as we'd asked for, and no pasta at all, despite it being the base for half our meals. The week before, the Foodies delivered at 8 p.m. instead of 8 a.m.; I discovered the boxes on the porch the following morning and had to throw all the meat and dairy out. The upshot has been a lot of unhappy customers who can't order what's on the menu and a significant cost to find more expensive replacement ingredients at the last minute.

The one thing keeping Crunch from becoming a serious threat to us is that their space is a lot smaller than ours. They have ten tables crammed into a space more suited to a corridor than a cafe.

In any case, I've asked Tom to take a look at the Flywheel's accounts to calculate the precise extent of our woe. Our profit margin has never been huge, so if I can't get the budget under control and business keeps dropping, I'm not sure what I'll do.

"Chorizo?" Charlie asks, offering me the plate.

Did I mention what Charlie's wearing tonight? Despite the fact that it's almost 8 p.m. and we're sitting in a shadowy corner of the courtyard beneath a wall heater, there are dark glasses and a trench coat involved.

I scoop a piece of sausage from its pool of oil. "Is the disguise really necessary?"

"Try the quail," deflects Charlie.

I look at the tiny bird quivering in butter and screw up my nose. "I'll pass."

"It's really good," he insists, pushing the plate at me.

"How good, on a scale of one to five? One being Hamish Creel's raspberry crumble and five being Catarina's flat chicken burger."

"I can't believe you would even put those two dishes on the same scale!"

"Oh, did I offend your delicate sensibilities? I didn't think someone who wakes up with encrusted drool on his chin would be so precious."

"I didn't realize that someone who eats Vegemite-and-Doritos sandwiches after dinner would be queasy about quail."

I hardly need to say things are a bit tense between us at the moment, and it's not just the fact we're sharing a bed. What's really got me fuming is that less than a week after the Rose Bay Bust-Up, Charlie McFarlane, Fugitive of Love, appears to have forgotten the woman he got into this mess for in the first place, and is breathless over someone else!

That's right. Sarah Jones, History Tutor, is history.

When June drove off on the back of Mungo Stevenson's motorbike last year, Dad was always listening to this song called "La Donna è Mobile," which means "The Woman Is Fickle" in Italian. I can understand why it spoke to Dad at the time but really, how totally sexist. What about the fickle men? Whoever wrote it certainly never met Charlie McFarlane.

To get past my fury, I have to remind myself that this is what Charlie always does. No matter what I say, he won't be listening. He'll wheel out his lame "The heart wants what it wants" excuse, as if that's really the organ he's listening to.

Who's the lucky woman to have captured his capricious heart, I hear you ask? Answer: a new customer who's been in twice since Charlie began to work in the kitchen. She spent most of yesterday and practically all of today at table seven, staring at him over a copy of *Stereo* magazine, taking care to eat toasted sandwiches without leaving crumbs on her face. Each half takes her about eight minutes. That's two minutes for Charlie to swoon behind the coffee machine, and six minutes for me to pick him up off the floor.

And this time he has the audacity to deny he's obsessed with her. In fact, to date, he has resisted all of Stereo Girl's efforts to win his attention. I suspect this is because he knows what I'd do if he showed an interest after what he put me through over Sarah. Kicking him out would be just the beginning.

Charlie readjusts his sunglasses. He looks pathetic in his stupid disguise, and I feel a pang of guilt about my ungenerous thoughts. We can't help who we fall for. I, of all people, know this. I just wish Charlie's love cycle was a bit longer than the life expectancy of a cicada.

Just then, the familiar strains of flamenco music begin inside the restaurant. My heart quickens, and we make our way inside. I follow Charlie through the crammed-in tables to the front of the restaurant, where we join a crowd of people standing at the bar watching the dancing.

The trio has just begun their first dance. They always start with a traditional flamenco number. Angeline, wearing a red skirt, black top, and red flower in her hair, is dancing around Ramon, who is looking very sharp in black high-waisted pants, a crisp black shirt, and shiny black vest. Beside them twirls the divine Rosa Barea, arms raised in front of her, fingers pointed to the ceiling. The blue flower in her hair matches her skirt. At her waist, a round of tassels quivers as she moves.

My heart quivers with it.

This close, I can see the shine of perspiration on her forehead. I can see the muscles in her arms flex and her chest rise every time she catches a breath. I am close to fainting from desire.

Soon it's time for each of the three dancers to choose an audience member to dance with. For this part of the evening they usually perform Latin dance numbers, which you need a partner for. I've barely had a chance to get nervous when Angeline picks a young girl here with her parents who's probably no older than ten. "Come on, niña!" says Angeline, and the girl grins shyly. When she takes Angeline's offered hand, the whole restaurant cheers.

My heart is pounding. I don't want to get picked by Ramon, because what if Rosa would have picked me? Do I even want Rosa to pick me? But Ramon coaxes an older woman out, guiding her deftly around the floor, his hand lightly but firmly on her waist. "No, no," she tells him, shaking her head, but she's grinning like crazy. At one point he spins her around and she trips, but he catches and steadies her and by the end of the dance she's blushing with pleasure.

Rosa is next. I can't breathe.

The thing is, the idea of dancing with Rosa on the Charada floorboards is one of my many Rosa-themed fantasies. In this particular fantasy the music is loud, the dancing is fast, and our bodies are close. I am always nervous at first, only to discover when Rosa takes my hand that I am actually an incredible dancer. We dance with our eyes locked and our hips pressed together, finishing in a tight, hot embrace to the sound of ecstatic applause. As the audience calls for more, Rosa pushes me through a door into a back room of the restaurant and, after adjusting the blue flower in her hair, ravishes me.

I suddenly feel like throwing up. Of course I want to dance with her, but as pretty much all of year eleven, if not a significant proportion of the world's population, knows by now, I am a terrible dancer. The experience of dancing in public could in fact cause me to suffer an acute heart attack and die.

It is with some relief then that I witness Rosa's gaze pass cleanly over me. My relief turns to horror, however, when it lands just a foot to my left—on Charlie.

Charlie grins and steps forward. The crowd claps. Rosa smiles at him and puts a hand on his waist.

I can't believe this is happening.

She leans forward to whisper something in his ear and in that moment I hate Charlie more than anyone on this earth. They begin to dance. Around me, the crowd claps in time to the music, cheering them on.

They dance effortlessly together, twirling from left to right. Charlie spins Rosa out toward the edge of the boards and gathers her back with a flourish. She is clearly impressed.

Next she pulls him against her chest and they dance cheek-to-cheek for a length of time that is basically unbearable. His hand sits low on her back. Anyone would think he's just won Oz Lotto from the way he's grinning. He's having the time of his life.

He's not the only one. When Rosa spreads out her arms and begins twirling her hands from the wrists he copies her and she laughs with her head thrown back. She shifts toward him seductively until they are face-to-face, so close their noses are almost touching. Her lips are an inch away from his.

I can't bear to watch any more. I push through the transfixed crowd, back to the courtyard.

I am finishing off the last of the zucchini fritters in a frenzy of misery when Charlie returns. "So? What did you think?" he asks cheerily. "The crowd loved us!"

I glare at him.

"What?"

"You practically had sex with her on the dance floor!" I growl.

"Come on! It was just a bit of harmless flirting."

"God, Charlie, is no one exempt?"

Charlie is brazen enough to look outraged for a moment. Then, seeing the misery on my face, he softens. "Come on. You might get a chance to dance with her in the second round."

"The second round?"

"Yeah, they dance out here next, for everyone in the courtyard."

I think he must be having me on, but Rosa and her cousins are already coming in single file through the courtyard doorway.

How could I not have known about the second round?!

The music begins again, and terror overwhelms me. Of course I want to dance with Rosa, but now I don't want to compete with Charlie. He made it look so easy.

Before I've had a chance to take it in, the dancing has begun again: the three of them twirling and stomping and clapping before the courtyard dinner crowd. Rosa and Ramon take the floor and perform a flamenco dance side by side. Each time Rosa turns to him, she meets his smile briefly with her own. All I can do is envy all the time they must have spent rehearsing together.

My head is a blur as Angeline and Ramon take turns choosing their audience members and dancing with them. When the time comes for Rosa to choose somebody, I am suddenly alert again. My heart begins to thump in my chest and my ears start burning. I slide down in my chair and watch her peruse the crowd.

The word "lovely" doesn't cut it. Rosa Barea is *rapturous*. She is still out of breath from her last dance. Her skin shines with exertion. Every face in the courtyard is turned toward her.

She raises a finger and draws a playful, imaginary line with it across the waiting crowd, her lips pursed and her brow furrowed in a mock agony of indecision. Her finger targets the other side of the room, swerves, and comes back slowly.

Someone behind me has caught Rosa's attention.

I turn. There's Charlie, bouncing madly up and down and pointing.

Pointing at me.

Rosa meets my eye, grinning. She signals for me to come forward. I stare at her, then down at myself, in horror. As usual, I'm slumming it tonight in a T-shirt and jeans. I now wish I'd put a bit more thought into what to wear.

She stretches out her hand to me. I have no choice but to take it.

She pulls me toward her, close enough to rest her other hand very lightly on my waist. I wonder if she's holding me as tightly as she held Charlie. She puts her mouth to my ear. Her skin smells like vanilla. Her breath smells sweet.

"Just copy me, Del," she says, and gives my waist a light squeeze. It's probably the same thing she said to Charlie. Even so, the sound of my name on her lips, together with her hands on my body, makes me tremble.

I float across the dance floor in her arms. I can't even hear the music. My attention is focused on every single part of her body that is in contact with mine.

Around us, people begin to clap in time to the music. The sound of it snaps me out of my dream state. I look around and see expectant eyes on us. I think of how awesome Charlie and Rosa looked together. Then I think about Mark Wellington spinning me violently in the corridor at school.

The thought makes me lose my concentration for one crucial second. As Rosa turns me around I lose traction and my hand slips from hers. All of a sudden, I'm on the floor.

The crowd gasps.

I've landed heavily on my side. Everyone is staring.

I slowly get up, a sob caught in my throat, avoiding meeting anyone's gaze. I don't want to see Charlie's face right now, or Rosa's—especially not hers. So I try not to notice her look of concern as she reaches out to me. I ignore the hand and push past Ramon and Angeline. "Del!" Charlie calls. But I'm done. I limp through the crowd toward the front of the restaurant, break into a lopsided run, and head for the door, the music soaring around me.

13. A CONVERSATION

Sunday morning.

Charlie: How are you?

Me: Fine.

Charlie: Really?

Me: Yes.

Charlie: Fine as in fine? Or fine as in you want to kill yourself?

Me: Fine as in fine.

Charlie: Truly?

Me: Yes.

Charlie: Where would you say you are on a scale of one to five, one being suicidal and five being having-the-best-day-of-your-life?

Me: [*a pause*] Probably a two.

Charlie: A two.

Me: Yes.

Charlie: Shit. Shit, shit, shit.

Me: It's okay.

Charlie: A two is not okay. A two is shit.

Me: It's better than a one.

Charlie: It's only marginally better than a one.

Me: A two is double what a one is.

Charlie: A two is shit and it's my fault. I made you do it.

Me: It's not your fault.

Charlie: It is.

Me: It isn't.

Charlie: You can say that but I don't believe you.

Me: Why would I lie?

Charlie: You just would.

Me: No, I wouldn't.

Charlie: Yes, you would. That's the kind of thing you would totally do.

Me: When did I last lie to you, huh? Tell me.

Charlie: How the hell would I know? You're really good at it.

Me: Is that supposed to make me feel better or worse? Because if it's worse, then congratulations.

Charlie: See? I'm a total prick even when I'm trying to be nice!

Me: Do you want me to beat you up? Is that what you want?

Charlie: [*contemplates this option*] That could help, actually.

I stick a finger up his nostril. "Urgh!" he cries and slaps my finger away. I smile. For once I'm really glad he's here.

14. STEREO GIRL OPTS FOR TURKISH

Despite how much I wish he wasn't sleeping in my bed, I have to confess that Charlie is proving to be an asset to the Flywheel. He has finally given up his kitchen hideout and started waiting tables. Since then, customer numbers have stabilized. There's been an increase in the giggly girl contingent, and more than a few punters have praised his interpretation of the Flywheel's peanut butter slice, which he makes with dark chocolate, roasted peanuts, and vanilla bean paste. It's not the only item on the menu that he's mastered. I don't know what Charlie does to make the pastry of our sweet potato and leek tart so crispy and light, but they're flying out the door.

As unlikely as it sounds, I have a deep suspicion that Charlie is actually enjoying the work. Every time someone compliments him about his cooking, he gets a goofy smile on his face. He's even started making up his own recipes and lecturing the part-timers about what they're doing wrong. All this just might be enough to save us from financial ruin, if only I can keep him focused on the job instead of the new Love of His Life.

I suppose I should be grateful she's a paying customer.

On this particular morning, while I'm thinking mournfully about Rosa, who will probably never enter the Flywheel again after my performance last weekend, Charlie's Stereo Girl sits with her legs crossed underneath her on her chair and her *Stereo* magazine open on the table in front of her. For the last half hour she's been transferring the dates and locations of music gigs into her phone calendar. She wears her dark hair tied up loosely and a white shirt with a lace trim at the collar. Her shoes are strappy and high, and her makeup looks like it's been applied by Maybelline herself.

"What a total ESP," Misch declares with disgust.

She, Lucas, and Lauren are lined up on the couch beneath the Flywheel's front window, checking out Stereo Girl. The couch is low to the ground, which means that Lauren's knees are up and the enormous stack of schoolbooks in her lap is pressing at her chin. Misch has her wide hips settled comfortably in the middle, leaving only a narrow space for Lucas at the end. He's balancing against the windowsill to stop himself from falling off.

"What's an ESP?" he asks.

"Eastern Suburbs Princess," Misch informs him. "They're like field-side girls but with more money. Will you check out what she's wearing? So disappointing. Why do guys always go for preppy anorexics?"

"Lauren is preppy and anorexic, and Charlie hasn't gone for her," Lucas reasons.

"Loz isn't preppy. And she only looks anorexic because she's too tall," says Misch.

"I'm right here, guys!" Lauren cries, looking longingly in Charlie's direction.

"Charlie doesn't have a type," I say to reassure her, stacking their empty coffee cups on my tray. "Maybe if he did he wouldn't fall in love with somebody different every five minutes."

"At least she isn't blonde," muses Lucas. "Personally I prefer brunettes, although generally ones with a bit more meat on them."

Misch sighs. "Don't, Lucas. I've told you no a hundred times."

Lauren shoves a piece of paper under my nose.

"What's this?"

"What does it look like?"

It looks like our next Geography assignment. "Lauren," I sigh. "I think I'm going to give school a miss for a while."

I decided this on the weekend. Even though I have Charlie's help with the Flywheel now, and a few of the part-timers are working regular shifts, we've got a long way to go to get a steady profit flow. I need to focus on the cafe, at least until Dad returns in September.

"That's a really bad decision, Del." She frowns.

"Can we not have another fight about this?"

"With something this important I'm more than prepared to have a fight."

I try to think how to explain myself in a way she'll understand. "Okay, look. You doing well at school is important to your parents, yeah?"

Lauren hunches her shoulders crossly. "I suppose so. But—"

"They want you to get into law."

She rolls her eyes. "Of course they do."

"And you care about your parents?"

"Yes, Del."

"So, I care about mine, too," I say. "Well, Dad at least. Which means I want to protect what's important to him. And this business"—I gesture to the room—"is his universe."

Lauren looks ready to launch into another argument but apparently changes her mind. "Then can you at least help me with the assignment?"

I shift the tray of empties from one hip to the other and snatch the sheet from her. "*Discuss one effect of tourism on the cultures of world cities,*" I read. "Okay. There are heaps of things you could talk about. The globalization of, you know,

113

food, fashion, and music. Or how tourism can increase the crime rate and damage the environment, that kind of thing."

Lauren smiles. "I knew you'd have some good ideas."

"I'm warning you—"

"I'm just saying," Lauren says defensively, and sighs. "You should know that Mrs. C asked to speak to me again after class yesterday. Now she wants to know where your parents are and how she can get in contact with them. She told me she's sent your dad two letters but hasn't had any reply. She even mentioned calling Community Services."

"What for?" I cry.

"If your parents aren't here then you're a minor without parental supervision. It's a child safety issue."

"You have got to be kidding." This is ridiculous. "What did you say to her?"

"I tried to be reassuring but not too specific. I told her your dad's been away for a couple of weeks but is coming home soon. And that my mum is keeping an eye on you. Which she's totally happy to do, by the way." She pauses. "I can only put Mrs. C off for so long, though."

I put the tray down. I know about the letters from the school. I've filed them away very carefully. In the recycling bin.

"Seriously, Del, she's on the warpath and I'm not sure I can hold her off much longer. Why don't you just speak to her?"

"I am *not* speaking to her," I say sharply.

"But what if she asks me again?"

"Just tell her you don't know anything."

I head across the cafe floor with the tray of empties, in the direction of Stereo Girl's table. Charlie is hovering beside it, notepad in hand. He may as well be wearing her name inside a love heart on his apron.

For her part, Stereo Girl has been doing everything in the Book of Flirting to get his attention: batting her eyelashes, angling her cleavage in his direction, touching him on the arm and hip at every possible occasion. Short of actually launching herself onto his face, it's difficult to imagine what more she can do to make her intentions clear.

"All right, that's one espresso," Charlie is saying as I pass, careful not to meet my eye, "and one toasted vegetarian . . ."

". . . on Turkish. Yes, please."

"Turkish? Are you sure?" Charlie asks.

"Yes. Definitely Turkish. Today I'm feeling . . . bold."

Turkish bread is an uncharacteristic choice for Stereo Girl. She's never ordered anything but toasted vegetarian on rye. As Charlie bustles behind me to wreak havoc in the kitchen on her behalf I glance back at her, suddenly curious, wondering what has prompted this sudden alteration. What does she mean she's feeling bold? Does this statement perhaps signify some broader change of approach toward Charlie?

Just then my attention is diverted. Seriously diverted. Rosa walks past the cafe looking unbelievable in my favorite Jenny Kee knitted dress, purple leggings, and knee-high boots.

I actually gulp. This is the first time I've seen her since fleeing Charada. No doubt she thinks I'm a total loser for falling over like I did, and a complete fool for abandoning the dance floor. That's probably why she's not coming in.

It's just as well. How could I possibly face her?

In the kitchen Charlie is making Stereo Girl's Turkish sandwich and whistling a Broadway number. He only ever whistles Broadway tunes when he's falling for a girl. At the beginning of one of his crushes it's usually something from *West Side Story*, but today he's hitting the heady notes of "I Dreamed a Dream" from *Les Mis*. This is a sure sign that the crush has moved to the next level.

"Turkish bread, hey?" I say pointedly.

"Where do we keep it? I can't seem to find it."

"It should have been in this morning's delivery. Didn't you unpack the box?"

Charlie nods. "There wasn't any Turkish bread."

"Of course there was," I say, rummaging through it. "God, Charlie! Where the hell have you put it?"

"Calm down, will you?"

"Do I have to do everything myself?"

"There wasn't any Turkish bread, I swear," says Charlie quietly.

I look up at him. He is staring at me with a worried expression.

"What?" I say.

"Are you okay?"

"Of course I'm okay."

"You seem angry in an out-of-proportion kind of way."

"I'm fine. But if those guys have stuffed up our order again . . ." I grab the phone off the wall, dial the Fresh Foodies' number, and ask to speak to Joel. I explain to him about the Turkish bread and everything else that appears to be missing from today's order.

"But you canceled the Turkish bread order yesterday," says Joel. "Same with the tomatoes, the bananas, the feta cheese—"

"No I didn't. I didn't cancel anything yesterday."

"Not you personally. Your kitchen hand."

"Charlie?"

"That's not his name. The other guy. The one who always places the orders."

"No one except me places orders. Not since Hamish . . ." Slowly the realization of what has happened dawns on me. "Do me a favor, Joel. From now on, only take Flywheel orders from me personally, okay?"

I hang up and find the number for Crunch. "If I wanted you to break someone else's nose for me, how much would I have to pay you?" I growl at Charlie.

He laughs uncomfortably. "How about instead I duck up to the bakery for the Turkish bread, free of charge?"

As he heads out I punch in the Crunch number and ask to speak to Hamish.

"What do *you* want?" he sneers.

"Stop messing with my orders or I'm calling the police."

"I have no idea what you're talking about," he says innocently.

"What is your problem?" I shout. "I sacked you! Get a life and move on."

Hamish clicks his tongue. "That's easy for you to say. I got kicked out of my apartment because of you. Did you know that? Couldn't pay the rent so I lost my room. I loved that place," he mutters, keeping his voice low. "Had my own balcony. Space for my record collection. I'd just started to get some gigs DJing as well. Now I'm living in a tiny place next to the highway. I had to put my records in storage."

"You're a thief, Hamish. If you want to blame someone, blame yourself. And stay away from my produce."

I'm off the phone and my breathing has settled by the time Charlie gets back, carrying the bread and the mail, which he hands me. I open an overdue notice from the gas company, an overdue notice from the water company, and one from the council demanding a late fee. I shove all three in the bottom drawer of the kitchen cabinet.

The next letter has my school crest on the front left-hand corner.

Dear Mr. Green,

I am writing to invite you to attend a meeting with the Vice Principal, Grace Hanrahan, and me, to discuss your daughter's absence from school in the last few weeks. While Delilah has reached the minimum school-leaving age, she is a student of significant potential and we would be interested in exploring the reasons for her absence with you.

Please contact the school to arrange a convenient appointment.

Sincerely,

Jane Cronenberg

Year 11 Coordinator

The last piece of mail is a postcard. On one side is a glossy photograph of a herd of horses with a snowcapped mountain in the background. I turn it over.

Dearest Del,

Greetings from Ulaanbaatar! I am having a terrific time, although the weather is freezing. How are things at the Flywheel? I have a great idea for expanding the drinks menu—fermented mare's milk! It sounds unpleasant but it is actually delicious!

I won't be able to call for a while—there's no reception where I'm going—but I am sure you're managing just fine without me. I'll call again when I'm at Lake Uvs Nuur (rhymes with "loves yer").

Who loves yer? I do.

Love, Dad xxx

Fermented mare's milk: Has the man gone completely crazy?

I leave the kitchen and tack the postcard to the wall behind the counter, beside the map I've put up to record Dad's trip: *Countries where Eugene Green has been.* Charlie's put up a second map beside it. He's named it *Countries where the girls think Charlie McFarlane is darlin'*. Naturally, he's colored in every country.

Back in the kitchen I slot a piece of bread into the toaster. Charlie is whistling happily and I feel a pang of the heart. How pathetic I must seem to Rosa after last weekend. Oh, to be happy in love.

15. IMAGINE

Imagine there's a girl in your English class, a girl you've never really spoken to before. She's one of those girls who cares more about fashion and makeup than school. She and her friends sit beside the sports field at lunchtime watching the boys play football. They swap lip gloss and eat kiwifruit with special kiwifruit spoons and braid each other's hair into tiny braids almost too small to see with the naked eye. You, on the other hand, prefer to eat lunch with your friends beside the main road in the traffic fumes, listening to podcasts and reading secondhand paperbacks and arguing about whether lentils work as a meat substitute in lasagna.

Imagine that one day your teacher divides the class for a book assignment, and rather than pairing you with one of your friends like he normally does, he pairs you with this field-side girl instead.

Initially you dread the two hours a week of project time in class. The field-side girl appears completely uninterested. When you try to talk to her about the book, she rolls her eyes and says stuff like "I don't see how this is, you know, going to help get me a job at *Vogue*?"

Her drawings are good, though. You have to admit that. What's more, in the third week, she also comes up with a pretty good idea: Rather than just handing in a map of the island where the book is set, the two of you should make a model of it out of papier-mâché!

Imagine you're both excited enough by this idea that you decide to work on it secretly at her place so that your classmates don't get wind of it and copy. You hang out in her bedroom after school, working—you on an essay about the nature symbols in chapter four and she on topographical illustrations. She admires your text analysis; you admire her color choices. You notice that, since starting on the papier-mâché model, she hasn't giggled stupidly or rolled her eyes at you once.

In fact, while you are working away she begins to ask you questions, as if she is keen to know more about you: what you were like as a kid; about your parents; how you felt when your mum skipped town. She begins to tell you things, too. She tells you about the time she got picked on in primary school for wearing the wrong sports uniform to a carnival. She talks about her favorite cousin who died in a bus crash when she was seven, and how it broke her heart. She confesses a secret passion for peanut butter and banana sandwiches.

Imagine, while she's talking, you begin to notice her excellent bone structure. If she didn't wear all that shimmery makeup all the time she'd actually be quite pretty. She has some other natural features going for her, you have to admit, like clear skin and a cute smile. Also, as far as necks go, hers is quite appealing.

Imagine that, rather than dreading the thought of spending time with her, you begin to look forward to it more than anything else in your week. You start arriving at her place early, so you can stay there longer. Some nights, rather than sitting on the floor in her room, you sit next to her on the bed instead.

Imagine one night you notice that, while you're both working, her leg is kind of pressing up against your leg. The sensation of her flesh against yours sends such a startlingly pleasant shiver through your body that you quickly move your leg away in case she notices. A few minutes later, though, you feel the warmth of her flesh again—she is pressing her leg right up against yours even though you are now squashed up so close to the edge of the bed that you're almost falling off it.

So you press your leg back against her leg.

And she presses her leg back against your leg.

And you press your leg back against her leg.

And she presses her leg back against your leg.

This all happens without either of you making eye contact.

Imagine that, after about two minutes of this, you finally turn to look at her. She looks back at you without breaking her gaze. Is that her hand beneath your thigh? The warm thrill of it opens a door inside of you. You decide to step through the door. You lean over and kiss her.

For a second you're shocked by your own action. A rush of blood to the head overwhelms you. You kiss her again, your mouth upon hers, and slowly, steadily, you begin to feel delighted. Because you realize she has come through the door with you.

She is kissing you back.

And then imagine that, because of that kiss and what follows, your whole life turns to complete and utter shit.

16. TORNBULL AND STOKE

Charlie's whistling is getting higher and more out of tune as he attempts the crescendo in the final verse of "A Heart Full of Love."

"Just ask her out," I say wearily.

He stops whistling. "Who?" he asks innocently, busying himself with buttering the Turkish bread.

"You know who," I say, making an effort not to shout at him. "The girl who's been sitting out there for a week and a half, trying to get your attention."

He stops buttering and looks at me. "But I barely know Karen."

"It's *Lauren*. And you know it's not her I'm talking about."

He places a beetroot slice carefully onto the middle of the bread. "You wouldn't be mad?" he says without meeting my eye. "You know, so soon after what happened with Sarah?"

"What's my opinion got to do with it?" I ask, annoyed.

Charlie puts the tongs down. "You're my best friend. I care about what you think."

"Yeah, right."

"I do." He is earnest now, and for a moment I am touched that he's worried about how I feel. "Go on. You can tell me honestly. I know you think it's too soon."

"Of course it is," I say crossly.

Once I've said it, I want to leave it at that. Sure, part of me wants Charlie to know how ridiculous he looks, falling in love at the drop of a hat, time after time. But I also know how unfair that is, because Charlie never judges me about how I feel, or who I feel it about. It's also possible I'm being snarky with him because of my own rotten luck in this department. So I add, "But so what? If it feels right, you should trust that instinct."

He looks at me, clearly uncertain. "I don't know. I think you were right the first time. It's way too soon. Forget we even talked about it."

He exits the kitchen holding Stereo Girl's toasted Turkish. I follow him out to make a latte.

As I pull a shot of coffee at the counter and ready the cup, Charlie goes up to Stereo Girl's table and places her meal in front of her. "Your lunch, miss," I hear Charlie say to Stereo Girl with awkward formality.

From behind a cloud of steam I watch carefully. Something is going on with her, I can tell, and it's more than just her change of sandwich order.

"Thank you," she says, gazing up at him. She takes a breath. "I was wondering," she continues, "if you were free for dinner sometime next week?"

Charlie freezes, clutching the cloth. He glances at me. Then he starts fiddling with his apron strings and ties them together in a knot. Then he unties them again. "I'd like that," he says finally, and beams.

For the next five hours Charlie is in a tip-top mood. That's five hours of whistling, laughing, and singing "Master of the House" at the top of his lungs. When Tom comes in at six o'clock for a take-away toasted sandwich, Charlie tries to rope him into performing the rest of the first act with him.

"But I'm here because I need to talk to Del," Tom protests.

"Not until intermission!" Charlie cries.

Charlie has just pulled a backpacker to his feet to sing the Javert parts when the cowbell chimes, and I look up to see two police officers standing in the doorway.

Everybody in the cafe falls silent. I imagine the thoughts whizzing through their minds: *Have I parked in a loading zone? Was I jaywalking? Did I remember to hide the body?* One cop is a tall and lanky woman, the other an even taller and lankier man. The woman has the predatory stare of a vulture; the man has large, round, vacant-looking eyes protruding from his narrow face and a pathetic comb-over consisting of about three hairs in total. I notice him staring hungrily at the cakes behind the glass counter.

I'm hoping they're only here for cake and coffee. I attempt to use mind control to direct them to a seat at one of the tables.

Instead they do exactly as I fear. They walk straight across to Charlie and me.

"Charlie McFarlane?" says the woman.

Charlie turns red, instantly giving himself away.

The cop gives him her best fake smile. "I'm Inspector Stoke and this is Senior Constable Tornbull. How are you today?"

I turn on the coffee grinder to drown out the sound of her insipid voice.

"We'd like you to come down to the station for a chat," she continues in a tone that is pretending to sound friendly.

"Oh," says Charlie, doing a very bad job of feigning surprise. "Has something happened?"

Stoke and Tornbull give each other a look.

"I think you might already know what's happened," says Tornbull, his large round eyes flitting back and forth between Charlie and our last piece of caramel slice.

"I think you might be mistaken!" Charlie says shrilly.

"Is that your car in the laneway?" Stoke asks.

My stomach plunges. Charlie is done for.

"Is there a problem over here?" asks Tom. His tone, coupled with his tidy collared shirt and sensible suit pants, is enough to command Stoke's attention. He holds her gaze with the steady calm of an assassin. Little does Stoke know that Tom always looks at people this way. "Do you have a warrant to be in here?" Tom says to her. "Or do I need to ask you to leave?"

Stoke clears her throat. "We're just making some inquiries," she says, stiff now.

"It's called harassment," Tom says without expression.

"Tell you what, Charlie, here's my card," Stoke suggests, reaching into a jacket pocket, all appeasement and charm. "We're just up the road. Big blue and white sign out front. Says 'Police.' Can't miss it."

The cowbell rings again like a death knell as the cops leave. As soon as they're out of sight, Charlie collapses onto a chair. Something tells me we won't be making it through Act I.

"Tom, you were incredible," I gasp.

"What the hell am I going to do?" Charlie cries.

"It sounds like you need an alibi," says one of the backpackers. "I've got a mate who could get you one for two hundred quid and a six-pack of Coronas."

"More like a one-way ticket to Majorca," I mutter.

"What you need," says Tom in his quiet, precise voice, looking from Charlie to me and back again, "is a lawyer. And you're not the only one. Del, I actually came in to speak to you about your accounts."

"What about them?"

"You don't have any money."

The words reach my brain slowly. "Money" is the first to hit the mark, and to this word alone I respond calmly. It's when the "you don't have any" bit slams into my cerebrum that my heart begins to pound.

I swallow. I look at Tom. He is not smiling. He never really smiles, but right now his facial muscles are as far away from a smile as Hanoi is from Hobart.

"When you say I don't have any money—"

"I mean exactly that. You have no money," says Tom impatiently. "Less than none, in fact. You're going to have to close the Flywheel."

17. MOURNFUL AND BROKE

"This situation," murmurs June in a tone of knowingness and exasperation, "is so typical of your father. Where did you say he was again?"

"West of Ulaanbaatar." With the phone at my ear, I let my head fall heavily against the Flywheel kitchen wall. From this awkward position I have a clear view of the cafe floor, where the breakfast crowd of one is enjoying his fried bacon and hash browns at table four. I haven't actually closed the cafe yet, despite Tom's advice to do so immediately. I need a few more days to think everything through.

The Marx Brothers stencil on the wall looks positively demonic today, Harpo's mad grin in particular. Beside it, our map of the world collection has seen better days. The tape has come off the top of *Countries where Eugene Green has been*, and someone's taken a Sharpie to Charlie's *Countries where the girls think Charlie McFarlane is darlin'*, putting a big red cross through New Zealand (I'm guessing this is the handiwork of Suzie the Kiwi backpacker, who made a pass at Charlie last night and was rejected).

"Ulaanbaatar?" June tuts. "Is that even a real place or does he make these names up?"

"It's in Mongolia."

"Mongolia, indeed," says June, stern with disapproval.

Listening to her, an eavesdropper might mistake my mother for a proper grown-up—a reliable, fully-fledged adult with responsibilities she takes seriously. The kind of person who would never, for example, abandon her husband and only child for another man in a fit of middle-aged passion. With her voice so stern and outraged, one could easily imagine her in an important job—obstetrician, fund-raiser, public defender—with the type of life experience that commands a daughter's respect.

This is the fantasy I chose to embrace when deciding to call my mother for advice about the Flywheel's finances. In my desperation I failed to recall that during the years she and Dad ran the cafe together, she demonstrated less business sense than a wild turkey.

"He didn't leave me in charge. He left Dominic in charge. It's just that Dominic—"

June sighs loudly into the phone. "Whatever he did exactly, it's not fair on you, my darling. Your father can be so selfish at times."

I thump my head against the wall in frustration. Charlie gives me a sympathetic look from across the kitchen, where he's sorting groceries.

"Del, darling. Are you still there?" asks June.

"Sorry. Yes."

"All I'm saying is that I don't know how you've been managing your schoolwork on top of the cafe."

"I'm doing really well at school," I tell her.

"I can't imagine how. When do you possibly find the time to study?"

Making this phone call was a mistake. "I told you already, Mum—"

"Call me June, darling. I know you feel the need to support your father, but the cafe simply can't come before school. I've said it before. You should come down here and live with Mungo and me. That way you could focus on what counts. You know we'd *love* to have you."

"I know, but—"

"Listen," she says, lowering her voice. "Of course you feel a loyalty to your father, but he's not even *there*. He's off gallivanting, without a care for how you're coping."

June's attempt to paint Dad as the villain is just not fair. "Did *you* ever think about how I might cope when you gallivanted off to Melbourne?"

There is a pause on the line. "Darling," June says at last. "That had nothing to do with you." She sounds suddenly weary. "It was about your father and me. I hoped you'd understand by now—" She stops. "Look, this is an important time for your education. Your father should be thinking about that as much as I am. At our place we could set you up in the second bedroom. Imagine, Delilah! Plenty of time to study. And you certainly wouldn't have to wait on tables."

The problem is that June has a knack for sounding reasonable. But how can I trust her? Besides, it would be a life without the people I love in Sydney. And it would break my dad. Fleeing to Melbourne? Then I'd be no better than her.

"I'll think about it," I say, just to get her off the phone.

"Good girl," says June.

I hang up and am about to sound off to Charlie when he slips something under my nose. It's a copy of the local paper.

Local Icon Fights to Save Library

You may not know her name, but many locals will recognize Rosa Barea. She is one of the iconic flamenco dancers who nightly grace the boards at the historic tapas restaurant, Charada.

Barea, a political science student at the University of Sydney, says she is passionate about flamenco, a style of dance that connects her to her Spanish roots, but it is not the only thing that excites her passion.

"Having grown up in this community, I am invested in protecting the rights of the locals," she

134

says. "Especially those vulnerable members who depend upon the ever-dwindling resources increasingly under threat from greedy developers and money-grabbing councils."

Barea is referring to the council's recent decision to close the Glebe branch of the City of Sydney libraries and sell off the sites to Maxivelle Constructions.

Councilor Donovan Verinder says the plan will provide much needed inner-city housing. But Barea argues, "The provision of new housing should not come at the expense of public resources."

She will take her fight to the streets next month in a public rally at the Glebe library site.

On the opposite page is a picture of Rosa standing in the library forecourt in her flamenco gear, looking very passionate indeed. I run my finger along her outline.

It's almost enough to quell my anger at June.

18. LEGAL EAGLE

Marina Bitar, the McFarlane family's lawyer, knows the *Crimes Act* inside out and has the darkest brown eyes. The combination, I have to admit, is more than a little distracting. Her office may be temperature-controlled with a calming view of the harbor, but I'm still feeling the heat.

"Assault occasioning actual bodily harm," she says indifferently. "That's section fifty-nine." She clicks the mouse a few times with French-polished nails. "Maximum penalty of five years' imprisonment."

Charlie whimpers. "*Five years?*"

"Correct." Despite what she's saying, the timbre of her voice sends a pleasant shiver down my spine.

Charlie is pale, and reaches out to grab my arm. I regard him briefly but I can't help gazing back at Marina.

"This is serious, Del," Charlie whispers.

"I know."

"Then why do you have that look on your face?"

"What look? I don't have a look."

We're here because yesterday Tornbull and Stoke sauntered into the Flywheel a second time, court papers in hand. After he was back from the police station, Charlie called Marina.

"What evidence do they actually have?" Charlie asks.

Marina slides her chair back from her desk. "The victim's statement, to begin with. I'll be able to tell you more once we have the full brief and I've talked to the prosecutor. But I can tell you this." She weaves her elegant fingers together. "These charges are no laughing matter, Charles. They're alleging that you broke that man's nose."

"I didn't lay a hand on him!" Charlie lies.

Out the window, the red light at the top of the Harbour Bridge has begun to blink in the growing darkness and right now, with Charlie's future on the line, it looks suspiciously like a laser point in search of its target.

"Can't you help him?" I say keenly to Marina. "Charlie can't go to prison. He can't."

Marina looks at me, at both of us, with a serious, lawyerly stare. "There are things I can do to improve Charles's chances. And if you're prepared to plead guilty, Charles, you're entitled to a reduction of your sentence."

"But if I plead guilty I have no chance of getting off. Also, I'm not guilty," he adds quickly.

"I've seen stronger cases," Marina concedes. "The victim's evidence is weakened by the fact he's described his attacker as six three with brown hair."

"That's good, isn't it?"

Marina purses her lips. "It helps. But victim descriptions are notoriously inaccurate, so the judge is likely to take that into account. Your bigger problem is that they've placed your father's car near the scene. If you did it, pleading guilty is the best course of action, I assure you." She leans back in her chair. "You don't have to decide right now, though. Have a think about what I've told you. You can make a final decision once we've seen the whole brief."

"Okay," says Charlie, but he's frowning.

We begin to stand up.

"Not so fast. There's something else I need to ask you about," says Marina.

Please, God, let it be my plans for Saturday night.

"My fee. Are you planning to pay it yourself, Charles?" she asks with a wry smile, "or were you hoping I'd send the bill to your father?"

Charlie looks suddenly shifty.

"If so, I'm assuming he knows about all this and is happy for you to be engaging my services?" The smooth skin at the top of her nose crinkles. "Before I see you again, I need you to tell him what's happening."

19. NO MORE EXCUSES

We exit Marina Bitar's office building into a laneway near Martin Place. "Let's find somewhere to eat," I suggest. "I need to absorb all of this sitting down."

Inside a restaurant on the next block, out of the wind that's blowing a chilly path between the tall buildings, we pull up a couple of chrome chairs at a scratched chrome table. "Decor?" says Charlie as soon as we're seated, playing the game we always play when we visit other restaurants.

"One star," I say, eyeing the furniture, the bad art behind the counter, and the sign above the door written in lowercase Comic Sans font.

A waitress sashays up and parks her right hip against Charlie's shoulder. "What can I get for you, darl?" she says to him.

"An espresso, thanks," says Charlie without looking up. "And something to eat." He studies the laminated menu, which lists a range of standard pastas and a single risotto dish for variety. "What about a toasted sandwich? Vegemite and cheese?"

"It's not something we normally do, but I'll see what I can rustle up for you," she says, pressing against him. She begins to sashay away.

"Hey!" I call out.

The waitress turns around, looking genuinely surprised to discover another person at the table.

"Make that *two* toasted sandwiches with Vegemite and cheese."

"Service?" Charlie asks when she's gone.

"Zero stars," I say coolly. "I'm hoping the place you went to with Stereo Girl last night was better than this."

"Alyssa," Charlie corrects me.

"Alyssa, then. Well, was it?"

"Marginally."

"Don't be coy. I want to hear how it went."

Charlie sits back, pushing the menu away. "It was good," he says neutrally.

"That's all you've got?"

"We had a nice time. Especially afterward in the car." He grins. "I never knew the seats in those SUVs could go so far back."

The waitress comes with his coffee, pressing her palm to Charlie's spine as she puts it down.

"I'm not sure I want to see her again, though," he adds when she's gone.

I drag his coffee toward me. "Ugh, you're disgusting."

Charlie sits up. "That's a bit harsh." He tries to grab the coffee back.

"It's always about the chase for you, isn't it?" I say, holding the cup away from him. "Some backseat action if you can get it, and then onto the next one."

"Hey—she chased *me*!"

I sip at his coffee, peering at him from over the rim of the cup. "So tell me, then. What is it about *Alyssa* that makes her so unworthy of a second date?"

Charlie looks up at the ceiling and down again. "She's okay," he concedes. "Just, I don't know. A bit dull."

"In what way?"

"Pretty much every way. She spent the whole time talking about low-carb diets and how many followers she has on Instagram."

"That does sound dull." I study him thoughtfully. "Maybe it's a good thing."

"How so?"

"Well," I say slowly, "perhaps instead of focusing on a girl, for once you can focus on sorting out the rest of your life." Charlie is about to protest but I keep going. "You heard what Marina said. You have to talk to your dad. Seriously. You have to tell him everything that's happened. He's back soon, isn't he?"

"Tomorrow morning," he says, gnawing at his thumbnail.

I tip the cup against my nose and finish the coffee. "Charlie," I say, placing the empty cup back in front of him. "I really mean it this time. No more excuses. You've got to go home."

Charlie disappears for a few days after that. After a fortnight of living in each other's pockets, it feels strange not having him around. Even though business is slow enough for me to manage the Flywheel and the staff on my own and it's a relief to stretch out on my mattress again, I find myself missing him.

That's not to say I haven't had other things to think about since he's been gone. Tom's been bugging me every day to shut up shop and rent out the space to pay off our debts. Dad's already mortgaged the building to the hilt, and Tom says the sooner I can start getting some decent money coming in, the better. Otherwise we'll not only lose the cafe but the flat as well.

I can't help but think there must be a way to turn things around, but when I try to figure out what, I draw a blank.

As if to bolster the arguments in favor of closing, even the regulars have been getting on my nerves. The other day I had to kick out some uni students because they decided to turn their poker game into *strip* poker. There's nothing like a college boy in Y-fronts to put a diner off her food.

I've told Tom I won't do anything about the business until I speak to Dad, and I can't get in touch with Dad right now. All the while I keep thinking about June's proposal that I go to Melbourne to live with her and Mungo. I wish I could dismiss it entirely and just forget about it. With the business failing and Dad away, though, I'm feeling vulnerable to June's persuasions.

I think about the second bedroom at June and Mungo's place. The window looks out across the street. An old plane tree sits outside, and on windy days the baubles hanging from the closest branch knock against the glass. When I visited them at the Easter holidays, I loved lying in bed in the mornings in the quiet, watching the dappled shadows roll across the duvet.

I could probably handle a life down south.

As if I needed more things to worry about, this morning as I'm slicing haloumi for a batch of HAT sandwiches, Mandy ducks her head into the kitchen. "There's someone here to see you."

"A customer?"

"I don't think so. She wants to speak to you personally."

I'm immediately suspicious. "What does she look like?"

"About my age, wearing an old jumper and carrying a pile of books. I think one of them is an atlas?"

Oh my god. "Okay, Dallas," I tell our Thursday part-timer. "Block the door. Mandy. Can you tell her . . . I've gone on a holiday. To—um—Kangaroo Island."

Dallas squares his shoulders across the doorway. Mandy looks confused. "But I just told her you were here."

"What did you do that for?" I whisper tersely.

"How about I tell her I couldn't find you? That you must have ducked out for something?"

I nod. "You're the best. Your sandwich is on the house."

From under Dallas's armpit I peek into the cafe. Sure enough, there's Mrs. Cronenberg standing at the counter. She shifts irritably on her feet. I watch Mandy approach her. She'll know what to say to get rid of her.

Apparently not. Before Mandy has even finished speaking, Mrs. Cronenberg steps past her and heads straight toward the kitchen.

"Don't let her in, Dallas."

I race out the back door and into the lane, cursing the woman's persistence. I look around for a doorway to slip through or a Dumpster to climb into. Nothing.

Then I spy Charlie's dad's tarp-covered Mercedes.

I hear a shout from Dallas, and Mrs. Cronenberg clomping around the kitchen, calling out my name. I duck beneath the tarp and try the passenger door. Locked. I check the other doors. All locked.

"Delilah?" I hear the door from the kitchen to the laneway start to open.

I have no other option but to slide underneath the car.

It's damp and oily and smells of rotting food. I squash a pile of decomposing lettuce scraps with my right elbow and a half-eaten kabob with my left thigh.

"Del?" Mrs. Cronenberg calls again. I put my hand across my mouth to stop myself from audibly retching.

I listen to her footsteps as she walks up and down the lane. She calls my name a couple more times. I breathe slowly through my fingers, concentrating on not vomiting.

Finally I hear her walk back through the Flywheel door. I stay where I am for another few minutes, just to be sure, before crawling out and heading upstairs for a long shower.

Now I'm in a state of permanent trepidation that Mrs. Cronenberg is going to show up at the Flywheel again.

After she leaves, I'm sweeping the floor of the Flywheel when I discover a spiral-bound notebook wedged in beside one of the couch cushions. The hand-drawn picture on the cover catches my eye: a woman in a ruffled skirt, her arms outstretched, a set of castanets in each hand.

I'm not going to pretend that I don't open it or that I even hesitate before flipping the cardboard over the wire curls to see what it contains. What am I hoping to find? A journal, perhaps. A record of Rosa's deepest secrets, a key to her heart.

But what I hold in my hand is not much use to me in that respect. In fact, it's full of fairly mundane notes about the library rally.

The first few pages are a to-do list. Rosa's writing is pretty scrawly, but if I squint I can just make out what she's written.

Set date

Talk to council

~~200 posters + 500 flyers: PosterBoy~~

~~Yolanda from NW Mail—touch base re article~~

~~Set up FB page~~

Screen-print T-shirts

Uni paper ad/article?

Speak to BH re sound equip

Distribute flyers: ~~Del@FW~~, Andy, ~~Bengt~~, guy at Tempest,
   Gleebooks + other cafs

Vollies—Angeline, Joss, Solomon, Nadine, Del(?), Saxon

Reading this list and noticing that I appear on it twice has quite an effect on my pulse rate. I tell myself to calm down.

Rosa wants my help with the rally, that's all. Anyway, she's probably rethought asking me after my display of crazy the other Saturday at Charada.

But for some reason finding the notebook fills me with an insane kind of joy. It's possible Rosa's forgotten all about my meltdown. Fleeing the dance floor mid-number is probably something diners do all the time!

Before I lose my nerve, I grab my jacket and the notebook and fly out the Flywheel door.

20. LATE-NIGHT DELIVERY

Outside, the last of the lights are starting to go off in the shops and restaurants along the street. Cars and pedestrians are thinning out, and I cross the road without having to wait for traffic. When I knock on the door of Charada, nobody answers.

I cup my hands and put my face to the window. The chairs are upturned on the tables. Everything is still.

I knock for a second time and wait. No one comes.

On the inside cover of the notebook in sprawling letters is Rosa's street address. Her house is a few blocks from here. A fifteen-minute walk at most.

It's almost eleven, and therefore not a prime time to pay a house visit. Charlie and I learned that lesson only too recently. Rosa will no doubt be back at the restaurant tomorrow night, so I could easily give her the notebook then.

Just wait, I think. *Be sensible. If you show up at her door in the middle of the night she'll think you're even more of a freak.*

I congratulate myself for such sound reasoning. Then I start off down the street toward Rosa's.

I decide to take the back way through the quiet streets, away from the cars and the blink of neon and traffic lights, along the footpath past rows of narrow terraces. It is a cool night and the moon is full. I walk quickly and quietly, listening to the gentle smack of my sneakers on the asphalt, the sound of coins bouncing in my pockets, the blood beating in my veins.

I reach the gated park and follow the fence line for a couple of blocks.

The house is at the end of a cul-de-sac. It is single-storied and wide, with a cream stucco front and arched windows. It sits behind a low brick wall lined with round-edged clay tiles.

I stand in front of it, hesitant. I make an effort to comb my hair with my fingers, then look down at my clothes and instantly curse myself.

As usual, I'm covered in food and milk stains. Even the coat I'm wearing has some kind of mark on the right arm. Is that mold? I spit on my finger and try to rub off the most disgusting stains. The effect I'm creating is one of having drooled on myself. I should have changed before coming out. I shouldn't be here at all. I should go back home and give her the notebook tomorrow.

I decide on a compromise. I'll leave the notebook on the doorstep. That way she won't have to witness the appalling state of my clothes, or be reminded about my meltdown at Charada, but she'll know I made an effort for her.

I open the gate, which squeaks softly, and make my tread as light as possible down a concrete path past a row of potted plants. I climb three steps into the alcove held up by twisted columns at the front door. Slowly and carefully I place the notebook on the doormat.

Success! I make a hasty retreat.

Right into the row of potted plants.

As it turns out, the sound of terra cotta smashing on concrete has a surprising musicality, possibly due to the curve of the clay and the varying sizes of the shards.

The volume of the sound is perhaps not so surprising. A chorus of neighborhood dogs start barking. Light brightens a number of nearby windows. The door of Rosa's house cracks open, and hot sweat breaks out on the back of my neck. A small boy rubs his eyes sleepily, looking down at me, sprawled on the path amidst clumps of soil and uprooted peonies.

"Hi," I whisper, giving him a friendly wave, not wanting to alarm him.

The face vanishes. I hear the boy's feet padding hastily down the hall.

"Back to bed now," a voice says. "Go on, into your room." The crack in the door widens again and suddenly there is Rosa, filling the width of it. She is wearing pajamas and a dressing gown and has traces of makeup around her eyes.

She peers into the dark and switches on the light. "Oh!" she says, spotting me. "Del! Are you okay? Are you hurt?" She hurries over.

I can't believe this isn't even the first time in recent memory I've found myself at her feet. Once again, she offers me an outstretched hand. This time I take it.

"I brought you your notebook," I explain, brushing myself off and moving toward where it lies on the doormat.

"Oh! Thank you," she says, and picks it up. "I've been looking for this for days."

I smile, still nervous. "You left it at the Flywheel."

"That sounds about right. You're a legend for dropping it over."

"I'm sorry I broke this stuff," I say.

"It was an accident," she says lightly. "It's really nice of you. I know this is out of your way."

"It's okay. I was passing by."

This is so obviously a lie that I bite my lip and stare at a fascinating crack in the brickwork. When I look up again she gives me a curious smile. I return it. We hold each other's gaze for a moment.

A wild idea flies into my head. Maybe Rosa doesn't mind about my dancing freak-out one bit. Maybe there's a reason

151

that I'm on her list twice. Maybe the fact that she comes into the Flywheel has nothing to do with coffee. Maybe it's to do with . . . me.

Invite me in, Rosa, I want to say. *Take me into your house. Your room. Your bed.*

But instead I clear my throat. "How's the rally prep going?" I ask. I know I should leave her in peace at this time of night but I don't want to go, not yet. "I saw you in the paper."

"You did?" She seems pleased. "Pretty well. I've managed to get a lot of flyers up, plus I've set up a Facebook page. And the article got a lot of interest."

"That's great!" I try to think of something smart to say about libraries or rallies or education. I remember one of my dad's favorite Groucho Marx quotes. "My dad always says, 'Outside of a dog, a book is a man's best friend,'" I say, grinning. "'Inside of a dog, it's too dark to read.'"

Rosa beams, and it turns into a laugh. "I like that one."

I wonder if there's a greater pleasure in the world than making Rosa Barea laugh. Other than getting locked in a broom closet with her, I can't think of one. "I'm really sorry. About your potted plants, and about the—the dancing," I stammer. "At Charada."

She looks suddenly mortified, and shakes her head vigorously. "*I'm* the one who should be apologizing. It was my fault. I spun you around too hard."

"No you didn't," I assure her. "I'm kind of clumsy, as you've no doubt already noticed. And I got nervous. I had a bad dance-related experience recently, you see. I know that sounds weird—"

"It's okay. I heard about it. My cousin goes to your school, so . . . I understand."

My stomach twists in horror.

"People are really cruel, Delilah. It's nothing you should feel embarrassed about. Actually, you should be proud. I think you're really brave."

I nod at her a couple more times than I need to, not sure what to make of this comment or the earnestness in her voice. "If you need help with anything else to do with the rally, just let me know," I say.

"Really? Because I was actually going to ask you . . ." She gestures at the notebook. Something passes across her face— the realization that I have probably read her list.

I blush.

Until I notice that Rosa is also blushing. "A few of us are going down to the park on the bay tomorrow to screen-print some T-shirts. Would you . . . ?"

"I'll be there," I say quickly.

She looks relieved. "That would be amazing. Really great. We have a lot of shirts to do, and a few people pulled out today."

"No worries."

"We're meeting at nine," she says, and then she hovers in the doorway for another moment. For a crazy second I really think she's going to invite me in. "Well, good night," she says.

Damn.

"Night," I reply reluctantly.

She closes the door with a gentle click.

I stand there in the glow of the porch light for as long as I can without it being too weird. I don't want her to think I'm a stalker or anything. Then, my chest pounding like a Rushmore drumbeat, I hurry down the steps and back onto the quiet road.

21. A BEGINNING

I'm at the entrance to the park on the bay just before nine, scanning the view for Rosa Barea as I've scanned so many views before this one. It's warmer than it's been for days, so hordes of people in shorts and T-shirts are out, walking dogs, jogging, pushing strollers, or simply wandering about in groups. In a dark-green hoodie and my cafe pants I feel extremely out of place. The spring-injected pastel people probably think I'm in mourning or something. But nobody has died. If all goes well, today is not an end but a beginning.

For one, Charlie came back this morning. Just as I was trying to figure out who I could ask to mind the cafe for a few hours he loped in, dumped two heavy-looking bags on one of the couches, headed for the coffee machine, and made himself a double espresso.

"Rough couple of days?" I asked, watching him scull the black liquid down. "Did you fess up to your dad about the assault charge?"

Charlie leaned against the counter, all his weight on his forearms, and nodded.

"And?"

"He was exceedingly pissed off." He hammered the grinder's On button and roughly tamped another round of freshly ground coffee into the filter basket. "He said he *wished* he was surprised, but that he was 'beyond surprise' by now. He said he's done everything he can to give me opportunities in life and that I've thrown them all back in his face."

That was a harsh blow. "What about how you've missed so much school? That couldn't have gone down well."

"He doesn't give a shit." Charlie slammed his cup beneath the filter. "Not really. He pretends to, but he's just angry that the latest school couldn't sort me out either."

"I'm sure that's not true."

Charlie grabbed the cup and threw back the shot. He wiped his lips dry with the back of his hand. "He said if I don't plead guilty he's going to cut me off."

I stared. "Cut you off?"

"Stop my allowance, disinherit me, kick me out. Cease all correspondence," Charlie laughed sarcastically. "He can go to hell. I'm out of there, anyway. I'm staying here, with you, and we're going to sort out a way to save this place, and I'm going to earn some money and then find a flat of my own."

"He's got a point, though, Charlie. . . ."

"I'm serious, Del. I'm through with him."

"But he's your dad."

"A mere technicality," he said, falling onto a couch.

I sat down next to him. We were quiet for a while. I know Charlie well enough to know this wasn't simple anger. There was grief mixed in as well. For all her faults, I knew he was thinking, his mother would never have threatened to cut him off, but she wasn't around to have a say.

"Did you go to Minnows?" I asked him.

Most people visit the gravesites of their dearly departed if they want to feel close to them, but this has never worked for Charlie. The place where he feels his mother most strongly is in a waterfront restaurant at Watsons Bay. She spent a lot of time there wining and dining her clients and eating her way through an ocean of seafood.

"Yeah," said Charlie softly. "I did. Yesterday."

"Did they let you in this time?" The place has a pretty strict dress code. He's been denied entry before for wearing sneakers, and another time for wearing a shirt without a collar.

"Got the table in the corner. She lived at that bloody table."

I grinned. "I'm glad."

Charlie peered at me solemnly. "Del, thanks for listening," he said. "I don't know what I'd do if I didn't have you to talk to." He looked like he was about to cry.

"You'll be okay!" I said, alarmed.

Charlie jabbed roughly at his eyes. "I don't know what's wrong with me today."

"Listen. If you need to stay again for a while, that's okay. We've just got to figure out a way to get this place back in the black."

"I'll help in any way I can."

"Well, I do have this thing at the park this morning . . . "

"Oh yeah?"

"With, ah, Rosa."

He punched me playfully on the shoulder. "I'll hold the fort while you're out."

I spy Rosa's cousin Angeline first. She and a girl I don't recognize are taping newspaper to the surface of a picnic table beneath a massive fig tree. I look around for Rosa and spot her crouched next to the table, pulling things out of a plastic container.

I start down the hill toward them with a stride that I really hope looks casual.

"Hey, Del," Rosa says when I reach them, with such warmth that my heart balloons. "So glad you could make it."

She introduces me to Angeline and her friend, Joss, a girl wearing a baseball cap.

"Have you done any screen-printing before?" Joss asks.

I shake my head.

"That's okay. I can show you how," Rosa offers.

It is a beautiful day to be down by the water. The breeze has a pleasant sharpness to it that makes everything distinct: the walkers, the cyclists on the bike path, the rowing crews skimming along the bay toward the university boat sheds.

"When you're making a stencil, you have to think of everything in reverse," Rosa explains, showing me the ones they've made already. "Big block images are best. Does that make sense?"

"Sure," I say, even though I'm only half paying attention. I am distracted by her outfit (a '60s psychedelic skirt with a white T-shirt and canvas slip-ons) but what is even more distracting is the fact that we're hanging out.

I'm so busy enjoying being with her like this—like we're a part of each other's lives or something—I keep forgetting to listen to her instructions.

"Once you've made the stencil you need to tape it to the frame, like this," I hear her say.

"Uh-huh." I lean closer, ostensibly to watch her draw the tape from its roll.

"Next—staple the shirt to the wood."

"Watch it!" I move her fingers away from the jaws of the stapler, and for a brief moment it's almost as if we're holding hands.

How long has it been since I held somebody's hand?

It makes me think of Georgina. Suddenly I'm remembering the few good weeks we had before everything went pear-shaped. After we finished our English project, we kept finding ways to see each other. I'd mention to her during class that I needed her advice about what color to paint my room. Or she'd approach me in the hallway when no one was around to ask for my help with one of her History essays. Excuses like this were necessary: People like Georgina and I weren't even supposed to be friends. After school she was supposed to be shopping for fascinators and heels with the field-side girls, and I was supposed to be in a video arcade playing air hockey with Lucas and Misch, or doing extra study with Lauren.

We never spoke about it, but every time we hung out, something would end up happening between us. We'd be standing at my bedroom window, say, examining the color of the frame, deep in conversation, when the wind would blow the blind against her arm. I'd reach across to pull it up and she'd turn toward me. Then we'd be kissing.

One Saturday, we made an almond cake in her parents' kitchen. It took us hours, because every time her mother left the room Georgina's hand would find mine. She'd wait for my smile, then prod me into the corner against the fridge and press herself against me. We'd kiss like that, our hands exploring beneath the bench, until we heard her mother's heels again on the slate floor of the hallway.

"Every T-shirt needs this stencil on the back," Rosa explains, showing me one with a "Save Our Library" slogan. "But you can put anything on the front as long as it's book-themed. We've got some paper and pencils if you want to draw your own design. Otherwise you can use one of Angeline's."

I flip through the stack of stencils. "Wow, these are really good."

Angeline shrugs shyly. "I like to draw."

"She's being modest," Rosa says, nudging me. "She's been winning art prizes for years."

"I'll try one of my own, but if it doesn't work I'd love to use one of yours," I tell Angeline.

"What are you going to draw?" Rosa asks.

"A girl reading a book. If you'll model for me, that is."
Am I flirting with Rosa Barea?

She laughs. "Where do you want me?"

I resist articulating any of the dozen suggestive responses that fly into my head, and instead direct her toward the bottom of the fig tree.

Drawing Rosa gives me the perfect excuse to study her face. It's crazy how different people appear when you get the chance to look at them properly. Occasionally our eyes fix upon each other, before I look down again at the paper.

It takes me five minutes to realize that the drawing is a disaster.

"Show me."

I protest, but she tears it out of my hands. She looks at it for a moment and then at me. "This is terrible," she says, bursting into laughter. "Let's get you one of Ange's."

"I guess I draw as badly as I dance. How come Angeline gets to be good at both? It's not fair."

"This family is too talented for words," Joss agrees.

"If only we weren't," says Angeline, looking knowingly at Rosa.

"What do you mean?" I ask.

Angeline and Rosa exchange glances. "We've just been doing it for a long time, that's all," says Rosa. "Sometimes it gets . . ."

"Tedious. Repetitive. Boring," Angeline fills in.

"Oh," I say, looking from one to the other. "But you're so good at it! And your article in the paper, Rosa, about the rally—even there you said how passionate you were about flamenco."

Rosa looks uncomfortable. "I used to be. I mean, I am. It's part of our family history. But we do it a lot, Del. Six nights a week—"

"For ten years!" Angeline cries.

"Then why not give it up?"

"Because it means so much to Mum and Dad," says Angeline. That would be Rosa's aunt and uncle, Adelina and Elvio.

"And it helps drum up business," Rosa adds.

"So you'd rather have another job?"

"I'd rather be studying for uni. And doing this," Rosa says, smiling. "Speaking of which, let's get you set up."

She holds out her hand. And with hope in my heart, I take it.

22. CRISIS TALKS

This afternoon we're having crisis talks at the Flywheel. I've invited Mandy, Tom, my school friends, and the least stoned-looking member of the backpacker clientele, a Californian named Buck, and I'm closing the doors for an hour in order to hatch a grand plan to save the cafe. If recent average sales are any indicator, an hour's closure will lose us the business of approximately one-third of a customer, amounting to a cost of $2.60. I'm hoping it'll be worth it.

The big news is that Rosa has agreed to come as well. When I asked her about it this morning at the park she looked pleased. She warned me that she didn't know how helpful she'd be, but I told her the more heads I could get together, the better.

Now everybody I'm expecting has arrived except for her. I wonder what's holding her up. Maybe she felt obliged to say yes but has no intention of making an appearance. Or maybe I am paranoid.

Our powwow is taking place near the cake counter so that sustenance is only an arm's length away. Charlie has made coffee for everybody, and I'm hoping that the combination of sugar and caffeine will stimulate positive ideas.

My hopes may well be dashed. About five minutes ago Mandy abruptly started bawling into a handkerchief, and I cajoled her into the kitchen in an attempt to sort her out. "What's this about? That ex of yours still giving you trouble?" I ask, hands on my hips.

Mandy's mascara has left black streaks all the way to her chin. "He's seeing someone else," she says, voice cracking.

"How do you know?"

"I saw them together yesterday, shopping for bath toys."

"Bath toys? How old is she? Four?"

A brief grin. "She did look young."

I try and get her eyes to meet mine. "He's not worth it. You know that, right? You're terrific. If he can't see it then he's an idiot."

"But I love him. What am I going to do about that?" Her eyes fill with tears again.

"What you're going to do is be sad for a while," I tell her. "You'll feel sorry for yourself every time you watch a romantic movie or see some dumb couple kissing on the street. And then, in time, you'll start feeling better. And that's when all those guys who've been waiting for you to get over the dickhead who dumped you will start coming out of the woodwork. And Mandy, one of them is going to be right for you. And you're going to fall in love with him, and then you'll make him the happiest, luckiest man in the world."

Mandy sniffles into her handkerchief. "Thanks, Del. That's good advice." She pauses. "If it can happen to me it can happen to you, too, you know."

I feel my face going red. "Maybe," I say quietly. But where is Rosa?

We rejoin the circle. It looks sort of like the Weight Watchers meetings June used to go to, except with a wacky points system given that Tom, Charlie, and Buck are each on to their third piece of cake. Charlie has equipped himself with paper and pen and is writing things down between forkfuls.

"What have you come up with so far?" I ask.

"Charlie, read Del the list," Misch demands, picking up her Margaret Atwood book from the chair beside her so I can sit down.

Charlie clears his throat and flicks back his floppy hair.

You know what that means.

"Now, Del," Charlie begins gravely. "We all know the Flywheel is hemorrhaging customers right now. Never has a business been doing well one minute and the next minute—"

"The list, Charlie," says Misch.

"Right you are. We thought it would be a good idea to start by making a list of positives about this cafe and then a list of things that could be improved, because how often in our lives do we get the chance to sit down and take stock, like a king contemplating his—"

"Just read out the list," Tom snaps.

"Don't worry about them, Charlie. Take your time," Lauren says, pressing a hand on his arm.

Charlie smiles at her gratefully. "*List of positives*," he reads from a sheet of paper. "*One: Wi-Fi. Two: food. And three: opening hours.*"

"That's a good start," I say. "What else?"

"That's . . . the whole list."

I look at Tom, who stares at me blankly, and at Misch and Lauren, who shrug in sync. I turn to look at Lucas, who grins sheepishly, and Buck, who is busy clipping his fingernails with the scissors of his Swiss Army knife. "You only came up with three positives?"

"So far," says Charlie at the same time Buck chimes in with, "You betcha, honey," and a piece of his fingernail flies into the air, landing on the table.

I swipe it off in disgust. "What's on the list of improvements, then?"

Charlie looks at the list. "Prices. Decor. Music. Hygiene. Service . . ."

"Hang on, hang on," I say, snatching the list from Charlie. "Music? What's that about? I play great music!"

"Your music *sucks*," says Buck.

"If you think I'm going to start playing crappy chart music—"

"Hell, play Dolly Parton if you have to," Buck says, "and mix her in with Patti Smith if you like, but enough already with the Rushmore!" He pushes back his chair and makes his way to the door. "All right. That's my great idea. I'm going back to the hostel to pick up a Norwegian."

"Well, a fat lot of help you were!" I shout after him. "With an emphasis on the fat! I hope you enjoyed the whole cake you just ate!"

"A perfect segue to the next point," Lauren says as the cowbell rattles violently. "Angry staff."

"Angry customers, more like it," I grunt.

There is silence. I realize that everyone is looking at me. "What?"

"*You* are the angry staff, girlfriend," Misch says.

"I'm not angry," I say. "Or hardly ever, anyway. I never raise my voice. I'm cheery and fun!" I add weakly.

"You raise your voice all the time," says Misch.

"Like when?" I demand loudly.

"When Hamish was working here, you pretty much shouted at him every day," Misch says.

"Well, who could blame me? The guy was a thief and a liar."

"And you snap at the part-timers all the time," Lauren adds. "Not to mention the customers."

"I heard you scream at a group of students the other night—" says Lucas.

"They were *in their Y-fronts.*"

"You shout at Charlie in the kitchen, too," says Mandy.

"And you're screaming now—" says Charlie.

"Enough! I admit it, okay? I get angry! Who doesn't!" I shout. "But you have to understand—"

"Um, hi. Is it too late to join in?"

We turn in our chairs. Rosa is standing by the door. My anger turns to nerves at the sight of her.

"Hi!" I say meekly.

"I'm so sorry. I meant to be here earlier but I got caught up," Rosa says, straightening her psychedelic skirt.

"We're just getting started," I say, quickly brushing the corners of my lips in case of cake crumbs. "Come in, come in!" I furiously brush down my apron and pat the chair vacated by Buck.

Lauren and Misch look at Rosa and me. Then they look at each other.

I quickly introduce everybody.

"Bus stop is the next item on the list," says Tom impatiently.

"Bus stop," I repeat dumbly. God, Rosa's hair smells incredible. Whatever shampoo she uses should win international awards.

"Right," Mandy says. "I've heard the backpackers complain about having trouble getting from here to the tourist attractions."

"It's easy enough to catch a bus into the city."

"It's Bondi they want to go to," Mandy says.

"Then offer transportation," says Tom. "A shuttle from the cafe to Bondi."

"Sounds expensive," I say.

"Can I interrupt?" says Rosa. "I don't know what you've already discussed. For my two cents, obviously improving your service and amenities is really important. But I wondered if you'd thought about other angles."

We look at Rosa blankly.

"Your biggest problem," Rosa continues, "is the franchise down the road, Crunch. It's backed by a huge corporation. You need to tackle it head-on."

I'm nodding slowly. "What do you reckon would work?"

"A strategic campaign," says Rosa, looking cunning. "One that emphasizes you as a local family business and paints Crunch as a fat-cat imposter on the strip."

Everyone's looking at each other uncertainly.

"It sounds pretty negative," Charlie says.

"It has to be," Rosa says simply. "Or you're going to lose the cafe. I'm sorry to be this blunt about it, but any other view is naive."

Charlie's face turns dark. Uh-oh. I recognize that look. Last time I saw it was just before he broke a man's nose.

"How about I promise to have a think about it?" I tell Rosa hastily, and something like dismay passes briefly across her face. "Thanks, everybody. These are all great ideas. Let's call it a day. Now, can I get you anything before you go, Rosa? A coffee, perhaps?"

"One of those sandwiches would be great," she says, pointing to a prewrapped baguette in the display cabinet. "Thanks, Del," she adds warmly.

"No problem."

I look beneath the counter for a paper bag for her sandwich. The cowbell clanks and the door opens mysteriously, as if by itself. A very short person with a shock of black hair has stuck his head through.

It's Rosa's little brother. "Rosa," he sings in his sweet, high voice. "Come over to the restaurant."

Rosa looks at me and rolls her eyes. "Coming, Franco," she calls to him, digging into a pocket for coins.

"Quickly," Franco sings back, as I slip the sandwich into the bag. "Your boyfriend's there."

That's when I stop moving.

The word is like a punch to the head: a punch of the Charlie McFarlane variety, which leaves you bleeding, broken, and willing to press assault charges.

Rosa has a boyfriend.

Why has this possibility never occurred to me before?

I pass her the bag numbly.

"He means Ramon," Rosa says, looking embarrassed.

Ramon, who she dances with in Flamenco Hour? "Oh. I thought Ramon was your cousin."

"He's not my cousin, exactly. He's—"

"It's fine, it's none of my business," I say hastily, waving her away, knowing now the precise depths of my stupidity. I saw them myself the night we went to Charada: Rosa and Ramon dancing so beautifully together. Of course! I was so distracted by Charlie and Rosa dancing that it barely even registered. But now that I think about it, the two of them never broke each other's gaze. I think again of all the rehearsal hours they must have spent together. It makes perfect sense. It's been in front of my eyes this whole time. I've been a complete fool.

Rosa hesitates, paper bag in hand.

"Go, I don't want to hold you up," I insist, short of breath. "Enjoy your sandwich."

Lauren comes up beside me, watching Rosa go. "She seems nice." Her voice sounds stilted, as if she's speaking in a foreign language. She doesn't meet my eye. "What was her name again?"

"I'm really busy right now." I grab a cloth and start wiping down the counter.

Lauren looks disappointed. But she doesn't know what disappointment is. Disappointment is watching Rosa Barea walk through the door and out of my life forever.

23. THE BLACK WAVE

At five o'clock I take a long walk down the cafe strip, past the pub on the corner and the ivy-scarred sandstone church. My heart beats madly as I go, a sad reflection of my fitness level as well as my emotional state. Cars roll blithely past.

Oh, Rosa.

Is it possible to feel the loss of somebody you've never even been with?

So she came to my meeting. As if that means anything. So she let me draw a picture of her underneath a tree.

I am such an idiot.

I sit in the park for a while to calm myself down. I understand how pathetic I am, being torn apart because a girl I like has a boyfriend.

After half an hour I walk home along the winding roads beside the water, past the endless terrace houses, and back to the main road.

It's when I turn the corner that I know for certain I'm on the leeward side of Lady Luck's benevolence today.

Because there outside the Flywheel, a pile of books against her chest, stands Georgina Trump, cute as a cupcake, her skin as pale as milk.

I feel an impulsive stab of yearning, followed by a wave of grief, which is quickly extinguished by anger. I remind myself that although she is pink of cheek and blonde of hair, she is black of heart.

I consider darting back around the corner and returning later. But who knows the depths of Georgina's patience? She might choose to stand there all day. Besides, when your fortune is taking a tumble, I figure there's nothing to do but ride out the black wave.

I approach cautiously, and am gratified to see she looks nervous. When I've almost reached her she rearranges her face, very carefully, into a smile.

"What are you doing here?" I ask her, making sure to keep my mouth fixed in a line.

She nods at the books she's holding. "Mrs. Cronenberg asked me to bring these over?"

"Why?"

"Because you've been missing school and she doesn't want you to get behind?"

I briefly found this habit of hers—turning statements into questions—kind of cute. That time has passed.

"I've dropped out. I'm not going back," I say, glaring. This is not something I have actually decided until now. Hearing the words hit the air like that, though, witnessing the firm shape of them, makes me sure.

"Oh," she says awkwardly. "Well, can you take them anyway? Mrs. Cronenberg made it really clear I had to give them to you. She says you're, like, really interested in Southeast Asia?"

I peek at the spines. One is about civil war in Burma. Another is about ethnic groups in Laos. I wonder if there's a chapter on the Arem people, but I push the thought aside. I'm not about to be won over by Mrs. C.

After the name-calling started last term, it was Mrs. Cronenberg's job as year eleven coordinator to counsel me about it. She poured us both a cup of coffee and I sat in the comfy chair in her office gripping the hot mug so tightly that it burned. I wished I were numb to it. Those days, I wanted to be numb all over. Maybe that way the Georgina-sized hole in my heart would stop aching. I could forget about her and move on.

I was glad it was Mrs. Cronenberg they made me talk to. I liked her more than any of the other teachers. She treated us like adults. If we failed to do our homework she didn't throw tantrums or hand out detentions. We were old enough, she said, to choose whether we wanted to do well or not. I never said anything to her about liking her class, but she gave me the odd article or paper "in case I was interested." I respected her, and she understood me. Or so I thought.

She sat across from me that day and watched me sip my coffee. "I'm sorry this has happened," she said.

I wanted to cry right then, my chest was tight with it, but I held it in.

"I guess you've talked to Georgina," I said.

Mrs. Cronenberg nodded.

"What did she say?"

A look crossed her face like she was deciding whether to tell me something. "That you had feelings for her and wouldn't accept that she didn't feel the same way about you," she said eventually. "So you kept showing up at her house."

I turned a sob into a snort. "She's lying."

Mrs. Cronenberg studied me.

I gripped the mug tighter. "She's lying," I said again. "Stuff happened between us, and it was her . . . doing . . . as much as mine."

It was important that she believed me. I needed her on my side.

"It's clear to me that something happened with Georgina that meant a lot to you," she said slowly. "I'm just wondering, Delilah . . ." Here she paused, as if contemplating an interesting dilemma in class, like whether New Zealand would do better to invest in sheep farming or coal mining. "Perhaps you should think about the possibility that you misread the situation."

I laughed.

"How can you be so sure you didn't?" she persisted, her careful gaze still fixed on my face. "You're a smart girl. You're comfortable with who you are. You have a fearlessness I greatly admire. But not everyone is like you. Not a lot of teenagers are so self-assured. Some are more . . . easily led . . . than others."

She was saying I'd pressured Georgina into the whole thing. I thought about Georgina standing behind me in her kitchen, running her fingers along my arm as I sifted flour into a bowl. I thought about her lips on my neck.

I thought Mrs. Cronenberg could go to hell.

So I slammed down my mug and walked out.

"Why did she send *you*?" I press her.

I'm pleased to see that the question makes her uncomfortable—she glances over her shoulder in the direction of the cafe door. That's when I notice Chief Bitch Ella loitering on the other side of it, slurping a Flywheel triple choc milkshake.

I glower in her direction and Ella glowers back.

Georgina looks flushed. "She wanted me to tell you . . . personally . . . that you should come back to school? That everybody's forgotten about—*you know*," she mutters.

"Yeah, right," I say, my face burning. "And anyway, what's any of that got to do with it?"

"How would I know?" she says back.

I can't work out what angers me more: the fact that she's assuming my dropping out has something to do with her, the fact that my dropping out doesn't have nothing to do with her, or the fact that she's pretending not to know that I love Southeast Asia. The last day we spent together was during the frickin' Southeast Asian film festival, when I'd talked her into coming with me to see a film about Cambodia!

When she'd finally agreed, I was ecstatic. It was the first time we were actually going out, *in public*, rather than just sneaking about behind closed doors in our own houses.

I don't remember much about the film. What I do remember is the taste of chocolate orange in her mouth. I remember her lips on my neck, and my intake of breath as she reached beneath my shirt.

When we came out of the Dendy I took her hand. After two hours of messing around in the dark of the cinema, I felt we had progressed to at least this. But Georgina snatched it away. "Are you crazy?" she whispered, and shoved both her hands into the pockets of her jeans.

The next day I saw her in the hallway at break talking with Clare Ando and Sophie Murray. I usually avoided the field-side girls, even since Georgina and I had become close. I never approached her at school. But after her sudden coolness the night before I wanted to make sure things were all right between us. All I needed was a look from her, a smile.

I started down the corridor toward them. But she immediately began walking in the other direction, Clare and Sophie trailing behind her.

At lunchtime I wrote her a note. Ella saw me slipping it into her locker.

"What are you up to?" she asked me suspiciously.

"Leaving something for Georgina."

She quirked her perfectly shaped eyebrows. "What makes you think Georgina would want to get anything from *you?*"

The field-side girls were always coming out with this type of remark, as if anyone who wasn't a part of their group was worthless. "Is that a serious question?" I asked, with probably more venom than usual. I knew how Georgina felt about me.

Ella's eyes narrowed. "It's sweet that you two bonded over your little papier-mâché project," she said. "But that's over now. Georgina doesn't want to be actual *friends* with you."

"Then why does she keep inviting me over to her house?" I said impulsively.

"You have got to be joking." And I could tell from her expression that she genuinely thought I was.

"We happen to really like each other," I said into her ridiculously symmetrical face. "Quite a lot, in fact."

For a second she looked unsure. Then she laughed. "We'll see what Georgina has to say about that." She turned on her heels.

Twenty-four hours later, I was a pariah.

Outside the Flywheel, on a day turning out to be one of the worst in modern history, Georgina purses her shimmery lips. "You're not still upset about that video? It was a joke, that's all."

"And how hilarious it was."

She flicks a strand of hair off her shoulders with a finger. "Whatever." As she hands me the pile of books she brushes her hand against mine. I register the heat of her skin. "There's some stuff in that pile from Ms. Shanker and Mr. Hammer too."

I stare at her as she hands them over, and for a moment the real Georgina looks back at me, radiating uncertainty. Then Ella steps out of the cafe and Georgina's eyes glaze over. It's like a television changing channels.

Ella blinks, unaccustomed to the light, as most vampires are, and tosses her hair back. "Ready?"

Georgina steps away from me quickly. "Well, bye!" she says airily.

They start off up the street.

When they're halfway to the end of the block, Ella turns around. "You could've thanked her at least," she calls out.

"What for? The public humiliation? Or the lousy snogs?"

Georgina's face falls and for a moment, remembering how I once cared for her, I feel bad.

But only for a moment.

"Lezzo loser," Ella sneers, and the two of them crack up.

Oh, how I want this crappy day to be over.

24. THE TROUBLE WITH VODKA

Something weird just happened between Charlie and me. Something very weird.

Let me explain.

After Georgina and her evil twin left, I had semi-imagined an evening spent indulging my misery with candles, my Rushmore *Unplugged* album, and a long hot bath. Instead I got very drunk with Charlie. We closed up the shop and went upstairs, me with misery in my heart, Charlie with a six-pack of vodka mixers, two cleanskins of red wine, and a longneck of beer in his arms. (Charlie being eighteen might be bad in terms of being eligible for adult prison, but it does have its advantages.)

Side by side on the bed, I tried to distract myself with Charlie's court case. "Have you thought any more about what Marina and your dad have said? About pleading guilty?"

Charlie fell back against the pillows. "I don't want a criminal record hanging over me."

"So you're going to lie? Under oath?" I asked, taking a swig of vodka.

"You make it sound so dramatic. I doubt it will come to that." He plucked a joint from his shirt pocket and lit it.

"Charlie, you did it. I saw you do it. They're going to be able to prove you did it. I can't see how it won't come to that. Why don't you just make it easier on yourself and admit it from the start?"

"You worry too much," Charlie replied.

It wasn't until after my third vodka and a few tokes on the joint that I gave up trying to get Charlie to change his plea and let him bring up my failed love life. That's when things began to get weird.

"What you have to remember," Charlie said, "is that the sea is big, and that there are plenty of fish." He wiggled his fingers to demonstrate the vast number of fish. But when he spread out his hands to demonstrate how big the sea was, he knocked the lamp off the bedside table.

The room plunged into darkness so I could only hear the bulb smash into a zillion pieces on the floor.

"Least of my problems," I said, dismissing the smashed lamp with a wave of my hand—the one holding the joint. I felt a trail of ash scatter across my knees. "Here." I held out a candle. "Light this. The sea might be big for *you*, and the fish plentiful for *you*, Mr. Straighty-One-Eighty. But for me we're talking about a significantly smaller body of water. Like . . . ever seen one of those plastic clam-shaped things that toddlers splash about in?"

"I think so. I'm not sure this is possible."

"Yeah, that's what I'm saying to you."

"I mean, lighting a candle with a spliff."

I felt around and tossed a box of matches at Charlie, hitting him in the chest. He managed to light the candle and placed it on the bedside table. The room was flickering and shaking in its dim glow.

Charlie took another toke and looked thoughtful. "I'm pretty sure Rosa likes you, Del," he said.

"I know she likes me. But I want her to *like* me, you know?"

"Maybe she does. How do you know if you haven't asked her?"

"She has a boyfriend. A *Spanish* boyfriend. With an accent and olive skin and a cute Spanish way of lisping every time he says 'Barcelona.'"

"Ramon doesn't have a Spanish accent. He was born here."

"Whatever! It doesn't matter! They're going out!"

"I still reckon she's into you."

I unscrewed one of the bottles of red and slopped it into two glasses.

"I've seen the way she looks at you," Charlie continued. "Which makes sense. You're very, you know . . ." He looked away.

"What?"

"Don't make me say it again."

"Oh. That I'm cute and have okay legs but bad shoes?"

"That's not what I said."

"I quote: 'You should retire those shoes.'"

"Who gives a shit about your shoes?" said Charlie earnestly. "I'm talking about the way you smile with your whole face: your dimples, your eyes. And when you tie your hair back from your face, these wispy bits sit on your neck—"

What the hell was he going on about?

Charlie stopped abruptly. "I'm just saying, she'd be crazy not to like you," he said quickly. "Hey, Del . . ."

"What? Why are you giving me that funny stare?"

"Never mind."

"No, go on. Say it, whatever it is. I'm pretty sure I can promise I won't remember it tomorrow."

"I was just wondering, that's all."

"About what?" I asked, feeling my gulp of wine run warmly down my throat.

"It's okay."

"It will only be okay if you spit it out. Come on."

"I was just wondering how you, you know, *know*."

"Know what?"

"You know."

"No. I don't."

"That you're into chicks," Charlie said. He took a long swill.

The question surprised me. "What do you mean? I've always known. Just like you've always known, I guess. I fall in love with girls. It's what I do. When I get crushes, they're on girls. When I fantasize about being with someone, it's with some beautiful girl. Same as you."

"But how do you know you got it right?"

"I used to have my doubts," I confessed, downing the rest of my glass. "I mean, it's not exactly encouraged so I've definitely questioned it."

"So when did you become sure?"

I shrugged. "It might sound stupid, after all she's put me through, but it was when I kissed Georgina."

"That's fucked up. She totally screwed you over."

"I know. But despite how much of a cow she's been, at the time we were . . . crazy for each other. And it was electric. Like a massive lightning storm passing through my body."

Charlie swallowed the rest of his wine and handed me his glass for a refill. "Have you ever wondered, though, what it would be like with a guy?"

"Are you serious?"

"I'm just saying, don't knock it till you've tried it." He grinned, but I could tell he was feeling awkward.

I held Charlie's glass in one hand and the wine bottle in the other. "What you're actually saying is that gay people have to try out straight sex before they know how they feel, but it doesn't work the other way around."

"That's not what I meant—"

"Have *you* ever done anything with a guy, Charlie? You should try it sometime. It might change your life," I said, pushing his shoulder with my shoulder. It was enough to make Charlie lose his balance. He fell off the bed, tipping the candle over on his way down.

"Ouch!" I heard him slam against the carpet and the sound of crunching glass.

I crawled across the mattress and peered over. He was lying on the floor in the fetal position, a red glow dancing across his face. "The glass. I'm cut," he said, wincing.

I, however, was more interested in the dancing red glow. The candle had rolled across the carpet and set fire to an overhanging bedsheet.

In a panic I grabbed the nearest bottle—the wine—and poured it on the flames.

The room plunged into darkness for a second time.

Silence, except for the sound of Charlie panting. The air reeked of red wine and ash. I slipped off the bed and hit the overhead light switch.

"Holy shit," I murmured as things came into view.

It was total carnage. The sheets were charred and stained with red wine. Wax was splattered across the bedside table. I could see shards of light bulb jutting out of both of Charlie's arms. Gingerly he crawled back onto the bed.

"Let me get the first-aid kit." I got it from the kitchen and sat back down on the bed next to Charlie, rifling beneath the bandages for some tweezers. Charlie gave me his left arm first and, focusing very hard on not fainting, I picked out three decent-sized pieces of glass. It was not an easy job given the state we were in, and I accidentally nipped his skin with the tweezers, making him wince. "Sorry."

"I'm sorry, too," Charlie said quickly. "About what I said before about you considering being with a guy. It was a joke. But it was out of line."

"I'm sorry I pushed you off the bed."

"I deserved it."

To show him I forgave him I mussed his hair playfully. His breath tickled my wrist. He squeezed my arm lightly and then tapped his fingers along it, like he was playing keys on a piano. Then I reached out and gave his cheek a brief stroke.

Now, it is important to remember at this point how drunk I was. I was very drunk. I don't really drink, and by this stage I'd had a serious amount of vodka and wine and no dinner. With all the alcohol and the joint it was surprising

I hadn't puked yet. I probably would have, had I not partially sobered up at the whole shattered glass and leaping flames fiasco.

But instead of puking, or passing out, or anything else vaguely sensible, what I did was this: I straddled Charlie's waist and kissed him on the lips.

I won't bore you with the details of what happened next. In summary:

Having Charlie's tongue in my mouth was like sucking on a worm.

Cheek stubble is scratchier than it looks.

Giving someone a hickey is an objectively hilarious thing to attempt. It's like being a vacuum cleaner for human skin. Why have I never noticed this before?

Charlie's bra-undoing skills are an inspiration.

In fact, he's pretty good with his fingers all around. But closing your eyes and trying to imagine that the person attempting to get you off (i.e., Charlie) is somebody else entirely (i.e., Rosa) only works up to a certain point.

A point that is reached pretty quickly in circumstances where the overhead light is on, you're busting for the loo, and the other person winces in pain every time you touch them.

After fifteen minutes we'd given up.

I was nowhere near drunk enough for this.

"I think there's still glass in my arm," said Charlie with an exaggerated wince as I let go of his shirt.

"The tweezers are on the desk," I replied, removing my other hand from his pants and searching quickly for my clothes.

"I'm kind of exhausted, actually," Charlie said, redoing his buttons hurriedly.

"And I've got a big day tomorrow helping out with the library rally." I snatched my bra from the pillow and turned away.

Charlie nodded vigorously. "Which means I'm holding the fort downstairs. I should definitely get some sleep."

"You can have this side," I patted the far side of the mattress. "I'll sleep all the way over here."

It's now after midnight. Charlie is snoring, the room stinks like a pub, and I wish Rosa was here. I drift toward sleep thinking about her, and looking forward to seeing her tomorrow.

25. TO SAVE A LIBRARY

It's a glorious day for a rally. The sun is out, the air is mild, and the only clouds are a couple of wispy white ones so high up that they're barely noticeable against the blue. It's almost enough to take my mind off my splitting hangover and the cringeworthy memory of what Charlie and I got up to last night. I look around the library courtyard and try to guess how many people have shown up. I reckon at least two hundred are crowded in between the library's two wings, all of them facing the makeshift stage.

My phone chimes with a message from Misch. *How are you going with saving the FW? Can I help?? School: I'm over it. XX*

Just then I see Rosa bent over a pile of flyers next to the stage with a number of empty donation buckets at her feet. I put my phone away. She's looking generally fabulous in jeans, sneakers, and one of the bright red rally T-shirts we screen-printed, emblazoned with the words *Save Our Library*. The sight of her fills me with confusion, though. Now that I know about her and Ramon, it's like an empty feeling spreads across the pleased part, threatening to cancel out the positive effect altogether.

"Del, fantastic! So glad you could make it. Joss is sick and can't come, and two of the other vollies haven't showed up either. I was going spare."

"No worries," I say casually, my heart thumping despite myself.

She passes me a bucket. "You have no idea how much it means to me that you're here."

I head back through the crowd, trying to quell my elation about what she's said, silently calling myself all manner of obnoxious names. I'd be a fool to read into Rosa's gratitude. Hope is a pathway to disaster. I decide that in order to retain what's left of my sanity I must make an effort to get over her. I compose a mental list of what's required:

Face facts.

Stop reading things into her every ordinary word.

Stop daydreaming about kissing her.

Stop fantasizing about her publicly confessing her undying love for me.

Stop loitering around Charada.

Stop watching Flamenco Hour.

⁓

Applause starts up in the crowd. I turn toward the stage and Rosa is there, microphone in hand.

"Could I please have your attention, everybody," Rosa says. "I have one quick thing to say before the speeches start. It's to a particular person in the crowd today, but it's something I'd like to announce publicly." She looks into the crowd and finds my eyes. "I love you undyingly, Delilah Woolwich-Green," she says, and the crowd cheers madly. "Now get up here so I can show you exactly how I feel."

Yeah, right.

Keeping to that list might be more difficult than I thought.

What Rosa actually says into the mike is that she is thrilled that so many people have come today. "As many of you will know, I was born and raised in this suburb. My family runs a local business. I attended one of our excellent local high schools. I go to the local university. I've always been proud that we are a community that looks out for each other—and, in particular, one that makes an effort to provide for those who are less fortunate."

A round of applause starts up in the crowd. Rosa waits (what an expert) until it dies down.

"The proposed closure of our library is an attack on our community values."

A number of people in the crowd whoop.

"It's an attack on our kids," Rosa continues. "On our elderly. This council's decision to sell off library land is greedy, and grubby, and strips community resources from those who need them most."

Most of the crowd is cheering and clapping now. Instead of throwing myself at her feet in worship, as is my inclination, I begin to roam among people with my bucket, pleased by the number of people who throw in coins and even bills.

Onstage Rosa runs through the list of speakers, which includes a member of parliament, a representative from a local retirement village, and an ex-councilor. Finally, she introduces the first speaker and sits down at the end of a row of chairs behind the mike stand.

Toward the back of the crowd I spot Rosa's aunt and uncle, Adelina and Elvio, who run Charada. It's been years since I've actually spoken with either of them, but we always smile at each other on the street. When I was a kid, Elvio used to bring over leftovers from the restaurant, the chorizo in particular, because he knew how much I loved it.

After the second speech finishes I end up in their part of the crowd. Adelina, who is a small woman with green eyes and a bun of gray hair, pulls me to her elbow without a word. I lean across Adelina to smile at Elvio. He waves back. Adelina pats my hand with her soft, plump fingers. "You have come to support Rosa, no?"

"Yes."

"You two are special friends."

This does not appear to be a question. "Ah, I guess so," I say, wishing it were truer.

"Look," says Adelina.

Onstage Rosa has taken the microphone again. She thanks the speakers and begins to run through a list of other thank yous.

"And a big thank you to Del from the Flywheel for helping with flyer distribution, screen-printing, and collecting donations. Where is she?" Rosa shades her eyes with a hand and surveys the crowd.

Adelina waves at Rosa and points at me.

"Thanks, Del!" Rosa says into the mike. "I encourage you all," she says, addressing the crowd now, "to support local business and visit the Flywheel this week. It's the best cafe in the neighborhood by a country mile."

I am possibly in love with this woman.

So much for my Get Over Rosa list.

26. THE FACTORY

Imagine my delight to find that since Rosa's rally speech, business at the Flywheel begins to turn around. My favorite flamenco dancer is apparently also a sorceress.

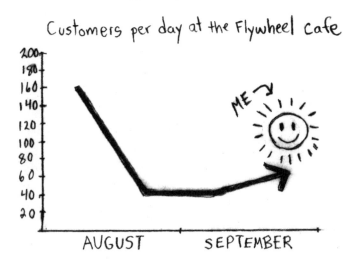

The other thing that's helped is Tom's suggestion of a daily shuttle service between the Flywheel and Bondi. It came into being after I was looking out my bedroom window the other day and noticed Charlie's dad's Merc still parked in the back lane, its tarp flapping lazily in the breeze.

It hit me like a flash. What could be better? For ten dollars you get to ride with the charming Charlie McFarlane as chauffeur. For fifteen you get a takeaway breakfast thrown into the deal. Who wouldn't sign up?

And so far things are going excellently. It means I've got to cover Charlie's kitchen shifts, but our backpacker clientele—especially of the female variety—has ballooned. Morning coffee and cake sales have doubled in a fortnight. What's more, yesterday, when dropping off a load at Bondi, guess who Charlie ran into?

As he was pulling up outside the pavilion with his carload of sunburned Brits, Alyssa stuck her head through the front passenger window. And yes, he said, she had a *Stereo* magazine tucked predictably under one arm.

"She seemed really pleased to see me," said Charlie. He looked shocked.

"That *is* kind of surprising, given you blew her off after one date. Did she give you the latest on low-carb diets?"

"No. As a matter of fact, she asked me whether I wanted to go to this." He held up a listing for Saturday's Local Line-Up night at the Factory. I was pretty familiar with it: Rushmore was second-billed.

I wasn't sure about this Alyssa girl, but to see that Charlie was increasing his relationship concentration span was encouraging. So I said, "That's perfect. You can come with me and Lauren."

"Lauren's going?"

"Yep. It'll be fun. If Alyssa turns out to be boring again, there's still the music. And you can always hang out with us."

So it is that at eight o'clock on Saturday night I find myself standing in a queue a block long on a street in Marrickville with Charlie and Lauren, wedged between a pair of thirty-somethings wearing goatees and trilbies and a bunch of giggling groupie wannabes in short skirts and heels. It's raining. Hard. I huddle against Charlie's back, holding a damp Factory brochure optimistically over my head. Yellow dye runs down my face and along my arms. Strange as it might seem, jaundice-chic was not the look I was going for tonight. In my trusty cafe blacks and Dad's old leather jacket, I was simply aiming to blend in.

Lauren is chatting to a guy from school who's here with some people I don't recognize. His name is Saxon, he's in her Maths class, and I know she thinks he's cute. Also, he has an umbrella.

Saxon doesn't acknowledge me, which is fine by me. It's not as if we've ever had a class together. It's also possible he has no idea who I am and that the term "dancing dyke" means nothing to him, which is even better.

"Here," Charlie says, passing me his hip flask.

I take a deep swig and swallow. The liquid burns at my throat. "Jeez. That is a strong mix."

"No mix," says Charlie through the strands of wet hair sticking to his face. "That's straight gin. I need a favor."

"So you thought you'd get me toasted first?"

"I've made up my mind about the court case. I'm going to plead not guilty," he says, very guiltily. "I know you think it's the wrong decision, but it's what I've decided. If you're willing to give evidence to say I didn't do it—"

"*That's* the favor?" I hiss. "To lie for you in court?"

"It won't be a *big* lie. We'll admit we were in the area taking a late-night drive. That will explain Dad's car. We'll just leave out the part where we knocked on the door of number thirty-four Faraday Avenue."

"And the part where you punched somebody, I suppose."

"Obviously we'll leave out that part."

"So what were we doing there?" I ask him, sarcastically. "Simply cruising around?"

"Searching for a quiet street to park and, you know." Charlie wiggles his eyebrows suggestively.

"Oh, that's just terrific," I snort. "Because that scenario turned out well when we tried it in real life."

"At least I've got the evidence to prove it happened if I need to. I can tell them about that birthmark on your—"

"This is how you try to win me over?" I interrupt him. "By promising to tell an open court what I look like naked?"

"It's my best chance," Charlie pleads. "Surely you don't want me to go to prison."

"If emotional blackmail was a crime, Charlie McFarlane . . ."

He pats my hand delicately. "I'll give you some time to think about it."

It's like he thinks it's no big deal.

The crowd offers a welcome distraction from Charlie's insanity. Beside me the groupie wannabes are shifting and jostling in the rain, legs tanned and smooth, bums encased in clingy cloth. No doubt they're here for the other bands. It is sad but true that the more likely Rushmore fans are the freaks in trilbies.

"No, no, no, no. *Victor Took a Trip* is far more consciously innovative than *Steamy Anemic,*" says Freak #1 to Freak #2.

Rushmore's second and third albums. How sadly right I am.

Finally the queue begins to move.

I'm seventeen and officially shouldn't be allowed into this gig, but I get in easily because I'm with Charlie, who gives the girl at the door a wink and a smile so dazzling she suffers momentary blindness. Blinking, unseeing, at my ID, she stamps our wrists with a pink Minnie Mouse and waves the three of us through.

We head straight to the bar. I snatch a pile of napkins and begin patting myself down with them in a lame attempt to get dry. Tiny bits of napkin come off all over my black pants and shirt. Wonderful. I now look like a lamington. Charlie orders us two beers each to save us from lining up later. I take one from him gratefully and gulp at it, and the fuzziness in my head from the gin intensifies.

Saxon comes up to Lauren. "We've got a spot near the stage if you want to stand with us."

"It's okay," Lauren says. "I should stay with my friends."

"Are you sure?" he asks, smiling.

She looks flattered but uncertain.

"Don't worry about us," I say. "We'll catch up with you later."

Lauren glances over at Charlie, paying for our drinks at the bar. "Tell Charlie I said bye," she says, then follows Saxon through the crowd.

The first act is a singer-songwriter from Redfern. As he starts to play, people begin to crowd at the front. Rushmore isn't on for another hour, but given the number of people still spilling through the door I wonder if we should also try to grab a spot farther forward.

"Lauren's gone down the front with some people from school," I tell him.

"Oh. Just like that?"

"We could try and join them if you like."

Charlie looks around for Alyssa as we edge sideways through the crowd, but there's no sign of her. Instead, to my great dismay, in a group loitering at the right of the stage is Adrian Hibbert from Crunch.

Before I can turn and sprint in the opposite direction, he flutters his hand in the air and pushes through the crowd toward us. "Hello there!" he cries, leaning in to kiss my cheek, lips puckered.

I reel back in horror right into Charlie, but not fast enough. Adrian plants his wet lips right on my skin and I almost lapse into unconsciousness at the overpowering scent of his aftershave.

"Nice tie," Charlie says. Tonight's beauty is emblazoned with miniature yellow trumpets on a navy background. Could not be lamer.

"Thank you!" Adrian beams. "I thought it suited the occasion. I suppose I have a bit of news to 'trumpet' tonight as well."

Inside my head I groan loudly. I think how well the Flywheel has been doing. What with Rosa's recommendation at the library rally and our Bondi shuttle, I wouldn't be surprised if some of our new customers had made the switch from Crunch. "You haven't found things have been a bit slow this week?" I ask, doing my best to keep my tone casual.

"We have seen a bit of a downturn, yes," admits Adrian with a suspicious amount of magnanimity. "But I'm pleased to report we've come up with a foolproof plan to turn things around. It was Hamish's idea, actually. He's convinced me to turn Crunch into a music venue as well as a cafe. He's a real asset. It's why we're here tonight, in fact—to celebrate."

"I wouldn't have thought you'd have enough space for that," I say, frowning.

"We're figuring something out," he says mysteriously. He swivels to indicate the group standing behind him, which includes Hamish Creel in his full dreadlocked glory, gesturing with his bottle of beer at an unfortunate girl to whom I intend to send a condolence card tomorrow.

I mumble an excuse, grab Charlie's hand and pull him away. We weave in and out of the crowd until I'm satisfied we've put enough emo kids between us and Adrian to ensure our safety. Given that most of them are on the puny side, this takes some doing. But now that we're in a decent spot, I'm reluctant to move. "Change of plan. How about instead of trying to find Alyssa, we wait for her to find us?"

"How about you mind our spot here, and I go and look for her myself?" says Charlie. "And if I see Lauren I'll tell her where you are."

I shrug like being abandoned at a concert by both my companions is no big deal, but Charlie's already taken off.

It turns out the singer-songwriter from Redfern has another six songs to go. Standing between two die-hards in jeans and tour T-shirts mouthing every word, I watch him belt out his tunes under the hot lights until his brown woolen vest is damp with sweat and his bushranger beard has wilted. When he's finally finished, the techs take off various pieces of equipment. Ten minutes later they're bringing different bits back on.

I begin to wonder where Charlie and Lauren are. Has Charlie found Alyssa? Has Lauren decided to stay with Saxon and his friends for the whole show? I haven't seen either of them for at least forty minutes. I stand on my tiptoes and peer across the top of the crowd.

A couple of guys come on to check the mikes and tune the guitars. Aaron Jarvis, lead singer and bassist of Rushmore, momentarily ducks his head out from behind the curtain, and a group at the front screams immediately. Excitement instantly fizzes in my stomach.

But still no sign of Charlie or Lauren.

Damien Kite, drummer and backup vocalist, steps onstage. More clapping. Jade Roth, lead guitarist, follows him out. She mucks about with her plugs and cords while Alice Wang and Leith Crouch, keyboardist and guitarist, wander on.

The applause of the crowd is gaining momentum. God, I love this band. I know from previous shows that any minute now Aaron will stride onstage clutching his bass, and that's when the show will begin.

I look around for my friends again. I wish at least one of them was here to sing along with me. It doesn't matter that I've seen the band live before. Every time is special.

Too late: Here comes Aaron, waving at the crowd. He belts out the first lines of "Movie About Your Life," and the crowd explodes.

It's my favorite of all their songs. And despite this, or maybe because of it—or because of the year I've had with school and the Flywheel, or because my friends have abandoned me in a crowd of happy noisy people—at the sound of Aaron's sweet, soulful voice soaring above the guitars, I begin to cry. I don't want to and I don't mean to, but there in the middle of the Factory I'm suddenly bawling.

I wipe my face with the back of my hand.

Jade Roth plays a high and solitary chord on her guitar.

I close my eyes and begin to dance.

I dance for the whole song, shifting my arms and head in time to the beat. For six and a half minutes, feeling lightheaded and boozy, I don't care what I look like. There's nothing to care about but the music. I dance the way I dance in my bedroom with the door closed. I dance as if Georgina never made that stupid video. I dance and sway and let myself be swept away.

The song ends. I sense someone watching me.

I open my eyes.

27. ROCKABILLY RAVISHED

Rosa Barea. She looks ravishing in a polka-dot top, black skirt, and white tights. Her hair is coiffed at the front and slicked back into a ponytail. Her lipstick is cherry red.

"How long have you been here?" I ask her, horrified.

"A while." But she doesn't say it in a teasing way, as if I should be embarrassed.

"Um. I didn't know you liked Rushmore."

She shakes her head. "I don't."

"Okay, so what are you doing here?"

"Hoping to run into you."

I stare at her. "Really?"

She smiles nervously. What is actually happening? Am I just drunk? "Is Ramon here as well?" I can't help but ask.

She nods. "And Angeline. We just finished up at the restaurant. They're parking the car."

"Right." Of course she's here with Ramon.

Jade Roth plays the opening chords of "Light Years Away." The crowd around us starts dancing to the music again. Rosa squeezes up next to me, facing the stage. This song is a boppy one, and Rosa bumps her hip against mine in time with the beat.

"Come on," she calls over the noise of the guitars and drums. "You love this music."

To oblige her I bump her back a couple of times, but now I'm hopelessly out of rhythm. She laughs and slips an arm around my waist to guide me. How am I supposed to concentrate on the rhythm now? She keeps her arm around me even when the song has ended.

The next song has fewer drums, a slower beat. Rosa slips her other arm around my front. She holds me like that for the entire song and I quietly go crazy. Part of me is pretty sure that something's happening between us, but how could that be right when I know she's with Ramon?

"Where do you think Ramon got to?" I ask lightly when the song ends.

Rosa lets me go abruptly. "Come outside with me where we can talk. It's too loud in here."

We get drinks at the bar and walk out together. I want to be back on the dance floor with Rosa's arms around me, but it's too late now. I wish I'd never asked about Ramon.

When we get outside it's only just stopped raining. The courtyard is cold and there's nowhere dry to sit. Finally we find a low wall under a dripping awning to perch on. There are about fifteen other people from the gig out here, smoking and chatting, but we sit a little way away from them.

"I hope it's okay I've dragged you away from the set," Rosa says. She sounds apologetic.

"It's fine. I've seen them, like, heaps of times before," I say, trying to be upbeat.

"Rushmore is your favorite band, I know."

"I play them too much at the cafe, don't I? Apparently I'm driving away customers." I laugh nervously. I'm jabbering. I don't want to be talking about any of this.

"That's ridiculous." She shuffles a few inches closer. "Have you thought any more about what I said? About tackling Crunch head-on?"

"To be honest, I haven't needed to," I babble on. "The plug you gave us at the rally on Saturday has really helped. That was so lovely of you. Although I just saw the Crunch guys back there, and it seems they've got some plan to turn things around. We've just got to keep up the momentum we have going now until Dad gets back."

Rosa looks like she wants to say something, but she stops herself.

"What is it?" I insist.

"It's just that . . ." She pauses uncertainly.

"Go on."

"I just wonder whether you should be doing it. Spending all your time looking after the cafe."

"What do you mean?" I ask, surprised. "I don't really have a choice right now."

"Are you sure about that?"

I frown. "I don't understand."

She studies me for a moment and then shakes her head. "Sorry. It's none of my business. I only ask because I know what it's like to be relied on by your family when you'd rather be doing other things with your life."

"The dancing?"

She nods.

"At least you get to do it with your boyfriend," I can't help but say.

"Del. I need to tell you something." Her voice sounds different.

"What is it?"

"I think you got the wrong impression the other day. About me and Ramon."

A lump forms in my throat: a lump that is one part embarrassment and two parts hope.

"He's not my boyfriend. We're just dance partners, nothing else."

"Your little brother seems to think you're more than that," I say. My heart is beating so fast.

"I know." Rosa shakes her head. "It's what I've let him think. And everyone: Elvio, Adelina, my parents. Ramon goes along with it because it's what our families want—for each of us to marry a good Spanish Catholic." She rolls her eyes. "It's hard to make them see how unreasonable that is. Ramon's girlfriend is Jewish, so pretending there's something between us is a good cover for him as well. But I wanted you to know the truth." She fumbles for my hand. "Because . . . I really like you, Del."

Oh god. "Really?"

"Yes, really. You're . . . gorgeous." She looks away, turning red.

I stare at her. My face feels as hot as hers looks. "You think so?"

She nods.

"You don't think I have short legs?"

She shakes her head, laughing.

I try to take it in. I am sitting in a courtyard with Rosa holding my hand and telling me I'm gorgeous.

"I mean, I'm pretty sure my torso is the length of a normal person's torso," I say in a rush. "When I sit down I'm as tall as everyone else sitting down, but when I stand up it's a whole different stor—"

"Del. Please stop," Rosa says with a hint of desperation, squeezing my hand. "I don't care about any of that."

And then she leans in and kisses me slowly on the mouth.

She smells of her shampoo and her lips are soft. I grab her wrist and pull her closer, my hand shaking. She lets me, and moves toward me, and opens her mouth onto mine.

I am kissing Rosa Barea, and it is incredible.

At first I'm aware of everything: the taste of her breath, the sound of our lips, the heat of her skin. The blood pounds in my ears like an ocean. Rosa presses her shoulder into mine and a sound escapes the back of her throat. I shiver. Then the details fall away and all I'm aware of is how much I want her.

Here. Now. Her hands on my waist. Her tongue in my mouth.

I lean in further.

I hear a snigger from behind us and the world rushes back. My blood turns cold. Rosa hears it, too. We pull away from each other.

"Getting a bit of fresh air, are we, ladies?" says Hamish Creel.

His dreads are in a jagged pile on top of his head. He's swinging his beer bottle by the neck between two fingers and grinning lewdly.

"Fuck off, Hamish," I tell him. I feel barely in control of my voice.

"Now, now," he says. "That's no way to speak to an old friend."

I give him a withering look.

He keeps grinning, refusing to move. I drop Rosa's hand and stand up. "You heard me. Fuck off."

"I was just being sociable," Hamish protests, backing away a couple of steps. "Which is pretty nice of me considering the unfair dismissal claim I could bring against you. But I'm willing to forgive all if you let me stay and watch you two. Oh, hang on." He looks behind me and around the courtyard, exaggerating his concern. "Where's your girlfriend gone?"

I turn to Rosa, but she's not there.

"Show's over," says Hamish with false disappointment.

I resist, with difficulty, the urge to wrench one of his dreadlocks out by its roots.

I look around the courtyard. Where the hell did she go so quickly? I don't see her anywhere. "I mean it, Hamish. Can you please fuck off?" But I'm faking my bravado now.

"Suit yourself," Hamish says. "But don't think I've forgotten how you screwed me over. You deserve everything that's coming to you. And believe me—it's coming." He saunters away.

I can't think about him right now. I have to find Rosa. She probably has a perfectly reasonable explanation for abandoning me. Food poisoning, perhaps. A sudden bout of diarrhea. I eventually find her around the corner near the outdoor bar.

"What happened to you?"

She looks upset.

"What is it?" I ask in a rush of worry, reaching for her.

She pulls away. "Hamish," she says, glancing about.

I look at her in surprise. "What about Hamish?"

"He might tell Adrian, and Adrian knows my uncle. They're on a small-business owners' committee together."

I stare at her. "*That's* why you bailed?"

She looks at me as if it's obvious. "I can't let my uncle find out about this."

"This? You mean, you and me?"

Hearing my resentment, Rosa gives me a pleading look. "Yes. This is all new to me, Del. Please."

I can tell she is trying hard not to cry, but my disappointment eats away at the warmth I've been feeling. This is Rosa Barea, defender of the young, the elderly, and the poor; the woman who is taking on the council single-handedly. And yet she won't stand up to a creep like Hamish Creel?

"Clearly you're not okay with this," I say, my chest thudding. "So why bother coming on to me in the first place?"

Rosa hugs herself with both arms. "You don't understand how difficult this is for me. It's easier for you."

Is she serious? I think of Georgina pulling away from me outside the cinema. I think of Ella's laughter. I remember Mark Wellington swinging me around the corridor at school. "Is that what you really believe?"

Rosa peers nervously around. "Keep your voice down. People are looking. Try to be mature about this—"

"I'm not mature enough for you, now?" I say, deliberately loud.

"You have more experience with this stuff than me, Del," hisses Rosa. "That's all I'm trying to—"

But I'm no longer listening. "Well I'm sorry that you don't think I could possibly understand. I won't bother you again."

"Del—" Rosa makes a grab for my arm but I push her away. I'm gone.

28. THE COFFEE MACHINE TELLS THE TRUTH

This morning the coffee machine is making a horrible groaning sound. I switch it off, wait a while, and switch it on again.

Idiot, it groans. *Idiot. Idiot. Idiot.*

What were you thinking, Delilah? Why are you even surprised? Why did you imagine that Rosa Barea would be any better than Georgina? Because she looks hot in a flamenco skirt, is that it? Because the sway of her hips makes your insides quiver?

I just never imagined Rosa would be like this. I want someone who is proud to be with me, someone who won't turn on me the moment anyone finds out we're together.

"*Here* you are!" Charlie says, far too cheerily, sliding a serving tray onto the counter. "I wondered whether we'd be seeing you before lunchtime."

"You should have woken me an hour ago."

"Don't worry, everything's under control."

A glance around proves Charlie is actually telling the truth. Breakfast customers fill most of the tables and a swarm of backpackers inhabits the couches. Most people have food in front of them. The Sunday part-timers are darting about taking orders like professional waitstaff. Charlie follows my gaze proudly. He's enjoyed taking charge. I try to remember the last time I felt as proud about the Flywheel as Charlie looks right now. It's amazing, and I wish I could care. But today my overwhelming feeling is weariness.

"What happened to you last night?" I ask. "I searched the whole Factory for you."

"Sorry about that," Charlie says, trying to conceal a smile.

My phone chimes. It's Misch. *Girlfriend! Long time no speak. What's happening with you?? XX*

I forgot she'd written last night too. I owe her a call. But I just can't deal with it right now. I slide my phone into my back pocket.

"You found Stereo Girl?" I ask Charlie.

He hesitates.

"Well, did you?"

"You could say that."

"And?"

"I ended up having a great time."

"That's fantastic. Are you going to see her again?"

"Maybe. Possibly," he says cagily. "I'm sorry I abandoned you." He does look genuinely sorry, despite the obvious joy that's radiating from his pores. "Did you end up having an okay night?"

I think about kissing Rosa, and the thrill of her lips.

I think about Hamish, and Rosa abandoning me.

"It was fine," I tell him, which, when I average it out, seems a fair representation of events. "I . . . ran into Rosa."

His eyes widen. "And?"

I give him a brief rundown. He whoops delightedly when I tell him about the kiss. Then I tell him about running into Hamish and about Rosa's sudden disappearance and his face falls. I finish with her lame explanation for abandoning me at the scene.

"Lame? That's a bit harsh," Charlie says.

"Oh, come on. I have encountered many types of lame in my time. Her explanation sits squarely within the range."

"Surely what she did isn't as bad as posting footage of you shaking your groove thang around a cafe kitchen?" he asks cautiously.

"Maybe not as bad, but definitely on the same scale."

"There goes your habit of putting things on the same scale that should not be on the same scale. Rosa not wanting her family to know she's into girls just yet is a long way from someone publicly humiliating you on the Internet." He pauses. "Del, I hate to change the topic because I think we need to explore this further, but remember last night I asked you for a favor?"

I purse my lips. "A court-related favor? Yes, I remember."

"Have you thought about it?" He pushes his hair back nervously.

I shelve my anger about Rosa for a moment to consider again what it would mean to lie in court for Charlie. I remember what Charlie means to me. He's not the love of my life and never will be. But I do love him, and I can always depend on him to be in my corner—more than Lauren, who lately wants to argue with me rather than support me; more than Dad, who isn't even here; certainly more than Rosa.

Then I remember the horror of watching Charlie punch a guy in the face, and part of me thinks he deserves to be punished for what he did.

"Sorry, Charlie. I can't do it."

"Del, you're my only chance," he pleads.

"I'm not the one who got you into this mess. And if you think you're going to get away with it just because I give some shonky evidence, you're crazy."

"I can't believe this," Charlie says bitterly. "I was sure you'd say yes."

The cowbell crashes against glass, loud enough to interrupt our argument. Charlie and I look around. At the sight of flapping dreads, every muscle in my body tightens.

"What the hell are you doing here?" I ask Hamish Creel.

He is holding a stack of postcards. He fixes me with a triumphant gaze. "Delivering on a promise," he replies, pivoting away from me, a literal spring in his step. "Hey, mate," he says to a backpacker lounging on one of our couches. "I've got an offer for you. The deets are all here." He hands him a postcard.

I rush forward. "You can't do that. This is private property. No soliciting allowed!"

But Hamish ignores me and hands out the stack of cards. The backpackers are already passing them around and reading them with interest.

Hamish turns back to me, gloating, clearly enjoying my outrage. The nerve of the guy, stealing customers from under my nose! No doubt it's a revenge fantasy he's been dreaming up for weeks.

"Out," I order him. My pointing finger is trembling. He shrugs and obeys, grinning. The damage has already been done and he knows it. The backpackers are on their feet and following Hamish en masse.

"Hey!" Charlie calls out to them. "I've got orders up for you guys! And you haven't paid for them yet!"

"Better deal down the road," one of them calls back, shrugging an apology.

"Hang on." I dance beside the doorway. "I'm sure we can work something out."

"Good luck with that. Have you seen what he's offering?" a backpacker says, handing me a card.

I skim it and freeze. Hurriedly I shove the card into my pocket. "You'll be back tomorrow, though, yeah?" I ask the backpacker, hating the whimper in my tone.

"Maybe," he replies, eyes sliding away from mine quickly.

It's robbery, plain and simple. What's worse, it took barely minutes to execute. I watch the cafe's future crumble to the sound of scraping chairs and a clanging cowbell.

Within seconds, the couches are bare.

The following day confirms it. When we go down for opening, no one's waiting outside. No one shows up all morning. It's so damn quiet you can hear the cakes in the cabinet going stale.

Hamish Creel may have struck the final blow.

29. COMFORT FOOD

I've always said that nothing brightens the spirits like a Flywheel caramel milkshake made with fresh milk, caramel syrup, and a generous dollop of panna cotta gelato. So sure am I of this fact that I've written it in capital letters in the margins of all the menus. It is therefore with embarrassment, as well as a sense of gloom, that I confess Charlie and I have just had three apiece and feel no better than we did before.

Actually, we feel worse.

"I don't think having that many in a row was a good idea," Charlie says gingerly.

Today's paper lies open on the table. I study the two-page *Good Living* spread again. In an oversized photo, Adrian

Hibbert stands before the Crunch shopfront wearing a red tie covered in miniature croissants (seriously) and gesturing toward a shiny new minibus. INNER-CITY CAFE ATTRACTS NEW CUSTOMERS WITH BEACH SHUTTLE, says the headline.

How they can afford it I haven't a clue, but there's no way we can compete with their ten-dollar beach and brekkie combo.

I push my glass aside. "I am actually going to choke him with my bare hands. That was *our* idea."

"Where should I put these chairs?" Charlie asks.

"Kitchen," I reply.

Out on the street the shop lights are coming on. The dinner crowd is milling on the footpaths on their way to other places. It's eerie to watch from the silence of the empty Flywheel, where Charlie and I, between milkshakes, have been sorting and packing.

Now that the backpackers, our main client base, have defected to Crunch, the Flywheel is "no longer a viable business prospect," according to Tom. He made that very clear, switching his voice distinctly from Monotone to Stern.

I told him we'd have to wait for Dad to get back before making any big decisions.

"There's no time for that," said Tom. "Can you call him? E-mail him?"

"Not for another couple of weeks."

"Then we're going to have to do what we should have done weeks ago."

"Which is what, exactly?"

"Close the Flywheel."

I'm carefully pulling the maps of the world off the wall behind the counter. I can't bear to throw them away, so I place them in a box instead, along with the order pads, sugar canisters, salt shakers, and pepper grinders. It's hard to get a good working rhythm going. We keep finding ourselves standing still, staring blankly into the gloom: at the couches beneath the window, the secondhand chairs, the Marx Brothers stencil—all of which will have to be sold or boxed up or painted over.

It was Dad's idea to name the cafe the Flywheel. He was inspired by one of his favorite Groucho Marx characters, Wolf J. Flywheel, a detective from a movie called *The Big Store*. As you'd expect, the film itself is full of great puns and madcap chases. But despite how crazy things get in Marx Brothers films, they always end well, usually with a big song-and-dance number. I guess Dad hoped naming the place the Flywheel would serve as a good omen.

"Don't worry," Charlie says, reading my expression. "We'll find a way to save this place."

I heave out a chest full of breath. "What was Dad thinking, leaving me in charge of all this?"

"He left Dominic in charge," Charlie corrects me. "And you talked him into it. Where should I put this poster?"

"Storeroom," I say without looking.

"Really? Don't you want it upstairs? I've always loved this poster."

The poster Charlie is holding is the promo poster for an obscure late-'60s comedy called *Skidoo*, in which Groucho cameos as a mob boss called God. It features a close-up of a woman's torso from just above her waist to her mid-thighs. Her stomach is bare and the fly of her corduroy pants is partly undone to reveal the smooth skin of her lower belly. It's pretty sexy, but it does little to cheer me up. "It's a farce," I say bitterly.

"Isn't every Groucho Marx movie?"

"I'm referring to my *life*. My life with *Dad*."

Charlie gives me a look like I'm being melodramatic, but I mean it. I'm thinking about how for seventeen years I've watched Dad bumble along like the silver screen clowns he so admires, not knowing his beak from his bum and dragging me along with him. He should just give in completely, start carrying around a honking horn and wearing oversized pants. "You know what I wish at times like this?"

"What?" Charlie asks, cautious all of a sudden.

"I wish . . ." I pause, feeling guilty before the words have even left my mouth.

"Spit it out."

"I wish that it was Dad who went to Melbourne," I say quietly. "You know? And that Mum had stayed instead."

Charlie stares at me like a bunch of daisies has just sprouted out of my nose.

"She might be crazy, but in some ways she's actually got it together," I continue, convincing even myself. "She and

Mungo have a comfortable life. She knew she'd never get that with Dad. *She* could see how hopeless he was. Why couldn't I?" I begin to cry.

"Come on, Del," Charlie says gently. "Your dad's great. He loves you for who you are. He knows you can handle things without him. He has enormous faith in you."

"Look at where that got us." I gesture at the empty room.

"What's happened with the cafe is not your fault. If it wasn't for Dominic running that red light—"

I shake my head. "I can't cook. I'm hopeless with money. How could I have been so deluded to think I could actually run this place?"

"You don't mean that," Charlie says. "You're just saying that because things are hard right now—"

"I should never have left school."

"School's overrated. Take it from me," Charlie scoffs. "I'd far prefer to be running the Flywheel. All schools care about is making sure you toe the bloody line. They don't even care if you learn anything. And you don't need that."

"That's easy for you to say."

"Why?"

"Because your family's loaded."

"What's that got to do with anything?" His tone has shifted. I've hit a nerve.

I frown at him as I swipe aluminum trays into a box. "Whether or not you finish school means nothing. Even if you screw around with your education, you can do anything, *have* anything you want." I'm getting worked up now. "In fact, maybe that's your problem, Charlie—you've been given too many chances."

"Oh yeah?" Charlie says, fully indignant now.

"Yeah. It doesn't matter how many times you screw up, because your dad will always bail you out. He's paid for the best lawyer, just like he pays for the best tutors, and just like he'll introduce you to all the best people so that you can get the best jobs. If I screw up, what have I got? What has my father got? If we can't sort out the Flywheel, we won't even have a place to live!"

"Jeez, Del, that's a bit harsh. I told you what my dad said last time we spoke," Charlie says, turning red. "He threatened to disinherit me. And I can't imagine that a criminal conviction is going to look very good on my résumé. Things aren't so bad for you. If you don't want to run the cafe then go to Melbourne and live with your mum, who you miss so much—"

"So I'm supposed to just walk out of my life, am I? Give up everything and everyone I care about?" I drop the box and kick it into a corner.

"You're only seventeen, Del," Charlie says. He's lost all patience. "Leaving Sydney for a few years is not going to make the sky fall in. Maybe it will even do you some good— have you ever thought of that?"

"Do me good?" I snort. "Well, it makes sense you'd say that. Abandoning people is second nature to you. You flit from one girl to the next. You fall in and out of love as often as most people change their underwear." I consider him for a moment. "You know the thing I liked most about you when we first met?" I ask.

"My charisma? My wit? My good looks?"

I smile thinly. "It was how passionate you were. You gave me your 'World History Is Full of War' speech and I thought—this is a guy who *cares* about things. About peace, for starters. About stamping out violence." I laugh. "What a joke that turned out to be."

"What do *you* know about passion, Delilah?" says Charlie, fed up. "You've been obsessed with Rosa for months, and then you get a chance to make a go of things with her and you chicken out!"

"Were you even listening when I told you what happened at the Factory? Me chickening out was not part of the story."

"Sure it was. Rosa laid her heart on the line. She told you exactly how she felt about you. And what did you do? You got all worked up about her not coming out to her family three minutes after you'd kissed. You chickened out rather than telling her how you feel about her."

"Oh, come on. If she's going to freak out about being with a girl, what's the point?"

Charlie sighs and gives me a look like I'm being a total sook. "Look," he says. "I get it. You're scared. Georgina burned you, so now you won't take a chance with anyone else. But just because you got screwed over once doesn't mean it will happen again. It sounds like Rosa's got a lot of family stuff to deal with—stuff you don't have to worry about with your dad. I'm just saying there are a lot of reasons why things might play out differently this time. Tell Rosa how you feel, Del! You never did that with Georgina, and maybe that was part of the problem. Why not talk to her about it?"

"It's not worth it."

"You're unbelievable. You accuse me of being a hypocrite, but at least I *act* upon my feelings, rather than sitting around and doing nothing. At least I fight for the ones I love."

"Yeah, for two seconds, and it generally involves breaking a couple of bones. Is it your dead mother complex, Charlie? Is that what makes you so hopeless when it comes to women?"

The darkened look on Charlie's face tells me I've gone too far.

"Oh god, I'm sorry," I say quickly.

He gets up from his chair.

"I shouldn't have said that. Come on."

A wry smile twists Charlie's face. "You know," he says bitterly, "I didn't understand loyalty for a long time. Sure, my family's loaded, but they've never been around. Not even Mum." His voice cracks. "I feel closer to her now when I go to Minnows than I ever did while she was alive. How pathetic is that?" He pushes his hair back roughly. "Your dad would come back from overseas in a second if he knew you needed him. *My* dad has spent nine months of every year overseas for *fifteen years*, and no amount of begging on my part has changed that. I've always envied you because you have a father who loves you and encourages you and who you're friends with. I never had that," says Charlie, brown eyes blazing. "And I thought I *had* shown loyalty to one person, though. Someone who I thought would stand up for me in return, like if I was facing jail time, for example. Someone I could trust not to accuse me of having a *dead mother complex*." He gives me a meaningful look. "But it looks like my loyalty was misplaced."

He marches to the door and wrenches it open. The cowbell rattles its hollow chime.

I kick the table leg and the table skids across the floor with a satisfying squeak. Bloody Charlie. Sure, I went a bit far bringing his mom into it, but he'll be back. He'll do a round trip via Catarina's for a couple of flat chicken burgers and return with dinner for both of us.

I sit waiting in the dark for half an hour.

He'll regret saying those things, and if he doesn't I'll bloody well make him regret it. He can't expect me to lie under oath for him. And how dare he accuse me of being scared to be with Rosa?

The room feels incredibly empty. I sit down at one of the tables and sob into a paper serviette. I feel better after a good cry, but hungry. In fact, I find I've worked up quite an appetite. I could really go for a flat chicken burger right about now.

Half an hour becomes an hour: long enough for me to think that perhaps there's a citywide flat chicken burger shortage.

My phone rings. It's about bloody time.

No name comes up but I recognize the number. Mrs. Cronenberg. Arghh.

I let it go to voice mail and then check the message.

"Delilah, it's Jane Cronenberg again. I'm calling to let you know that I've managed to track down your mother in Melbourne. I'm planning to call her to discuss your absence from school. I wanted to let you know to give you a chance to talk to her beforehand. Anyway, I hope you're well."

What is the woman's problem? June is going to have a fit! And what's my response going to be? That quitting school was totally worth it? That the Flywheel is raking it in?

I close my eyes. I feel a headache coming on.

It's nine o'clock.

Where's Charlie?

30. ACTING OUT

With the help of one of the part-timers, I finish packing up the cafe on Tuesday. On Friday Mandy assists with the final clean. I mop the floors while she scrubs the skirting boards.

"What's Charlie up to today?" she asks. "I thought he'd be here."

"He had something on," I say vaguely.

Mandy catches my eye but says nothing.

"Okay, we had a fight," I confess.

"Oh Del. I'm sorry," she says. "What was it about? Unless that's prying," she adds quickly.

I slap the soaked mop against the floor. "Not at all. It was about what a spoiled brat he is."

"Oh?"

"You know what he told me? That I shouldn't bother going back to school, even now that the Flywheel's toast."

"I'm sure he was trying to—"

"His problem is he has no idea what it's like to need an education in order to earn a living. Making a living by Charlie's standards is lounging poolside while the hired help brings out hors d'oeuvres on a tray. If he cared, he'd be honest about what a mess I made of things. Anyone could see how crap I was at running the cafe."

"You're *not* crap, Del—"

"A real friend would have pointed out to me that I'd be better off staying in school."

"Someone like Lauren, you mean?" Mandy asks. "Hasn't she been doing just that?"

I mop vigorously at a sugar stain. "Believe me, Lauren has her own agenda. She's under pressure from her parents to get into law, so she puts her obsession with school and good marks onto everyone around her."

Mandy dips her brush into the bowl of soapy water carefully. "But isn't that what you're angry with Charlie for not caring about enough?"

"You know, Mandy, I'm so angry that I'd rather not talk about it. I wish you hadn't brought it up. Can we please change the topic to something else?"

So we chat about the new assistant at her physiotherapy practice until Tom slips through the doorway, a manila folder under his arm. I lean my mop against the wall, and Mandy gets up from the floor. Tom opens his folder and hands me the papers inside.

It's a rental application. "You found someone already?"

I know I should be grateful. A tenant who pays rent is exactly what we need. Even so, I can't quite believe things have come to this. Trying to picture another business in the shop that my family has run for so many years is painful. I can't imagine what it will be like to live above a place that's not my own cafe. I suppose I imagined I'd find a way out of this mess before it reached this point.

"Who are the tenants?" I ask.

"Another cafe," Tom says.

"That makes sense. The space is set up for it. Anyone we know?"

A peculiar sound comes out of Tom's mouth—something between a cough and the squawk of a dying bird. I look at him sharply.

"Tom, are you okay?" Mandy asks with concern.

But Tom has his lips pressed so tightly shut you'd think the air had been flooded with poison.

I flip through the pages of the application and let out a wail. "Oh, no. No, no, no."

"It makes no sense," says Mandy, looking over my shoulder. "Why would Adrian Hibbert want to rent the Flywheel when he's already got a cafe down the road?"

"Because the space they have down there is too small," I explain. "Especially when you have plans to turn your cafe into a music venue, complete with dance floor. I can't do this," I tell Tom.

"I think you should," he says.

"We're not renting out the Flywheel to Adrian Hibbert."

"I think . . ." Tom begins.

"What?" I demand.

". . . that you're being a bit, ah, melodramatic. Under the circumstances—"

"I hardly think it's melodramatic to get upset about my rival blatantly basking in my tragedy—"

"Okay, can everyone please calm down for a minute?" Mandy pleads.

"The rent he's offering is better than any offer you're going to get," Tom continues. "It's a three-year lease, and he's willing to pay double the usual down payment, which is the only way you're going to settle your current debt."

"Unless we reopen the Flywheel and come up with a strategy to . . . to . . ."

"You've tried that already, Del," Mandy says gently.

My head is pounding. So Hamish will finally have his revenge. He stole from my till, screwed with my orders, took my customers and now my premises. He's landed a music venue and settled his score with me in a single bound. "But I'd have to pass them every day on the way upstairs to the flat. Hamish's smirk and Adrian's smarm! And listen to Hamish's crap music through the floorboards . . ."

"It's up to you," Tom says. "We won't be able to formalize things until your father gets back, of course, but they're interested in moving in as soon as possible."

But suddenly I wonder why I'm fighting this. Tom is right. It makes perfect sense to rent out the Flywheel. Why am I so resistant when running the place has become such a nightmare?

I think about the room in Melbourne June has promised me, the one with the plane tree outside the window. It would mean time to study, a fresh start.

Right now, the Flywheel is the only thing keeping me in Sydney. What else is there to stick around for? I don't want to go back to this school. It's clear I've been wasting my time with Rosa. Charlie's had enough of me, and Lauren is driving me crazy.

"Let's do it, I guess," I say at last.

Mandy grips my arm. "Del, you don't have to decide right now."

"You've got till, well, tomorrow morning," Tom says.

"Tom," Mandy says in warning.

He looks at her, and something funny happens to his otherwise expressionless face. "It's their deadline, not mine," he says apologetically.

I take a deep breath. If I don't decide now, I'll lose my nerve. What difference does it make whether I decide now or tomorrow morning? "Do what you need to do," I tell Tom.

After Tom has left to seal the deal with Adrian, Mandy and I mark the occasion with a couple of glasses of Dad's cellar wine. It feels wrong getting stuck into the grog that he's saved for a special occasion, when that special occasion is my decision to rent out the Flywheel from under him. But Mandy insists he won't mind.

When she's gone home, I call Lauren and tell her what I've done. She'll be pleased, at least.

"It's the decision you had to make," she assures me. "This way you can come back to school. That stuff you e-mailed me for my Geography assignment last week—it's really good. You'll have to work a bit to catch up, but you'll be fine. You've got to think about your future."

I wanted this reassurance, but her certainty makes me angry. "It's not as simple as that."

"It is, though. It's what you need to be doing right now. Del, there's something I need to tell you—"

"But what about Dad?" I wail, cutting her off. I realize I'm slurring my words from the wine. I try to compose myself. "What is he going to do now that I've taken away his livelihood? How is he going to support us?"

"He could always break the lease if he really wanted to. Or start a cafe somewhere else. You're the kid! You need to think about what *you* want as well."

I laugh bitterly.

"What?" Lauren asks.

"It's just that it's pretty funny coming from a girl who spends her whole time trying to please her parents."

"What are you talking about?"

"How you study your butt off to get into law because your parents want you to," I say, exasperated.

There is a pause on the line. "Is that what you really think?"

"Don't tell me you dress like a paralegal and study up on contract law by *choice*."

Lauren hangs up on me.

I tilt the wine bottle upward and finish it off.

Five minutes later she calls back. "I didn't want to tell you like this, but I think you should hear it from me. Charlie and I are seeing each other."

"Oh, very funny."

"It's true," she says defensively. "We got together at the Factory the other night."

"That's ridiculous. Charlie was with Stereo Girl that night."

"Her name is Alyssa. And actually, he blew her off and spent the night with me."

I can't believe how delusional she's being. Even if Charlie

did end up hanging out with Lauren that night, there's no way anything happened between them.

"Lauren," I say firmly, and swallow the final gulp of wine. "He thinks your name is Karen. Besides, you're taller than him. Guys hate that. They find it very unattractive. Anyway, I've been with Charlie myself and let me tell you, he has great bra-removal skills but he's a very wet kisser. You can do better than him."

That's when Lauren hangs up on me for the second time.

I am so sick of people today. I'm glad I've decided to spend the night in by myself.

For dinner I order tandoori chicken pizza and eat it in front of the television. It feels strange to have a night free of Flywheel chores. I have fantasized about this kind of free time. But it doesn't feel as great as I thought it would.

First of all, there's nothing on but pathetic reality shows, and I'm not in the mood to watch someone try to reinvent the power ballad or cook an ocean trout tostada. Secondly, when eight o'clock draws near I find myself gravitating to my usual spot at the window.

Twice I get up and try to start on something else—making the bed, sorting my books by spine color—and twice I return.

It's when the flamenco music begins that I give up on the farce of finding something else to do. I settle in, my arm resting on the sill. I watch Rosa on the dance floor with Angeline. They spin gracefully around, Rosa's skirts flapping. My heart leaps as she readjusts her bra strap.

Oh, Rosa.

She's too beautiful *not* to watch. Kissing her was incredible, and that's part of the problem. But if she's not strong enough to be true to herself then how could things possibly work between us? I wish I could forget about her altogether.

My mind stays on her kiss, though, and the memory of holding her. I think again about what Charlie said during our fight.

Sure, Rosa could have shown more spine, but was I right to dismiss her completely? Maybe Rosa Barea is the kind of person worth waiting for. Maybe she's worth a little compromise.

Thinking about my argument with Charlie brings me to wondering about him and Lauren. Could it be true? Could my two best friends be seeing each other? It would mean Charlie lied to me about that night at the Factory, and the two of them deliberately kept their relationship from me. The thought makes my chest tight.

I stay at the window in the dark, long after Flamenco Hour ends. I watch the diners in the restaurant finish their meals and start on dessert, thinking all the while. I watch them eat dessert and order dessert wine. And when they've finished the wine I watch them leave, table by table.

I wonder if Rosa is still out the back, taking off her makeup, eating leftovers. I could go over, try and talk to her.

No, I argue with myself. *It would only end in heartbreak.* Besides, I'm moving to Melbourne, so what's the point? As soon as I've organized things with June, I'm out of here. She's probably gone home anyway.

I look back to the restaurant. One table of customers is still lingering.

Then again, maybe if I hurry I could catch her.

By the time I cross the road all the diners are gone. Rosa's aunt is at the cash register and Elvio is putting chairs onto tables. I tap lightly on the glass door just below the sign that's been turned to display the word "closed" so recently it's still swinging on its string. Adelina looks up from the register. She smiles and waves. She says something to Elvio, who ambles over.

He peers through the door at me. I see him recognize me.

"Is Rosa here?" I call through the glass.

His brow turns dark.

Rosa's aunt has disappeared into the back of the restaurant. "Go away," he murmurs, flicking his hand in the direction of the Flywheel. "Shoo."

His reaction surprises me, especially after his friendliness at the rally. "I just want to speak to Rosa," I call.

"You're no good for her," he mutters, still motioning for me to leave. "Rosa needs to stay away from girls like you."

This stops me dead. Girls like me? Elvio has known me since I was a kid. He's never had a problem with me before. "What the hell do you mean by that?" I shout, clutching the handle and shaking the door. The glass rattles in its frame. I'm a little wobbly and I can feel the wine rising to my cheeks.

"Go!" Elvio spits.

I think about how Rosa behaved at the Factory because she was scared Adrian would tell Elvio about us. Could one of those lowlifes have said something? I lean against the door and try to push it open but it won't budge.

Elvio stands on the other side, arms across his chest. "Get lost!" he hisses in a half-whisper.

There's hatefulness on his face, and I've seen it before. In Ella's eyes. In Mark Wellington's smirk. In Hamish's sneer. It's a look that says *You're worthless.*

I feel a pressure build in my chest. And suddenly it becomes too much to bear. Like a stream of hot lava, it bursts forth, and I let out a scream. "Let me in, you homophobic prick!"

31. CLUTCHING AT STRAWS

Elvio steps back as if he's been hit. He actually puts his hand to one cheek. His surprise is so great I feel the pulse of it there on the footpath, on the other side of the glass.

Adelina appears from the back room, her face drained of color. She heard me.

That's when I turn and run.

When I get home, I sit on my bed for a long time, too exhausted to move. I need to talk to someone, but I don't know who, or what I'd say.

Dad would make me feel better. *We'll fix it, darl,* he'd say. *Don't worry about a thing.* Charlie's right: Dad'll never be a great provider, but one thing I'm sure about is how much he loves me.

If only he wasn't in bloody Mongolia.

I think about Elvio's face, its stunned stillness. It won't leave my mind.

I can't talk to Lauren, not after our phone call earlier today. She wouldn't understand, anyway. It has to be Charlie. He'll know how out of control I feel, better than anybody.

I pick up the phone.

I put it down again. Am I out of my mind? I can't call Charlie. Not after our fight. Not now that he and Lauren are together, a fact he chose to lie to me about.

That's when the truth sinks in. I've lost everybody who's ever cared about me.

Except for maybe one person.

"Darling?" says June when she hears my voice on the line.

"Mum!" I say, stifling a sob. I'm so relieved she's home. I'm imagining her on the couch beside Mungo, listening to opera or watching a late-night BBC murder mystery. The kinds of things normal parents do. Scrubbing leftovers off chipped crockery and stumbling to bed in a haze of exhaustion is reserved for abnormal parents. Moving cities to spend some quality time as part of a regular family is exactly what I need.

I picture myself in my new bedroom, sitting at my desk writing an essay on the economic legacy of the Khmer

Rouge, working better than I ever could squashed at the upstairs kitchen table above the Flywheel. I wonder how long it will take to book a moving van. I'll probably have to stick around for a week at least, to finish packing up everything, but I should be able to get a flight to Melbourne next weekend.

Then I picture Dad coming home to our empty flat, putting his rucksack down with a thud. And realizing I've abandoned him.

I shake the image free. He's the one who got me into this mess. And anyway, I'll only be an hour's flight away. I can visit him every few weeks.

"I've told you, darling, call me June, *please*." My mother sounds put out.

The edge comes off my relief. "Is this a bad time?"

"Of course not, darling. It's just late, and I'm tired."

"I have some news," I say. "I think you'll be excited."

"That's a coincidence," June says slowly. "Mungo and I have some news as well. I've been meaning to call you."

My stomach tightens. Please god, don't let her be pregnant. "What is it?"

"No, you tell me yours first."

"It's okay. You go."

"We're moving!" she announces brightly.

"Moving?"

"To America! Mungo got a job at the University of Chicago, starting in September. Isn't it wonderful? We've found a little apartment in the downtown area, right where all the action is."

"Wait. For how long?"

"The contract is for two years to begin with, so we'll see how we go after that."

The scene of southern bliss I had imagined, complete with plane tree at the window, disintegrates. Moving to Melbourne is one thing, but to the other side of the world?

"They say it's a wonderful city," June carries on. "It's very cold in winter, of course, but it has a great cultural vibrancy. Just imagine, Delilah, once we've set up you can come and visit us there! The place we've found is really very small—you'll have to sleep on the couch, but that would be okay for a couple of weeks, wouldn't it? Delilah? Are you still there?"

"That's great," I mumble.

"You mean it? We'd love you to visit, you know. We really would. I'll miss having you in the same country *terribly*."

"It's great, June. Really."

"But I've been rattling on. What was your news, my darling?"

I suddenly feel incredibly tired. "Don't worry about it. I'll call back when it's not so late."

"Are you sure?" she asks after a brief pause.

"Yes."

"Promise?"

"Yes."

"Okay, darling. Night-night, then."

The line goes dead.

32. BROKEN SHADOWS

By midnight the street is almost deserted. Except for the 7-Eleven, every shop window is dark. From my absent father's bedroom window I watch the headlights of occasional cars flood Charada. Elvio's upended chairs cast long shadows on the floorboards.

Uh-oh. When I start noticing the length of shadows on floorboards, I know I've entered that psychological state my father likes to call the Self-Pity Parade. It begins with a hypersensitivity to tacky clichés of despair like long shadows and howling dogs. Next I'm having tragic-romantic thoughts about being subjected to extreme violence. Slumped alone here in the darkness I begin to think about how if a bomb exploded right this instant, right in this room, I would welcome it. I actually say that sentence in my head: *I would welcome a bomb right now.*

After that, I'm on to my funeral. I take pleasure in seeing the sad faces of all the people who have let me down: Lauren sobbing on Rosa's shoulder; Charlie doubled over in grief beside the cemetery plot; Dad howling with regret in the arms of the priest; June prostrating herself across my coffin as it's lowered into the ground.

The Parade isn't over yet. I mentally carve in stone all the bad things that have happened in my life, and now I'm picking up that stone and beating myself about the head with it.

My parents have practically orphaned me.

CRACK.

I've ruined my chances with Rosa.

CRACK.

I've destroyed the family business.

CRACK.

I'm penniless and friendless.

CRACK.

I think about Hamish, who has somehow managed to ruin my life despite his apparent lack of talent in any field of human endeavor. I think about my classmates chanting *dancing dyke* at me in the corridors. I think about Georgina Trump leading the call. Then I moan and swing that imaginary rock at my frontal lobe.

But even as I'm thinking this, with tears streaming down my cheeks (if nothing else, self-pity is a brilliant excuse for a bawl) I hear a no-nonsense voice in my head.

"You're being a bit, ah, melodramatic," it says. And I recognize Tom's familiar monotone.

I blink.

"You're *not* crap, Del," says another, more soothing voice: Mandy's.

I sit up in my chair.

I look out again toward Charada. I don't see shadows anymore, just plain uncomplicated darkness. The seal of gloom is broken. I begin to remember words of reassurance from other people I love.

"You're my wingman, Del," I hear Charlie say.

"You're my angel," says Dad.

"You've got so much potential," says Lauren.

"I think you're really brave," says Rosa, and with that one, it's as if my imaginary rock has dislodged some blockage in my brain, because remembering those words of hers gets me thinking again about what Charlie said. All this time I've been blaming her for her lack of courage, but now I'm not so sure Rosa was right when she called me brave.

What if what Charlie said is true? What if I was the one who really chickened out? What if I reacted the way I did because I was afraid of getting hurt?

Perhaps true bravery is not punching out the stranger who insults you (Charlie, take note), or swearing at a bigoted old man—maybe it's taking risks with your heart.

If Rosa thinks I'm brave, then I owe it to myself, and to all the people I love, to genuinely act like it.

33. CONFESSIONS OF A LUNATIC

The first person I decide to share my epiphany with is Mandy. I find her the following morning in the waiting room of her physiotherapy practice. As it happens, Tom is there as well. They have their heads together and a box of croissants between them. When they see me, Mandy sits up and Tom jumps out of his seat so quickly that for a second he is actually airborne.

"Del!" cries Mandy, too enthusiastically. "What a lovely surprise!"

Tom's usually blank face shows clear signs of embarrassment.

I look from one to the other. "What's going on?"

"What do you mean?" Mandy asks. "We're just having a bit of breakfast."

"Some croissants," says Tom, stating the obvious.

"Don't you look lovely!" Mandy claps her hands together. "What's the occasion?"

I glance down at my outfit. It's true I've made more than my usual effort this morning. There's an ironed shirt and makeup involved. I may have even brushed my hair.

"I've got some people to apologize to. Starting with you guys."

"What on earth for?"

"For putting up with me! With my melodrama," I say, looking at Tom. I take a deep breath. "You've helped me out so much, and I haven't thanked you enough. You've both been so good to me since I started managing the Flywheel. Tom, you've helped with the accounts. Mandy, you've listened to all my crises so patiently. You both helped during the crisis talks . . ."

"You know this is not an awards ceremony, right, Del?" says Mandy.

"I just wanted you to know I'm grateful." My voice wavers and Tom looks alarmed.

Mandy gives my hand a squeeze. "Anytime, dear girl."

I take a breath. "Thank you. Now if you'll excuse me, I have a long list of people to apologize to today."

"A croissant for stamina?" Tom asks, proffering a limp pastry.

"I'll pass. You guys enjoy your breakfast."

It's a five-minute walk back down the road to Charada. I time my arrival perfectly. Rosa is just dropping off her parents as I reach the restaurant. I loiter surreptitiously beside a wheelie bin until they have gone inside before making a quick dash for the passenger door.

As I land in the seat beside her, Rosa jumps. "Del!"

She looks stunning. With a white tank top, black combat boots, and a silver bubble skirt that matches her silver eye shadow, her theme today seems to be Intergalactic Battle, and I can't help thinking that she'd win just by dazzling the enemy.

"Hi," I greet her breathlessly.

There is a definite intimacy about sitting in a car next to somebody: being together in a small space, shut off from traffic noise with nothing but a handbrake between you. Being this close to her reminds me of our kiss at the Factory. I am certain she feels it, too.

"What the hell are you doing?" she says angrily.

Of course it was never going to be easy. She's still upset about our fight, and it's likely she knows about my confrontation with Elvio last night. I take a few deep breaths in time to the thudding in my chest. "I just want to talk to you for a minute."

"I don't have a minute. I'm in a loading zone."

So things are going to be trickier than I hoped. *Why did I expect more from her?* I wonder angrily. I reach for the door handle.

Then I remember my resolve last night, and what Charlie said.

Tell Rosa how you feel.

The thought of doing so terrifies me. If Rosa ends up betraying me just like Georgina did I might have to live the rest of my days on an iceberg in Antarctica until my heart freezes over once and for all. But she hasn't yet. I have to do what I'm here for.

"Perhaps we can drive around the corner and park," I suggest.

Rosa doesn't say anything, but she pulls out carefully into the traffic.

What follows is the longest five minutes of my life.

Seriously, semitrailers should be banned from suburban streets. And whose bright idea was it to have rubbish trucks make collections during peak hour? As Rosa negotiates every possible obstacle ever encountered on a road, we sit in silence next to each other, my right arm mere centimeters from her left arm, the scent of her shampoo making me light-headed.

We finally make it around the corner, and Rosa pulls over.

She takes off her seatbelt and turns to face me. I see her notice my lipstick and ironed shirt. "I have to be at an appointment in ten minutes, so you'd better make it quick," she says, but halfway through the sentence her stern tone wavers and it gives me hope.

"I wanted to say how sorry I am about my tantrum last week," I begin. "You're right. I overreacted. You see, the thing is . . ."

Just say it, Delilah.

I clear my throat nervously. "I know I've been playing it pretty cool—well, except for the time I spilled coffee on you. And when I fell on the dance floor. And the time I smashed your potted plants. Anyway, the fact is, I began noticing you ages ago. I've, um, I've watched you dancing at Charada more than a couple of times. That's a bit of an understatement, actually. I've basically watched you every night through Dad's bedroom window for months. It's become a joke at the Flywheel." I attempt a laugh.

I wait for a response. She doesn't say a word.

"And the way you spoke at the—at the library rally," I stutter on. "Your passion. I almost fainted. Not literally," I add hastily. "What I mean is that . . . okay, ah, I'll put it another way. You know how sometimes you come into the cafe wearing that denim jacket and then you take it off and you just have that leotard on that's cut really low at the back? Well, it's the highlight of my week."

I study her face for a reaction but it is blank.

Get it together, Delilah. This is all coming out wrong. "I guess what I'm trying to say," I carry on, "is that I think you're incredible. You're an incredible dancer, an incredible activist. An incredible person. I'm not as brave as you think I am, or I thought I was, but I'm trying to be. I should have told you all of this last Saturday—but, well, I got scared." I inhale deeply. "I know I've made mistakes. I acted like a moron at the Factory. And you probably heard from Adelina about what happened last night. What I said to your uncle was . . . appalling. I'm dealing with a lot of anger. From my mum leaving, from what's been happening at school. But also because you make me a little bit insane." I swallow hard. "What I want, more than anything, is to be with you," I finish in a whisper.

Everything is quiet. Rosa lowers her eyes briefly, and her silver eye shadow flashes like a promise. When she looks up again her expression has softened. I try to read what's going on behind all that silver-edged green.

I can't. So I reach over and grab her hand. It is warm.

Her voice is shaky. "You're not the moron, Del. I'm the moron," she says. "I wish I wasn't so scared about all of this. About you and me. About people finding out. I shouldn't care so much what my family thinks, but I don't want to hurt them, I guess. And I know that it *would* hurt them. This situation has already hurt them." She looks at me. "Adelina did tell me what happened last night—"

"I acted like a crazy person. I know that. I can't tell you how sorry I am."

"I just wonder . . ." Rosa smooths a hand over her skirt. "I mean, I told you how delicate things are on this issue with my family. And still you go and make a scene like that!"

"I will make it up to you. To them."

"Elvio is a very proud man, Del—"

"With some very old-fashioned views that he needs to update," I blurt. "Come on, Rosa, you can see that, can't you? You shouldn't be so hung up on what he thinks when he's living in another century. Anyway, does it really matter? He's your uncle, not even your father. And you're nineteen—"

She shakes her head. "You don't seem to understand how important this is to me. My uncle is a huge part of my life. He and my father are like that." She holds up two crossed fingers. "Elvio's older than my dad; he's the head of the family. It doesn't matter that he seems out of touch to you and me. Everyone listens to him. My dad. My mum. My little brother—especially him. He thinks Elvio's a god. Believe me, I'd love to be able to show up with you at the next Barea lunch and introduce you as my girlfriend, but it's never going to happen."

A bus swoops past within an inch of the driver's side mirror and the car shudders. I try to digest what she is saying. "Never? You're saying that if we were together, you'd want me to keep our relationship a secret?"

Rosa looks conflicted. "Del, this thing between us, it's barely started. I can't say what I might want down the track, but right now that's all I'm comfortable with, yes."

I try to see it from her perspective, to remember what Charlie said. I can't help but think, though, that if she cared enough about me she would be offering me more than this. I feel like we're back to where we were at the Factory.

"I just don't think I can agree to a secret relationship," I tell her. "Being honest about who I am is *part* of who I am, regardless of the consequences. How can you say you want to be with me if it's not important enough to tell your family about?"

I watch her. She is visibly struggling with her emotions. "I just can't, Del," she says at last, her voice breaking. She unlatches my hand from hers.

"Rosa—"

She looks straight ahead through the windshield, her eyes fixed firmly on the road.

I slam the door behind me.

34. ALL THE WAYS
I'VE RUINED MY LIFE

I'm sitting in the foyer of a courthouse, reading an article on my phone. There's a photo of a figure standing tall: her gaze steady, her skirts flowing.

LOCAL ICON SAVES LIBRARY, I read for the thousandth time.

Rosa did it. She won the battle. Her protest against the new development has succeeded—for now, at least. Last night the council voted against the plan to demolish the library.

Part of me wants to call and congratulate her. Another part of me shrinks at the thought. I think again about kissing her at the Factory. The moment plays in my mind like a video on a loop—the way she pressed against me with her mouth, with her whole body.

A court officer opens the courtroom door in front of me. I switch off my phone, stand up, and go inside.

It's my first time in a courtroom and frankly, it is a disappointment. I was hoping for high ceilings, cedar paneling, and an air of doom. Instead, it's a lot like Mrs. Cronenberg's classroom—with cheerful blue carpet, fluorescent lighting, and a magistrate's bench where Mrs. Cronenberg's desk would be. I take a seat in the back row, hoping to avoid detection. The idea of seeing Charlie after two weeks of estrangement is nerve-racking. After how things went down the last time we met, what right have I to rock up to his big day as a casual spectator?

I probably shouldn't even be here, given everything I have to do to be out of the cafe in time for Adrian Hibbert to move in. I should be putting stuff in storage. But the whole process is far too depressing.

An intoxicating scent diffuses the courtroom. I turn to see Marina Bitar striding through the door.

Charlie and Lauren trail behind her. Charlie looks uncomfortable in a suit and patent-leather shoes. Lauren, on the other hand, looks right at home in her pencil skirt, collared shirt, and heels. She's holding Charlie's hand firmly and smoothing the creases from his jacket with her other hand. She sees me and says something in his ear.

The smell of perfume wafts closer. Marina stops by my chair. "Are you here to give evidence for Charles?" she asks in a low voice.

I look up to where Charlie and Lauren are hovering behind her. They both meet my gaze: Charlie with a slightly pleading look, Lauren with a blank expression that swiftly slides off me.

I shake my head quickly.

Marina turns around and whispers something to Charlie. They pass by me without another glance.

The magistrate, who to my further disappointment is not wearing a wig, calls through the matters. Solicitors rise one at a time from the bar table to address her about the cases being heard before Charlie's. Charlie and Lauren are sitting in the row of chairs directly behind them, their heads together, talking quietly. Charlie turns and glances at me. He turns back quickly.

I look around the courtroom. I wonder if Sarah, who started all this, is here. I still don't know for sure if the man he punched was her father. I decide to ask Charlie later if he's seen her. If he'll talk to me, that is. And if he hasn't been sent to prison.

After about thirty minutes the magistrate calls Charlie's name. Charlie sits straight in his chair. The magistrate and Marina exchange a few words about the case.

"Please stand up, Mr. McFarlane," says the magistrate eventually. "How do you plead?"

Charlie straightens his jacket as he stands and clears his throat. "Not guilty, Your Honor," he says.

My best friend, the lunatic.

The police prosecutor begins to outline the facts of the case. Lauren clutches Charlie's shoulder and whispers something to him urgently. Charlie glances again in my direction.

Oh god. He's going to beg me to give evidence.

He leans forward to the bar table and speaks into Marina's perfectly proportioned ear.

I'm getting ready to flee.

Marina rises from the bar table. She places four fingers lightly on Charlie's arm. She turns, not toward me, but toward the magistrate. "Excuse me, Your Honor," she says, her white teeth gleaming. "I'm so sorry to interrupt my learned friend. It's just that my client has advised me . . ." She pauses. "My client, Charles McFarlane," she begins again, drawing it out, "has, just this minute, in fact, stated that he would like to change his plea."

The magistrate regards Charlie over her glasses. "Is that true, Mr. McFarlane?"

"Yes, Your Honor."

She gives a perfunctory nod. "Let's deal with the matter of sentence, then."

Far-out. I can't believe he's actually changed his plea. I'm pleased, I suppose. It's what I've wanted him to do from the start. But now that he's actually fessing up, it means he's going to have to face the music.

Seeing Charlie being sentenced is more than I can bear. Instead I wait outside in the foyer, nervous about his fate. For twenty minutes I squirm on a plastic seat, tearing a drunk-driving pamphlet into a thousand little pieces.

Finally Marina strides out, alone. Where's Charlie? What have they done with him? I knew prison was a possibility, but somehow I refused to believe it would come to that.

"He's not—they didn't . . . ," I stutter.

Marina shakes her head. "Three hundred hours of community service. He's a very lucky boy," she says grimly. "Be sure to remind him of that, emphatically and often."

Charlie emerges from the courtroom and Marina goes over to them. Lauren's arm is through his and they're talking to a well-dressed man who is old enough to be his father.

It takes me a second to realize that it *is* his father. He has the same eyes and nose as Charlie, and probably once had the same color hair, too. Even though I hate everything I know about him, I'm glad for Charlie's sake that his father has come.

"I don't care if they have you cleaning the Central Station toilets," Marina says. "If you miss a single hour I will call the police myself."

She shakes hands with Mr. McFarlane. While they're talking, Charlie takes Lauren's face in his hands and kisses her lips.

My two best friends are getting it on. The phrase runs on a loop in my head for a whole sixty seconds, along with that *whoop whoop* alarm sound you hear in buildings when it's time to evacuate.

I give them another minute before I figure it's safe to look up again. When I do, Lauren and Marina are heading together toward the lifts. Phew. But Charlie and his father are walking in my direction. By the time Charlie sees me it's too late for him to take another route.

"Dad, this is Delilah," he says reluctantly when they reach me.

"The famous Ms. Woolwich-Green," Mr. McFarlane smiles and stretches out his hand. "He talks a lot about you."

Charlie clears his throat loudly.

But his father is already deeply involved with his phone. "I'll let you two catch up," he says, distracted. "See you tonight, Charlie. Eat without me. I'll probably be late." He heads quickly for the stairs.

As Charlie and I watch him go, we stand side by side without speaking. I try to work out what to say first.

"He seems nice," I say at last, even though I don't really mean it.

Charlie grunts. "He can be very charming when he wants to be."

"I know someone else like that."

"Oh, really?"

We give each other hostile looks and it becomes a staring competition. Charlie breaks first and strides away toward the lifts.

He's halfway there when I call out his name.

He turns around and starts walking slowly back.

"I know you think I'm a bad friend for not giving evidence," I say.

Charlie shakes his head and mumbles something.

"What was that?"

"I said I shouldn't have asked you to lie," he sighs. "And it was good of you to come today. Even though you were a total bitch to me the last time I saw you," he adds gruffly.

"You think I'd miss your court hearing, just because *you* were a complete prick to *me* the last time I saw you?"

Charlie grins in spite of himself. "You coming today made all the difference, in the end. How could I spin my bullshit in front of you, when you witnessed the whole thing? I would have felt like even more of a prick."

"Oh, come on. On a scale of one to five, one being Mother Teresa and five being Hamish Creel . . ."

Charlie tilts his head expectantly.

". . . you're not so bad." I smile.

"Even for a wet kisser?" he asks.

I pause. "Lauren told you?"

"Don't worry. It was only after I told her you give a shithouse hand job."

I whack his bum. He cries out in mock horror.

"I missed you," I tell him plainly. "And believe it or not, I'm glad you don't have to go to prison. Those forest-green tracksuits they make you wear? Totally wrong for your complexion."

Charlie flicks my ear.

"So, when were you going to tell me about Lauren?" I say.

He looks guilty again. "I was planning to. Promise."

"Oh yeah?"

He looks thoughtful. "I guess I wanted this thing between Lauren and me to become, you know, the most it could become, before I told anyone."

"That is disturbingly poetic of you, Charlie. You've changed."

Instead of laughing, he's quiet. We walk together down the courthouse steps in silence.

"Well, has it?" I ask when we've reached the bottom.

"Has it what?"

"Become the most it could become?"

Charlie shrugs. "It's definitely moving in that direction. She's been amazing, you know. Through all this court stuff. She's just really . . . I mean—"

"Don't tell me," I say. "You're madly in love with her. You've never felt like this about anyone before."

But he hasn't flipped his hair once. And rather than coming back with some clever remark, Charlie just looks ahead and smiles.

"I hope you're aware Lauren's had a crush on you for ages," I say seriously, stopping at the traffic light and pressing the button. "If you don't treat her better than the others . . ."

He looks at me. "She's missed you just as much as I have these past few weeks, you know."

"Don't, Charlie," I warn him.

"So other than picking fights with your friends, what have you been up to, anyway? Keeping out of trouble, I hope."

I pause. I'll pretend I didn't notice that blatant change of subject. "Does renting out the Flywheel to Adrian Hibbert qualify as keeping out of trouble?"

Charlie halts midstride. "You did *what*?"

"And the things I said to you and Lauren combined aren't half as bad as what I said to Rosa's uncle."

"Del!"

"I went crazy," I confess. "Elvio looked at me like I was scum when I asked to see her, and I just lost it. *You* know how that goes. Then I tried to explain myself to Rosa, and made a mess of that, too."

Charlie grabs my arm. "We don't speak for two weeks and you go and ruin your *whole life*? I don't believe this."

"This is what happens when you abandon me, Charlie McFarlane."

"There's a way to fix all of it. There has to be. Especially with Rosa."

As much as I want to believe him, I feel obliged to set him straight. "I don't know this time, Charlie. I don't think we're compatible. I've got to face it, that's all."

And even though Charlie bangs on in vigorous disagreement during the entire walk to Central Station, I know I'm right. For the first time since I fell for her, I've resigned myself to a future without Rosa Barea.

35. TOO FANCY, TOO FREE

They serve breakfast like this to the stars. Truffled eggs on sourdough. Citrus salad. Black quinoa waffles with organic yogurt, attractively positioned on the plate. I hover my knife and fork over the waffles, not wanting to disturb the symmetry.

"Some more orange juice, Delilah?" Petra, the McFarlanes' housekeeper, asks.

"Just a little, thanks."

There's a breeze coming off the nearby water. I place a corner of my serviette under a potted orchid to stop it taking flight.

"What's on the agenda for today?" Petra asks cheerily.

On the other side of the McFarlanes' garden, at the deep end of the swimming pool, is a wall of wisteria. Beyond it you can just see the harbor. "Maybe a walk along the beach," I say. "And a nap this afternoon, after I've done the crossword."

"Lovely," she murmurs, stacking plates. "Why don't you take Charlie with you? Otherwise he'll sleep all morning."

I take another sip of juice and try to feel pleased. Why wouldn't I be? I'm in a beautiful garden on a sunny day being served gourmet breakfast with nothing to fill in the hours until dinner.

Maybe it's the adjustment that's proving tricky. I've spent the week and a half since Charlie's hearing packing up the Flywheel.

When I told Charlie how much I was dreading Adrian moving in downstairs, he convinced his father to let me stay at their place for a few weeks to get away from the whole situation for a while (he owes me big-time on the free accommodation front, let's face it). The upshot is I'm here, without school or the Flywheel to worry about, and a lot of time to ponder the big questions, like: Should I get Charlie out of bed? Should I have another waffle? And how the hell am I going to sort out the mess that is my life?

I've just woken up from my afternoon kip when my phone rings.

"What's going on?" Misch sounds hysterical. "I keep texting you and you never reply so I go to the Flywheel and it's empty!"

I ease myself off the mattress. "You'd better come round to Charlie's."

Three hours later Charlie, Lucas, Misch, and I are sitting on the McFarlanes' back porch, eating moussaka and drinking vodka from Charlie's dad's liquor cabinet. I fill in Misch and Lucas on the Flywheel's finances and my decision to rent it out. When I tell them about Hamish Creel messing with the orders, Misch is so angry that the whole table shakes with her fury. Then I mention how Crunch stole our Bondi shuttle idea and Lucas actually has to hold her down to stop her upending our dinner.

When Misch has taken some deep breaths she updates me about what's been happening at school. Highlights include Mr. Hammer choosing Georgina to read out the role of Lady Macbeth in English ("Even *he* can see she's an Evil Bitch," Misch declares) and Carl MacDonald setting Sophie Murray's hair on fire in Chemistry. Lucas does an impression of Sophie trying to slap Carl and put her head under the cold tap at the same time. Charlie is in stitches by the end of it, and he doesn't even know Carl or Sophie.

I watch my friends from across the table and realize how much I've missed seeing them every day. For a moment a feeling of well-being sneaks in. Not even the mention of Georgina has dampened my mood.

Then I wonder briefly what Rosa's doing now.

"Would it be okay if I kidnapped Petra?" Misch asks Charlie, helping herself to more food. "This moussaka is epic. Lucas." She nudges him with an elbow. "Remember to breathe when you eat." Lucas snuffles into his plate.

"It's not Petra you need to kidnap," I tell Misch. "Charlie made it himself. I watched him with my own eyes."

Misch gapes at him. "Incredamaze," she says with genuine feeling, and Charlie beams.

"This is the perfect night," I declare. I swig my vodka and lemonade and it warms my chest. "Good food, good drink, good friends. What more could a girl want?"

Then Charlie says, "You know, there's someone else who would have loved to be here tonight."

Lucas shifts uncomfortably, and Misch avoids my gaze.

I glare at Charlie. "Someone by the name of Karen, I presume?"

36. MY OLDEST FRIEND

In the months before June abandoned us for Melbourne, she became fanatical about my well-being. This was in such contrast to her previous laissez-faire attitude toward me that it came as a surprise. I've since supposed that she'd begun her affair with Mungo and figured that if she was leaving, the opportunities she had to set me on the right path were limited.

Whatever her reasons, she started me on a crash course of leg waxing, eyebrow plucking, and fake tanning. She attempted to teach me some basic cooking skills. I endured these humiliations calmly, figuring it was just one of June's phases. But when she insisted on enrolling me in tennis camp for the school holidays even though I already had plans to attend an art class at the community center, my patience with her frayed. (It wasn't the art I was interested in; it was a girl called Melissa who I'd met at one of the center's courses the year before.) I refused to go to the tennis camp, but June insisted. We fought about it for days.

And the whole time, it was Lauren who stood up for me. She knew how much I'd been looking forward to the art class, even if she didn't know why. I can still see her standing in the kitchen of our flat, her face earnest, her high ponytail swinging. She told June how passionate I was about art, how good it was to develop that side of the brain, and that nobody played tennis anymore anyway. June liked Lauren, considered her a positive influence, so June eventually backed down.

Good old Lauren.

I call her when Misch and Lucas have left and Charlie is watching television. I have to call twice before she answers her phone.

"I'm not sure I'm ready to talk to you," Lauren says stonily, but I can tell she's bunging it on.

"Just come over, will you? I won't take up much of your time. Besides, Charlie's desperate to see you."

The bait works. I suggest eight o'clock, figuring that's seven forty-five Lauren Time. When she arrives at half-past seven, an evening storm is battering the coast. I let Charlie meet her at the door and wait for them to finish their pash session, the sounds of which not even the five-inch-thick mahogany sitting room door can muffle. When Lauren comes to find me at last, her hair is damp with rain and her buttons are mismatched. She redoes them quickly and slips off her heels, all without meeting my eye.

"Cup of tea?"

She frowns stubbornly.

"We've got Russian Caravan." Her favorite.

"Well, I suppose in that case . . ."

I make the tea and coax her onto the couch. The swooping soundtrack of the cooking show Charlie is watching in the next room crescendos through the wall. Lauren sits stiffly, sipping the tea daintily, like she would in the company of someone she's never met.

I decide the only way forward is to fetch her a plate of Charlie's moussaka and fall on my sword.

Here goes nothing. "I'm sorry I said what I said," I tell her. "About your parents putting pressure on you."

Lauren takes a bite of cheese-covered eggplant. It has the lip-loosening effect I hoped it would. "Then why *did* you say it?" she asks.

"Because I'm a cow."

"No, you said it because you believe it." She takes a few more hungry bites before putting the food aside. "You can't actually understand that I might want to study law regardless of what my parents think."

"I thought they wanted you to go to law school," I protest.

"They want me to go because that's what *I* want, not the other way around! Jeez, Del, why is that so hard to understand? I understand the things that interest *you*, even when they're not the same as those that interest me. Why can't you pay me the same respect?"

"That's not true at all! Ever since I stopped going to school you haven't stopped trying to get me to go back. How is that understanding what interests me? Maybe running my family's cafe is what interests me."

"Come on, Delilah." She clenches her jaw and hunches forward and I recognize the look from when she was twelve and wanted to win our year seven spelling bee, and when she was fourteen and fought to get onto the first netball team, and every time before or since, when Lauren Crawley has been determined about anything. "I know you," she says. "I know what you love. You love learning about tectonic plates and high rainfall and the cities of the world. You love dancing to Rushmore. You love hanging out with Charlie. You love your parents, even though you're mad at your mum for leaving and your dad drives you crazy. And you love that flamenco girl from the tapas bar across the road." She shrugs. "I'm not stupid, you know."

"That's another thing." I look down. "You've avoided every conversation about my sexuality since I came out to you," I say. "I would have told you about Rosa, but you've never wanted to talk about that kind of stuff with me. Not once have we had a discussion about how hard it's been for me to be ridiculed by Georgina and her gang. Not once have you asked me why she might have started doing it."

"I didn't think you wanted to talk about that kind of stuff with me," Lauren says, seeming surprised. "Whenever I brought it up you changed the topic. After you told me you liked girls, I kept waiting for you to tell me about crushes you had, or the girls you'd kissed, the way we used to tell each other about what guys we thought were cute. I tried to ask you about Rosa the day of the crisis talks but you wouldn't talk to me and I figured it was something you didn't want to share with me. It's like ever since you became friends with Charlie, you don't need me for that kind of thing anymore."

I'm silent for a moment, digesting everything she has said. I have to admit that some of it is true. I remember why she is my oldest friend, and wonder how I was so close to forgetting.

"You could have just been straight with me and told me you felt left out, you know."

"I thought my being straight was the problem."

I gasp. "Lauren Crawley, did you just make a joke? A terrible, terrible joke?"

She grins.

"Listen," I say, serious again. "I'm sorry about what I said when you told me you and Charlie were going out. It was cruel. I was nervous for you because of Charlie's track record at breaking hearts. But I needn't have worried. I can tell it's different this time."

"It's okay, Del. I imagine it's pretty hard when two of your close friends get together. Suddenly they're off with each other instead of making time for you. You probably think we've divulged your deepest darkest secrets to each other."

I wait for a "but." "Well? Haven't you?"

"If it's any consolation, Charlie didn't find the story about you losing your bra during gymnastics tryouts in year eight particularly interesting."

"You didn't!" I grab her plate and try to hold it out of her reach, but it's a tactic that never works with Lauren. Reaching up with ease, she grabs the plate and forks some moussaka into her mouth.

"Charlie!" she calls beguilingly, dancing on her tiptoes as I swipe at her from below. "Babe, this moussaka is *delicious*!"

37. THE VERY CHAIR I'VE BEEN AVOIDING

I can't believe I'm sitting here. The chair is comfy, yes, but it is the very chair I've been avoiding. It is the Comfy Chair of Doom.

Opposite me on her ergonomic swivel seat sits Mrs. Cronenberg. Beneath a map of New York City's subway, she is spilling the crumbs of a blueberry muffin down the front of her hand-knitted jumper and studying me as if I were a mysterious land formation that has burst through the floor of her office overnight. The sound of banging lockers travels through the window and my stomach somersaults. Not so long ago I was in the cut and thrust of all that noise myself, my thoughts jumping among quadratic equations, the Persian Wars, and Othello, readying myself for lunch on the Road

Lawn and impatient with a million things to share with my friends.

"I'm only here because I promised Lauren," I begin. I also don't want anyone ringing June, and Mrs. C said she'll hold off on that phone call on the condition that I see her. "I'm not coming back to school."

"Muffin?" Mrs. Cronenberg offers.

I eye the bribe with suspicion.

"I have two. I'm not going to eat them both. Do you want it or not?"

I take it from her and peel back the corrugated paper.

"I'm glad you came, even if it is only for Lauren," she says. "You and I are long overdue for a talk."

I feel like telling her that I'm done with her talk. But I stay silent, partly for fear of that phone call and partly because I have a quarter of a muffin in my mouth.

"I think I understand why you don't want to come back even now your family's cafe has closed," Mrs. Cronenberg continues. "It has something to do with Georgina and the treatment you got from your classmates after that video. But that's not the whole story, is it?" She looks at me questioningly. "You can handle the other kids; I know you can."

"Because I'm so self-assured?"

"Yes," Mrs. Cronenberg agrees.

"Which means I lead other, weaker people astray?" I say stonily. It's the same conversation as last time. I don't need to hear her potted theory again, about how I pressured

Georgina into being with me. I will not be convinced by the chair's cushiony seat or well-positioned armrests into buying her crap. I stand up.

"Sit down, Delilah."

"Why should I?"

"Because I haven't finished. Look. I know I'm partly to blame. Will you at least hear me out?"

I look at the chair and at Mrs. Cronenberg. "Fine. But I am not sitting down."

"All right. Have it your way." She stands up herself and leans back against her desk. "When Georgina came to see me last term I took what she said at face value," she says, brushing crumbs off her jumper. "I realize now that things were probably more complicated than the way she painted them." She pauses, meeting my eyes.

"I'm listening."

"I had no right to make assumptions about what went on between you two, especially how you felt about each other. It was out of line. I leapt to a conclusion because . . . well . . ." She looks uncomfortable. "You remind me of myself at your age."

I snort, eyeing her cagily—the toothpaste drips on her jumper, the mess of her unbrushed hair. I glance down and rapidly flick the muffin crumbs off my shirt.

"I mean it. I was smart and headstrong, like you. Don't look at me like I'm telling you something you don't already know. I used to get into trouble for being a strong influence

281

on others. I was hauled in to see the principal once when I convinced a whole section of the choir to boycott the musical festival. Honestly, though, the choirmaster's arrangement of 'Oseh Shalom' was criminal." She pauses. "Anyway, I assumed you persuaded Georgina into something she didn't exactly want. I see now that I made a mistake. I let you down."

Of course she made a mistake! Part of me wants to shout this at her, but strangely I also feel relieved. Teachers aren't supposed to be wrong about anything, and when they are they hardly ever admit it. I'm glad that she has. The air feels strangely lighter.

I'm also glad she told me this story, because the thought of her being a bad influence is hilarious.

"What are you smiling at?" asks Mrs. Cronenberg.

"Nothing."

"There is one thing I'm not taking back, though."

Here we go.

"Because you *are* sure of who you are—which is a wonderful thing, don't get me wrong—it might mean that you place unreasonable demands on people who aren't so sure," says Mrs. Cronenberg, shifting on her desk. "It's just a suggestion. But maybe have a think about how things might have been different if you'd given Georgina a bit more time to figure things out for herself before, well, declaring to the world how you felt about each other."

"I only told Ella!"

"And you want to argue that's not the same thing?"

"I didn't even tell her anything specific!"

"I think we can agree you said more than enough for her to figure out what was going on."

"Are we done?" I grumble, folding up my muffin wrapper.

Mrs. Cronenberg slides back and stretches her legs out. "There's one more thing. Lauren tells me you've been helping with her Geography assignment. If you decide to come back I'm prepared to give you credit for it. That way you won't be as far behind."

"I already said—"

"It's just a thought."

The woman knows how to get under my skin, damn it. On my way back to Charlie's I think about everything. I'm not changing my mind about school, but the stuff she said about how demanding I can be of the people I care about sticks in my throat.

So I text Rosa after dinner, before I lose my nerve. I congratulate her about the library. I tell her I'm sorry for being unreasonable. I say that I'm willing to see her on her terms, even if that means keeping whatever happens between us to ourselves for the time being. I press Send and wait, but nothing comes. I keep checking my phone, but still nothing. I barely sleep all night.

38. AN AMAZING
GIRL I KNOW

The whole next morning passes without a reply from Rosa.
I check my phone so many times that it runs out of battery
and I have to plug it in. It's warmer today than it's been since
March and I think about having a swim in the McFarlanes'
pool, but decide against it on the grounds that the pool is too
far away from the wall socket.

"Maybe she's in the hospital," Charlie suggests brightly
when I tell him at lunchtime.

I probably shouldn't be discussing any of this with him
given that I'm wooing Rosa on the promise I'll keep quiet
about our relationship, but it's only Charlie, and since Rosa
and I don't yet *have* a relationship, I figure it's all right.
Charlie needs a distraction anyway. His dad is due back from

his latest trip to the States tomorrow and plans to drag him around to new schools in the hope that one of them will agree to enroll him next year (he's missed the boat for this year's exams). After the community service order, his last school has finally drawn the line.

"That's a terrible thought! Anyway, they have phones in hospitals, Charlie."

"She could be in a coma," he reasons.

That afternoon I call for reinforcements. Lauren, Misch, and Lucas agree to keep a lookout for Rosa near Charada on their way home from school. "I just want to know if she's in the country and in mobile range," I tell them.

Lucas makes the first sighting. He calls me. "You will never guess where she was." He sounds scandalized.

"Where?"

"Don't you want to guess?"

"Just tell me!"

"Eating a burger and milkshake with *Hamish Creel*, at *Crunch*."

With Hamish Creel?

"Can you believe it? She seemed to be having a great time."

He must have it wrong. That scenario is simply not plausible.

"Are you sure it was Hamish?"

"He's the dickhead with dreads, yeah?"

"That's him."

"Positive."

Maybe it was some other girl. "What was she wearing?"

"I don't know! A kind of crazy-patterned dress? With boots, I think."

Oh god. I know the dress he's talking about instantly. It's the Jenny Kee one that makes her legs go on forever.

I spend the next hour under the covers, not moving. What is the point of moving when Rosa is spending her time with Hamish Creel? What is the point of life?

At six o'clock a text comes through.

My breath catches in my throat. With the tip of my finger I touch Rosa's name on my screen.

What she's sent me is not exactly a message: It's a URL.

My stomach flips. I haven't been on YouTube since Georgina posted the dance video. What on earth has Rosa sent me? Surely not some other life-destroying footage complete with commentary from the gutter-mouths of the world?

No. Rosa wouldn't do that. I know that much.

In which case maybe someone *pretending* to be Rosa sent it. Someone who managed to get ahold of her phone at some point today.

Someone who ate a burger with her, for example.

I switch off the phone and throw it across the bed.

I have a shower, help Charlie with dinner, and try to forget about it.

Then I remember it approximately twelve times a minute for the next four hours.

It's impossible to sleep. I lie on the mattress listening to the date palms shift in the breeze, running through the possibilities in my mind.

The link *must* have come from Hamish. It's exactly the kind of heartless trick he'd play, in which case I should just delete it.

But if I don't check it out and it's something like Georgina's dance video, I'll find out soon enough from some sniggering idiot who Hamish sent the link anyway. At least if I look now I'll have the opportunity to skip the country before the public humiliation begins again.

Chicago's probably beautiful this time of year.

Then again, if it *is* some form of attack on me I shouldn't give Hamish the satisfaction of my attention. I should go through with my original plan: Delete the message at once.

I am going insane.

I turn on the light. I get out of bed. I turn on my phone and scroll to the message. For a full three minutes my finger hovers between the link and the delete button.

Then I click on the link.

Sure enough, up comes a video box. I scroll down to the description beneath.

Uploaded by **RosaB** on Sept 6

Glebe Library Rally. Check out 1:15–1:40 for an amazing girl I know.

All Comments (15)

Sign In or **Sign Up** now to post a comment!

RosaB 9 hours ago
Hi Del, this is a video a friend of mine took at the library rally. Take a look.

RosaB 9 hours ago
No one else has the link. I posted this just for you.

RosaB 9 hours ago
I wanted you to see a *good* video. One that shows how incredible you are.

RosaB 9 hours ago
See how at 1:24 the man is smiling as he talks to you?

RosaB 9 hours ago
As he's throwing the $20 note into your bucket?

RosaB 9 hours ago
That's how I feel when you talk to me.

RosaB 9 hours ago
You make me happy.

RosaB 9 hours ago
Thank you for helping at my rally.

RosaB 9 hours ago
Thank you for the message you sent yesterday. It means

the world to me that you're making the effort to understand where I'm coming from.

RosaB 9 hours ago
I'm sorry I freaked out when you came to see me the other day.

RosaB 9 hours ago
I want to be with you too. Of course I do!

RosaB 9 hours ago
I can't get in touch properly right now but I'll let you know what's going on as soon as I can.

RosaB 9 hours ago
You're an inspiration to me.

RosaB 9 hours ago
Not to mention an amazing kisser.

RosaB 9 hours ago
And Del? I LOVE the way you dance.

---

39. LOVE ON WHEELS

I could float out the window. Rosa Barea wants me, and the thought is intoxicating.

She said she can't get in touch right now, but it doesn't matter. I have to see her, as soon as I can. I have to make it to Charada in time for her daily drop-off.

I get up at seven, having barely slept. I leave Charlie's house with what I think will be plenty of time, but I'm not used to this commute, and the peak-hour gridlock foils my plan. I arrive precisely fifteen minutes too late. Rosa is probably well on her way to uni by now. I loiter outside the restaurant for a while in the hope that she might miraculously appear.

Across the street the Flywheel sits dark and empty. After another fifteen minutes of gazing mournfully at the symbol of my failure I decide it's unlikely I'm going to bump into Rosa. The higher powers clearly have no miracles planned for me today.

Except that when I'm walking past the hair salon two shops down from Charada, the door opens and one of the stylists calls out to me.

"Delilah?" She waves her comb in the general direction of the salon interior. "I've got a client in here who wants to talk to you."

I look inside doubtfully.

There are four people sitting in chairs along a row of mirrors. I recognize none of them.

Wait. Who is that underneath the pedestal hair dryer, head wrapped in foil and plastic wrap?

A sudden mad beating starts up in my chest.

Rosa's entire body is covered in a black hairdressers' cape with just her divine face sticking out. "Tonia, is there any chance you could wheel me into the back room for a minute?" she asks the hairdresser who has ushered me in.

"Sure thing, darl." Tonia unplugs the pedestal hair dryer from the wall, grabs the pole, and gives the chair a prod.

I watch Tonia wheel her away. What is going on?

Rosa twists in her chair. "Are you coming?"

"Oh!" I follow them through a narrow door.

The back room is a storeroom. Boxes of hair products sit stacked against the far wall and the smell that wafts from them is the smell of Rosa's shampoo. I breathe it in giddily. I wish Rosa wasn't covered in a cape. I wish Tonia wasn't rummaging at her feet.

"Did you get my message?" Rosa whispers.

I nod mutely.

"Well? Did you like it?" she asks weakly.

I look at her gravely. "I loved it."

She grins with relief. Her gaze lingers. "I'm sorry I didn't reply right away. I wanted to send you the video, and it took me a while to get it from Tonia."

"You made the video?" I ask Tonia, who has finally found the plug and is back on her feet.

"I thought someone should record the occasion," Tonia says, smiling. "It was a great day. You want me to close this?"

"Thanks." Rosa waits until the door is firmly shut. "There's one other thing I want you to have." I hear a rustle from underneath her cape. She produces her phone and hands it to me. "Check out the playlist called HC."

I was not expecting this. "What are they?"

"Audio files I recorded. Proof of the shitty things Hamish did to the Flywheel after you fired him. He told me all about the food orders, and about stealing the idea for the Bondi shuttle."

"This is why you saw him yesterday?" I ask, chest tight.

She nods. "I was nice to him. I built up his trust. Said some horrible things about you," she adds, looking uncomfortable. "I really want to help you save the Flywheel, Del." She reddens. "I thought if I could get Hamish to talk and record what he said, we could use the evidence to start a grassroots campaign. People will turn against Crunch after we expose what Hamish has done. It might not be illegal, but he's been pretty underhanded. And Crunch represents the big-money franchises, whereas you guys are local. It's just enough to cause a scandal, if we do it right. With the publicity you get from it you should be able to reopen the Flywheel."

Could we actually be in with a chance? "You honestly think it will work?"

"When everything Hamish has done comes out, you'll have people beating down the door." Rosa grins. "I've saved many a library in my time. You think I can't save one little cafe?"

"I can't believe you'd do all that for me."

She looks at me steadily. "There's no one I'd rather do it for."

That's when I kiss her, so forcefully that her chair starts rolling backward and the pedestal hair dryer with it. She laughs and grabs onto my shirt; her other hand grabs her plastic-wrapped hair. I stagger after her, kissing her still, almost tripping on the cord. I pursue her chair across the floor until the chair, the pedestal hair dryer, Rosa, and I are all backed up against a stack of boxes.

Once steady, we slow things down a bit. Our kisses become longer, deeper. She slides her arms around my waist and pulls me closer.

Ten minutes later there's a tap on the door. "How's your treatment going?" Tonia calls out. "Not too much heat?"

"The perfect amount," Rosa calls back, a hand over my grinning mouth. She waits until Tonia's footsteps fade, then clutches my collar and draws me down again.

40. A TASTE OF VICTORY

Rosa Barea is a woman of her word. She said she would run a campaign to save the Flywheel and she's doing just that. Ten days we've been at it. So far, so good.

It took her just a week to build a website and create a massive Twitter storm. She's managed to leverage the exposure to secure a string of web and radio interviews as well.

Notice how I just used the word "leverage"? Rosa taught me that one. Have I mentioned how incredible she is?

And today we were chalking the footpath up the road from Crunch with the words "Eat Local. Save the Flywheel." when we heard shouting nearby, and the sound of a door being wrenched open.

Hamish Creel was standing on the street, his dreadlocks swaying. He gave the Crunch door a shove with his foot and it slammed shut.

He stood fuming for a few seconds, fists clenched. Then he looked up the street and saw us.

"Happy now?" he cried angrily.

Had Adrian really chucked him out because of us?

"Keep your head down," Rosa murmured. "Just keep on chalking."

So I did. I scraped the chalk in vigorous lines, waiting for more abuse or for Hamish's shadow to cross the footpath in front of us.

But when I looked up a few minutes later he was gone.

41. THE NEWS GETS OUT

We hold our rally on a Saturday and almost a hundred people show up. There are a lot of familiar faces but a lot of unfamiliar ones, too. I am cautiously excited. If people we don't even know have made an effort to support us, I figure we have a shot.

The following Monday is when Crunch is due to take over the Flywheel lease. I've agreed to hand over the keys myself. I let myself into the empty space and find a spot on the floor to wait.

I try to imagine Adrian Hibbert in here, serving customers, but it's too depressing to think about.

I carry on waiting.

And waiting.

No one shows up.

I could call the real estate agent, but I don't want to jinx anything. Maybe Adrian just got the day wrong. I'm certainly not going to call him to find out.

The following morning I wait for him at the same time. Nothing.

The morning after that, Rosa and I are sitting side by side with our bums against the skirting boards, drinking bad coffee from Charada, when Charlie strides in.

"I have some news," he says, smiling. He pushes back a hunk of golden hair and clears his throat.

"It's been a long fight, a bitter fight," he begins. "There have been highs as well as lows, and the lows have taken their toll on all of us." He paces back and forth across the floor in front of us, his eyes bright. "We've fought corporate greed with determination, naked ambition with passion," he continues. "We've held off the storm of Goliath with a David-sized umbrella."

This is a Rousing Speech on steroids. I'd tell Charlie to cut to the chase but he's enjoying himself too much.

"Just like David, though, our precision has paid off. Our campaign has hit its target!"

Rosa grabs his ankles. "What are you trying to say, Charlie?"

Finally he tells us what he's heard. As we suspected, Adrian sacked Hamish, but it hasn't been enough to save Crunch. After our campaign and rally, customers have been deserting in droves. And rather than weathering the storm, Adrian has decided to close the shop.

"My sources tell me he plans to give up the Flywheel lease and move to another neighborhood altogether," Charlie reports. "Which of course leaves the Flywheel—Sydney's new favorite underdog—in the perfect position to reopen and recover its debt!"

We've been celebrating all morning.

When Mandy heard the news she showed up with a case of champagne. Rosa draped streamers from the ceiling fans. Tom fetched some glasses. Charlie dragged the couches out from the storeroom and I turned the stereo up loud. Rushmore, of course.

Now I'm crossing the road to the restaurant with Rosa, getting takeaway food to bring back for everyone. I feel heady from our victory and the pre-lunch champagne. I feel exhausted from the effort of the campaign.

But I feel something else, too; a dull weight that I try to ignore.

As we slip between the traffic, Rosa's arm brushes mine. It's twenty days today since we kissed in the back of the salon, and I'm still not used to being with her. Will I ever get used to it? To entering a room and seeing her green eyes light up? To reaching out to touch her face the moment we're left alone? Nobody knows about us except for Ramone, Angeline, my school friends, and Charlie. Rosa's promised, though, to work toward being more open about who she is. In return, I've promised to be discreet for as long as she needs, even though now, as we cross the road, all I want to do is hold her hand, to grab her waist and draw her to me, just to prove that this thing between us, this thing that has been a fantasy for so long, is real. I want to pull her close right here between the honking cars.

But I know I can't. Not out in the open, not with Charada across the road. So I resist.

Inside the restaurant, Adelina is at the bar polishing glasses. I haven't seen her since the night I screamed at Elvio. I freeze.

I sent them both a note of apology a week ago, which Rosa helped me write. I hope it's done the trick. Adelina gives me a friendly nod. I breathe out slowly.

Elvio is not so welcoming. We pass him in the back court-yard and when I say hello, he just grunts. Rosa shoots me a worried glance. I shake my head to say it doesn't matter. But I'm swallowing my anger.

We head to the kitchen, where her parents are preparing for the dinner crowd, and suddenly I feel sick. We've seen each other around the neighborhood but we've never actually met. What if Elvio has told them about me and Rosa or about my freak-out? What if they hate me on sight?

I smooth my pants and check my face for stray crumbs. Always a must for me.

We walk in and they look up.

"Mi niña," murmurs her mother. She holds out her long, slender arms to Rosa. She has her hair combed back from her face. She is beautiful like Rosa, even in an apron and washing-up gloves. Next to her, Rosa's father is chopping onions and looks up. Rosa inherited his eyes.

Rosa's kissing them both on each cheek. "Del, these are my parents, Antonia and Geraldo."

I am relieved when they smile at me. So Elvio hasn't told them anything, thank god. "Mama, Papa, this is Delilah, my good friend."

My good friend. It's a start.

It's Friday, which means tonight my school friends are at Lauren's house doing their English study thing. I decide to surprise them with a few bottles of the leftover champagne. When I arrive, Misch is in a mid-lecture trance, geeking out over Shakespeare's use of irony.

"Del!" Lauren and Lucas, who have been nodding off on the couch, leap up, and my heart swells. I tell them the good news about the Flywheel. Lauren raids her parents' china cabinet for glasses.

Within the hour we're tipsy and full of pizza.

"We need music!" Lucas bellows. "Any requests?"

"Don't you know anything?" Misch scolds. "Put on some Rushmore and make it snappy, boy."

"You know he's in love with you," I say to Misch when Lucas is hunched over the computer. "Don't be so hard on him."

"That's exactly why I am hard on him," Misch says firmly. "It's a lot less cruel than leading him on." She looks pointedly at Lauren, who glares back at her.

"What?" I ask. I'm clearly missing something.

But Lauren changes tack. "My question exactly." Lauren studies me for a moment. "You have your depressed face on."

"Me?" I laugh. "Why would I be depressed?"

"It's true," Misch says. "You do look kind of bummed." She plants her hands on her hips. "Did something happen with Rosa?"

"No! Things with Rosa are great." I tell them about meeting Rosa's parents—how well it went. I admit this is mainly because they don't know we're together. "It's okay, though. It won't be like this forever."

"Are you sure there's nothing else bugging you?" Lauren asks.

I sigh. The truth is, when we popped the champagne this morning at the Flywheel, I didn't experience the total elation at our victory I thought I would. I was half expecting a great weight to lift off me if we won the fight, and it hasn't.

I try to explain this to Misch and Lauren. "Having to close the Flywheel made me feel like I completely failed in life. It was like, I was failing at everything else, but if I could save the cafe I thought things would be all right. Then I failed that test as well."

"Until today, you mean," Lauren says.

"Well, yes. Except that until Dad gets back I have to run things. And even when he does get back he'll need me to help out as much as I was before he left, if we're going to make it profitable. And I was helping him out a fair amount. But it turns out there are other things I'd rather be doing with my life," I say quietly.

"Such as?" asks Lauren carefully.

"Studying, I guess." I bury my face in my hands and groan. "Going back to school."

"I know you don't want to face those horrible bitches," Lauren says, and then blushes because she's used the word "bitches."

"I think they got to me more than I admitted." I scoop up a piece of pizza and chew miserably.

"You can handle them," Misch assures me. "As for the Flywheel, why not use Charlie as cheap labor for a while? He still owes you. And he's just freed up the rest of his year, hasn't he?"

I look at them blankly.

"He didn't tell you?" Lauren asks.

"Oh, so this is how it's going to be from now on, is it? I get to find out all Charlie's news secondhand?"

"I have no intention of being his conduit, believe me," Lauren says crankily. "You could ask him yourself, you know."

"Just tell her, Loz," says Misch.

"His dad has said he doesn't have to go back to school," Lauren explains. "Charlie finally convinced him he wasn't suited to it. Especially not the disciplinary stuff you get at the type of schools his dad wants him to go to. So they've been talking about other options. It's not settled yet, but one idea is for Charlie to go to culinary school next year. Which means he's kind of at loose ends until January."

"That's awesome. And he really has been doing a great job at the Flywheel," I say, considering it.

"He *adores* the place," Lauren says. "Anyway, I think it will do him some good."

"What do you mean?"

"Never mind," Lauren mutters.

But the edge to her tone makes me wonder.

42. WHAT HAPPENS NEXT

I take our things out of storage. I unpack the chairs, the couches, and the tables. I drag them all back to their regular places. I stick the world maps up again behind the counter. I put the Marx Brothers stencil back on the wall.

I give Charlie the keys. Charlie, my manager.

I go back to school.

Three things happen on my first day back that are worth mentioning.

The first is my conversation with Lauren on our way there. I bring up the topic of Charlie, a task made tricky by the fact that as usual, she's half a block ahead of me for most of the walk. I want to remind her about the shortness of my legs, but decide the state of her relationship is a more pressing issue.

"Are you guys okay?" I call out. "You and Charlie? He's not being a dick, is he? Has he been flirting with other girls?"

Lauren swings around and paces back to me. "Definitely not," she mutters crossly.

"Then what's going on? You seem annoyed with him or something."

She readjusts her backpack and casts a glance up and down the street. "I don't feel comfortable talking to you about this."

"Because he's my friend? Come on, I know what he's like."

"You don't know what he's like with me," she says, pulling at her hair distractedly.

"So tell me."

We start walking again, side by side this time: Lauren at an amble, me at a light jog. She furrows her brow. "He's just kind of . . . intense."

"How?" I ask.

"The way he looks at me," says Lauren. "In this goofy, glazed way. Plus he told me he loves me, which I know he's said to other girls before, but I think, like . . . he really means it."

"That's good, right?" I nudge her lightly with my elbow. "I mean, you like him, don't you?"

"Of course."

"And how are things, you know, physically . . ."

"Oh, fine," Lauren says casually. "Great, actually."

"So to summarize. A hot, sexy guy who you've had a crush on for ages is in love with you, and you're having hot sex. You poor thing," I say with fake sympathy.

We reach the school and turn into the gates. Even though we're early and there's hardly anyone around, I begin to feel queasy. Everything looks exactly the same. Of course it does. Why would anything have changed? I'm going to have to deal with the same old crap, and I need to be prepared for that.

Breathe, Del, I tell myself, and remind myself why I'm here. Not for Lauren, or for Mrs. Cronenberg, or anyone else. I'm here because I want to be, and because I've decided not to let Georgina or her sidekicks sabotage my life. I take a deep breath and try to feel okay about it all.

"I just . . . I don't know," Lauren continues. "Charlie's my first boyfriend, if you don't count the pash I had with Carl MacDonald at the year nine dance—"

"The *what*?"

"—it just seems that things are moving really fast. I mean, what do we even have in common? Besides you, of course. He's not exactly academic. He has no idea what he wants to do with his life. Sure, he's fun to hang out with. And sexy. But is that really enough?"

"You're overthinking this," I say as we climb the front steps. "You're seventeen. You don't have to marry him."

She looks unconvinced. "He's just so sure about me. About us. I don't feel that certainty. It's hard to feel certain when he's the first guy I've been with."

"Not counting Carl MacDonald, apparently."

"And then there's the problem of Saxon."

I slow to a halt. "Excuse me?"

"You know. Saxon," says Lauren, as if it's obvious. She dumps her bag in front of her locker and begins taking out books. "We're in Maths together, and he was at the Factory that night, remember?" She smiles to herself. "I think he likes me," she murmurs. "And he's cute. And so smart. He answers all the questions in class—"

"So Lauren Crawley's breaking hearts now?" Maybe things have changed, after all. I'm trying to keep it light-hearted, but I feel a twist of panic for Charlie. I grab her arm. "Listen, Lauren. I know Charlie, and I've seen the way he is with you. He's never been like this about anyone before. He's never been with anyone for as long as this before either. This relationship? It's a breakthrough for him. *You are his breakthrough.*"

"But, Del." She looks at me steadily. "What if he's not mine?"

The second thing worth mentioning happens at break. I run into Georgina Trump in the hallway. Her blonde hair is bouncing. Her eye shadow is twinkling. She's clutching a hideous leopard-skin purse.

Our eyes meet, and her cheeks turn the color of her bright pink lipstick. I do an awkward half-swivel away from her and almost crash into the wall.

I swivel around again a few moments later, expecting her to be long gone. But she's not. She's standing there staring at me.

"Hi," she says. She looks nervous.

"Um, hi?" I reply.

"So, you're back," she says.

"Clearly."

"That's good. I mean, I'm glad."

"Okay," I say slowly.

She gives me a shy smile. I remember that smile. I haven't seen it for a while. It makes me remember the time we spent together, something I haven't thought about for some time now. We had our good moments, there's no denying it. We understood something about each other that no one else did. We made each other laugh. I felt connected to her in a way I'd never felt with anyone before. Briefly, I wonder whether Mrs. Cronenberg was right. Maybe things really would have worked out differently if I'd kept my mouth shut. If I'd given Georgina more time.

There's a shout behind us.

"George Porge!" Ella cries, slinging an arm around her neck. She has glitter in her hair and her tunic hooked up on one side in what I can only presume is a deliberate display of fashionable asymmetry.

"Oh dear," she says upon seeing me. "The little lezzo is back in town." Her voice is saccharine, but she's grimacing. "But I suppose I shouldn't say those sorts of things, should I? In case you go crying to Mrs. C? Whoops." She leans into my face and curls her lips. "*Sorry.*"

She giggles and turns to Georgina.

There is a long moment when nothing happens, when I hope that for once Georgina will stand up for me. I watch her carefully.

She looks at Ella and giggles back.

As they march away arm in arm I resign myself to the fact that this won't be my last encounter with the field-side girls. I feel like kicking Ella's head in and make a mental note to tell the counselor that the school has organized for me to see. She's been helping me with my "anger stuff," as we're calling it. We meet every Thursday and I get a full hour to bitch about my week. It's actually very soothing.

As for Georgina? Watching her head down the corridor, what I feel for her is closer to pity than fury. And that's how

I know I'm over her and that she is no longer a powerful force in my life.

The third thing happens after school at the Flywheel. Just before I go up to do my homework I check in to see if Charlie and Dallas need a hand. It's four-thirty and the place is still teeming, even though we normally close at four. Charlie is making changes to the specials board in preparation for tomorrow. Dallas is madly printing out bills to encourage some of the customers to pay up and leave.

I've just donned an apron to set about clearing plates when the door opens and I wonder if we should be letting in another customer.

But it isn't another customer.

It's Dad.

He's got his rucksack on and he's wearing the flannelette shirt he left in. His beard could do with a trim, but other than that he looks exactly the same.

I run to him.

"Hello, darl," he says, smiling, and I burst into tears.

Shaking himself free of the rucksack, he pulls me into one of his bear hugs. He smells of peppermint Tic Tacs and aftershave, just like he always has.

"Blow your nose on my sleeve," he says as I snot up the front of his shirt. "I don't mind."

We hug for an age and when we've stopped he takes a good look around, at the secondhand vinyl furniture, the Marx Brothers mural, the crowded tables: everything back in its place. Charlie, grinning, comes over for a hug as well. Then Dad parks his bum against the counter and runs a callused hand lovingly across its surface. He breathes out a satisfied sigh. "Seems like everything's in order. A full house this arvo, that's for sure. No dramas while I was gone?"

Charlie and I look at each other.

I open my mouth, and close it again.

"Nah," says Charlie, and grins.

43. AN OPENING

I am lying on my bed gazing out the window to the laneway below. The branches of a camphor laurel shift against a blue sky. There is sunlight on the carpet and Rosa Barea has her arms around my waist. It is a perfect morning, a perfect moment. I want to lie here forever, in the sunlight, with snatches of traffic noise filtering in and Rosa beside me.

She sits up on one elbow, slides a hand along my hips, and presses her mouth to my neck, slowly. Her open lips move against my ear, my jawline, my mouth. I run my hands through her hair and we're kissing, and my chest is thumping so loudly it echoes against the walls.

"Del! It's time!"

Or maybe the thumping is Charlie's fist against the door. Rosa groans and buries her head against my shoulder. "Do we have to?"

The answer, unfortunately, is "yes." Today the Flywheel reopens after two weeks of renovations and it's time for the opening party. We clamber off the bed and straighten our clothes. We've both dressed up for the occasion. Rosa is looking hipster-lush in Buddy Holly glasses and a fitted T-shirt beneath suspenders, baggy pants, and winklepickers. I'm wearing a collared shirt with skinny jeans and neither item has a single stain upon it.

I'm a bit nervous about the reopening. Charlie talked Dad into quite a few changes and I hope people like it.

Today is the first time I get to see the whole new look, properly spruced. Halfway down the stairs I pause to take it in.

A long, restored wooden table is the centerpiece. It sits under a row of low-hanging Edison bulbs. Benches run along each side, dotted with cushions covered with vintage fabric. On one wall Charlie has built a floor-to-ceiling bookcase, which acts as a display cabinet for all sorts of knickknacks: a nautical lamp, a giant china hedgehog, and a Darth Vader mask. Beside it he's put up the *Skidoo* film poster I almost threw out. Shelves along each windowpane are lined with succulents in terra cotta pots.

I can't believe this is the Flywheel.

"Decor?" Charlie asks.

"Definitely five stars," I tell him, giving him a hug. "The place looks amazing, Charlie."

To mark the reopening Dad has decided to serve coffee on the house, so he expects the place will pack out. Sure enough, within an hour of opening, half the youth hostel population is sprawled across the couches by the wall. Buck is working his way through a piece of chocolate cake the size and weight of a doorstop. The uni students have set up a poker game in the back corner. Lauren is helping wait tables. She comes out of the kitchen laughing at something Charlie has said.

I haven't told Charlie about the conversation Lauren and I had. I suspect she hasn't either. I think she's taking her time to work out what to do. Charlie is in love with her, that I'm sure of, but time will tell whether that's too much for Lauren right now, I suppose. I want things to work out between them, for Charlie's sake. But knowing how Lauren feels, I'm not actually convinced that it will.

Dad calls out to me from the open kitchen. "We're out of vanilla ice cream and I've got iced coffees on order."

"Okay, no worries," I call back. "I'm on it."

I scan the floor for Rosa. She's trying to extricate herself from the poker players, who want her to join their game.

She sees me looking and smiles. I still buckle at the knees at the sight of that smile.

I walk over. "Any chance there's some vanilla ice cream in the kitchen over at Charada?" I ask.

Rosa is thinking seriously about cutting back her dancing, but at the moment she's still working there six nights a week, which has its privileges.

"I'm happy to check," she says.

I watch her swing her hips out the door and have to grip the nearest table.

Mandy and Tom arrive. "Why is it you two always turn up together these days?" I ask them.

"We don't," says Tom.

"Pure coincidence," says Mandy at the same time.

I give Mandy a sideways look and she laughs. It occurs to me she no longer looks pale or drawn. She hasn't for a while.

Rosa is back ten minutes later. She hands me a bag. "Two liters of vanilla ice cream. There wasn't any at Charada so I went to the servo. The guy from there sends his regards."

"But I don't know the guy at the servo."

She gives me a significant look. "Long, filthy dreads? Big frown? Although I think the frown's a new feature."

"Hamish is working at the *servo*?"

I can't help but feel bad for him. I think about his DJ dreams and his record collection in storage. He won't be getting his music venue now. I've heard Adrian has already found a new cafe space in Alexandria, but I doubt he'll be taking Hamish on again. It's almost a shame. He's not a bad barista. I wonder if I should suggest to Dad that we give him another go.

That thought lasts approximately two seconds.

Music blares suddenly from the stereo.

I look across the cafe floor. Charlie is moving chairs and tables to create a clear space. He starts to swing his hips and clap his hands, and motions for Rosa and me to come over.

Rosa joins him on the makeshift dance floor. She moves beside him, her arms in the air. Patrons turn to watch them and some get up to join in. Soon there's a whole crowd of people moving to the music.

When the song ends Rosa finds me on the sidelines. She grabs my hand.

"What are you doing?" I ask in horror.

"Don't be such a wimp. It won't kill you."

"I don't know about that."

"I won't drop you this time. Promise." She grins.

I have no idea what the music is, but it is fast and melodious and it has a good beat. Rosa leads me into the sea of bodies. Beside us, Charlie and Lucas are trying out bad hip-hop moves. Misch is doing one of her Beyoncé hip rolls and

Lauren is swaying with her eyes closed. Rosa spins me around, and to my surprise I stay on my feet.

And in this moment I am happy. I don't know what's around the corner but it doesn't matter, because what I feel right now is enough. My friends are here, my dad is on the other side of the room, and there is music in the air. I'm with a beautiful girl I'm crazy about. And we're dancing.

OZ GLOSSARY

I'm told not all Americans are up to date with the latest Aussie lingo, so here's a list to help you out.

ALL-ROUNDER: One of those annoying people who is good at everything

ARVO: Afternoon. Which is far too long to say in full. Who's got time for three syllable words like "afternoon"? Or "syllable"?

BANGS ON: Talks too much, fails to shut up, goes on at length like those actors at the Academy Awards who thank so many people that the organizers play loud music to get them off stage.

BLOODY: A swear word that's been around for so long it's not even rude anymore. To water it down even further some people replace it with *bleeding*, *blinking*, or *blooming*, which are so far from swear words they're practically compliments.

BREKKIE: Breakfast

BUNGING IT ON: Faking it, pretending to be hurt when you're not, generally to gain sympathy when you don't deserve it. I don't know how you live with yourself, frankly.

BUSH BALLAD: A rhyming poem about things that happened (usually boring) in the Australian bush a long time ago. Sheep are often featured, as are horses. Also regularly mentioned are billabongs, which are a type of lake, not marijuana-related, sorry Charlie.

BUSHRANGER: An outlaw with straggly facial hair of the kind you often see on hipsters. Australia's most famous bushranger, Ned Kelly (you guys had a movie about him, remember?), wore a mailbox on his head so that will be the next trend no doubt.

CLEANSKINS: Cheap wine, referred to as a "clean skin" because it comes without a label. Not to worry though: you may not get a label but a hangover is *guaranteed*.

COMMUNITY SERVICES: The government department responsible for child welfare.

GROG: Plonk, brew, sauce, hooch, hair of the dog, giggle juice, nightcap, the hard stuff, to name a few variations.

HAVING ME ON: Putting me on, tricking me, pulling the wool over my eyes

HIGHER SCHOOL CERTIFICATE: The hellish exams we're forced to take in our final year of school to ensure a place at university. *Also:* HSC, short for "Holy Shit Crap."

KIP: Nap, a.k.a. something I haven't had time to do for approximately 138 days. Thanks, Dad.

KNOCK SOMEONE BACK: To reject somebody. This is generally done without actually knocking them, but physical violence is always an optional extra in these types of situations. Just ask Charlie.

LAMINGTON: Possibly the most Australian cake in existence. They should serve it with a little national flag and a koala. Coconut-dusted, covered in chocolate with sponge in the middle, everyone's aunt has a recipe for it, and no school fete is complete without it.

LONGNECK: A large bottle of beer, called "bombers" in the States. Very classy blokes like to stumble around the streets after football games carrying them in paper bags while showing their bums to passing cars.

LOO: Toilet

NOT KNOWING HIS BEAK FROM HIS BUM: Having no idea. I mean, if you're human and you think you have a beak then you're in trouble to begin with, aren't you?

OZ LOTTO: National lottery

PASH SESSION: Make-out session. Hella kissing, basically.

PEAR-SHAPED: When a situation goes horribly wrong, we say it goes pear-shaped. Which, come to think of it, is a bit unfair to pears. They're a lovely shape. Potatoes on the other hand . . .

POTTED (AS IN A "POTTED THEORY"): A superficial, shallow analysis. Nothing at all to do with marijuana. Sorry again, Charlie.

RANK: Horrible and disgusting. *See also:* sexism, racism, homophobia, xenophobia, and Charlie's breath before he's brushed his teeth in the morning.

SCULL: Chug, or what one does with a beer after having done something embarrassing.

SERVIETTE: Posh people like Lauren would say "napkin," which makes no sense to me, since "serviette" clearly comes from the French and what could be posher than that?

SERVO: Short for service station, which Americans call gas stations, because apparently what Australians call petrol Americans call gas, which is the word Australians use for farting. It's all very confusing.

SHITHOUSE: Terrible, awful, completely horrid. For example, imagine if your house was made of poo. That would be shithouse.

SKEW-WHIFF: Crooked or twisted

SNOGS: Kisses, of course

SOLICITOR: Lawyer. As boring as it sounds.

SOOK: Someone who acts like a big baby

SPORTO: A person who is into sport in a big way. I take it you call these people jocks. They play sport, they follow a team, they go to matches, maybe they even put money on who will win. What would I know? These people are aliens to me.

STUFFED UP: Messed up

TUCKSHOP: School cafeteria, but heaps cuter-sounding

TURKISH BREAD: Turkish-style bread, or if you are in Turkey: bread.

VEGEMITE: A dark brown food paste made from yeast extract that pretty much everybody else in the world thinks is disgusting. In Australia though, it's a rule that parents indoctrinate their children from a very young age so we grow up completely obsessed with the stuff.

VOLLIES: Short for volunteer, another one of those words that is *way* too long to say in full. We have lives to lead, you know.

WINKLEPICKERS: A pointy-toed shoe, first worn in the '50s by British rock-and-roll fans. In some parts of America they're called "roach stompers," which is gross.

Y-FRONTS: Men's underpants. You can imagine why, can't you?

ACKNOWLEDGMENTS

Thank you to the readers who provided feedback on early drafts: Rachael Cann, Lilly Gerlach, Cathy Hunt, Kate O'Donnell, and Rani Young. Thank you to the Australia Council for the Arts for its generous support. Thank you to my marvelous editorial teams: especially Karri Hedge, Hilary Rogers, and Marisa Pintado at Hardie Grant Egmont, and the managing editorial team and Taylor Norman at Chronicle Books. And thank you, most of all, to Emma Kersey.

Erin Gough is a Sydney-based writer whose award-winning short stories have appeared in a number of journals and anthologies. She wrote this book because she wanted to write the sort of book she would like to have read when she was a young adult working out who she was and what she wanted to be. It was the winner of Hardie Grant Egmont's Ampersand Prize, which selects one unpublished manuscript per year to award with publication. This is her first book. Find out more about Erin at www.eringough.com.

TOM HAS PLANS TO VISIT THESE LANDS

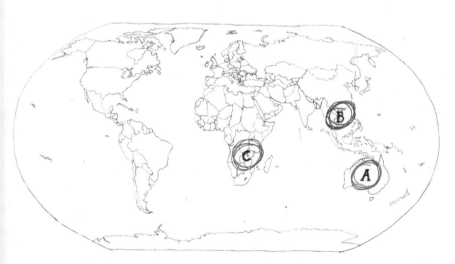

Eye Candy Endorsed by Mandy

① Uluru, NT, AUST
② Halong Bay, Vietnam
③ Victoria Falls, Zambia

Countries where eugene green has been